Adrian was born in South Africa and lived there most of his life. He immigrated to the UK eight years ago with his family and settled in Somerset, where most of his wife's family live.

Adrian has been involved in business all his working life and has run his own businesses as well as having worked for major corporations. He specialises in sales, marketing and IT, although he has wide business experience.

Adrian is a forward thinking individual who has been responsible for the introduction of many innovative ideas during his career. While in the UK he completed ten years research into new management measurement models, which provided the kernel of an idea for this book.

Adrian is an ideas person, who loves writing, having written technical books and manuals throughout his life. This is his first venture into the world of fiction, which he thoroughly enjoyed. He assures us he has many ideas for more highly topical subjects with exciting, though provoking storylines. He believes a good book is about a good story, one which is interesting, exciting and easy to read, while provoking thought by challenging popular perception.

Apart from writing, Adrian loves computer programming, oil painting and the beautiful English countryside. He is married to Paula and has two sons, Jonathan and Jeremy.

A SILENT WAR

Adrian Dore

A SILENT WAR

Vanguard Press

A CIP catalogue record for this title is
available from the British Library.

ISBN 978 1 843866442

Vanguard Press is an imprint of
Pegasus Elliot MacKenzie Publishers Ltd.
www.pegasuspublishers.com

First Published in 2010

Vanguard Press
Sheraton House Castle Park
Cambridge England

Printed & Bound in Great Britain

To my family and Paula – thank you.

Chapter One

I stand at my study window deep in thought as I look out over the beautiful Somerset countryside. It's late October and the autumn leaves swirl around the garden, driven by high winds and lashing rain. It's cold and bleak, but strangely beautiful, reflecting the ambivalent feelings I have for the phone call I have just received. Matt Todd, Chairman of the Global Marketing Association, an organisation representing the interests of some of the leading international marketing societies and institutes, has just phoned and told me he has been served papers by a leading business school, indicating their intention of taking legal action, on behalf of the business community, for what they claim has been the wilful misappropriation of business resources by marketing professionals. It appears that the gist of their claim is based on the poor financial accountability by marketing, which results in marketing squandering resources which are directly and indirectly under their control.

It's an interesting hypothesis and one which is frequently banded around corporate corridors. However, bringing an action like this against a profession is both unique and audacious, to say the very least. The ramifications of this action could have dire consequences, not only for marketing, but the entire international business community.

Matt has asked me to represent the Global Marketing Association in this matter, but I face a huge dilemma in accepting, as I've only recently gone into semi-retirement after a long, and dare I say, fairly successful career as a London solicitor. My early retirement was prompted, to a large extent, by the need to enjoy quality time with my wife which, unfortunately, I was unable to do during my career. And furthermore, I've started to enjoy my new life as a semi-retired 'country gentleman'. However, this will be a landmark case which could change the course of business forever, and have a major effect on the world economy. Hardly an opportunity one allows to pass by, but then, at my age and juncture in life, do I want the pressures and demands such a case will extract?

Just then the dinner gong rings impatiently and immediately thereafter, my wife storms into my study with an annoyed look on her face. "Haven't you heard the dinner gong?" she asks.

"Yes, I have, my dear," I reply.

"It's the third time I've rung it," she said.

"Oh, I'm sorry, I've just heard it now."

"What's wrong, you look a little pensive?" she queried.

"Oh, nothing much," I say. "I've just received a call from Matt Todd of the GMA who has asked for some advice on a rather pressing matter."

"Nothing which concerns you, I hope?" she remarks.

"Perhaps," I reply.

"No more of this," she says, grabbing me by the arm and leading me off to the dining room. "Lunch is getting cold and it's your favourite."

During lunch, I get chided several times. "You seem to be a million miles away. Why don't you just come out and tell me that Matt has offered you another one of his 'big cases', and you've accepted it?"

"I can't hide anything from you can I," I remark.

"No, you can't, but that's not the point. You're a workaholic and this semi-retirement thing will never work, as I've said so many times before. Taking a long weekend for you represents semi-retirement."

"That's a little harsh," I say. "I haven't spoken to anybody in the office for over two weeks."

"Big deal! I believe some people take annual leave of more than two weeks, but would hasten to qualify this by saying its only hearsay," she remarks with a twinkle in her eye.

"I know you too well, James. You have already made up your mind and are just wondering how to break the news to me as gently as you can."

"That's not entirely true," I say, interrupting her. She continues.

"I also know that if I resist, you'll become moody, irritable and totally intolerable, so it's entirely futile for me to suggest otherwise. All I would ask is that you try to work from home as much as you can, rather than returning to the office, as you know how I hate staying in this mansion on my own; I get totally spooked!"

"It's hardly a mansion my, dear."

"I know," she says interrupting me. "It's only a manor house, but with seven bedrooms, four reception rooms, etc, etc, we are lost in all this space and at night I find it too spooky. We should have bought that quaint little cottage in the village as I suggested."

"Let's not go through all that again – you, and I, agreed that the house and its exquisite countryside setting fulfilled our lifelong dream."

"Yes, but you don't have to stay here on your own, and you aren't frightened by the house at night!"

"I understand," I said, getting up from the table and walking over to her, putting my arms around her. She is such a good person! Throughout our thirty-five years together she has been nothing but supportive, allowing me to pursue my dreams, often at the expense of quality family time. She's right when she joked about hearing that some people take annual leave of more than two weeks. I can't remember when last we took a holiday of more than a few weeks because of the demands of work. Sometimes I wonder if all the hard work has been worth it. Did I give my sons, who have both flown the nest, enough quality time? I know I haven't given my good wife enough quality time. Since going into semi-retirement almost six months ago, I have tried desperately to extract myself from work and spend more time and money on my loved ones, hoping to make amends for my past errors. She's right, if Matt wants me to take this case then it's going to be on my terms and conditions – working from home as much as possible and not taking on too much myself.

"You're right – if I accept this case it will be entirely on my own terms and conditions," I say.

"If you accept! Oh, James, we both know you've already done that. Let me chat to Matt – I'll give him a piece of my mind. Offering you work is like offering an alcoholic a drink! He should be ashamed of himself after all you've done for him."

"No, no," I protest. "I've told him I'm going to sleep on his offer and discuss it with you first."

"Knowing Matt, he expects decisions there and then, so I bet he'll be phoning you this afternoon for your decision."

As if on cue, the phone rings.

"I wouldn't be surprised if that's not him right now," she says, heading for the phone in the entrance hall. She lifts the receiver and without pausing starts to speak, "Hello Matt, I thought you were James's friend? How could you be so cruel as to entice him back to work... oh, it's you, Dorothy."

I turn and walk back into the dining room with a huge grin on my face.

True to form, Matt phones me first thing in the morning.

Matt is a self-made multi-millionaire who, from humble beginnings and a poor educational background, went on to amass a small fortune through his strategic insight and astute business acumen. He specialised in turnarounds, spotting businesses with potential but in trouble; acquiring them for a song, turning them into highly successful businesses and then selling them for huge profits. At forty-five, Matt decided to retire from active business and plough some of his fortune, estimated at over three hundred million pounds, back into business for the benefit of the wider business community. As a passionate marketer, Matt thought that marketing's influence was on the wane, and that he could repay his debt to the business community, which had made him so rich, by dedicating his resources and time to help re-establish marketing as a leading business force. As a consequence, he formed the Global Marketing Association over ten years ago to represent marketing societies and institutes interests on an international basis. His objective has been to invest extensively in research and lobby tirelessly for the advancement of marketing's role in business.

Matt is a born and bred American, but five years ago he decided to emigrate to the United Kingdom and to settle in London, as he felt the European Union would become one of the most influential players in the future world economy, and he wanted to be 'closer to the action', as he put it. It was during this period that I came in contact with him, doing work for him and the Association. Over this period, he and I have become friends rather than business colleagues. However, I classify him as a 'high overhead friend' because he's such a dynamic person, always on the go, always very demanding. He's also a little brash, loud and pushy and lacks certain social refinements. It is these qualities which have not endeared him to my good wife; they tolerate each other at best.

"Hello, James, I've scheduled a helicopter flight for this morning…"

"Hold on, Matt," I say, interrupting him. "I haven't decided to take the case yet! There are still a few issues I need to discuss with you first."

"Okay, James, but let me tell you that over the past twenty-four hours while you've been sleeping or milking the cows – whatever you country folk get up to, I've been drumming up some serious support for this case. I've been able to get some of the big boys to stick their hands deep into their pockets. I've got a pot full of cash to fight this case, so much so, that we're going to blow Professor Asshole and his case so far away he'll think he lives on Mars."

"Matt, it isn't just about the money."

"Hey, the money is the least of my concerns. Lawyers are two-a-dime. I don't want any lawyer, I want the best, and you are the best! I've been telling people that I have the sharpest brain and best lawyer money can buy working for us, and that you'll make mincemeat out of this stupid Professor and his team; so don't back out on me now chum!"

"I'm most flattered you think so highly of me…"

"Cut the crap, James, you know you are the best, and I want you on my team. I know this semi-retirement bullshit is important to you, but I've got the money to give you a retirement package that will make Bill Gates happy."

"It's not the money," I say, grabbing an opportunity to present my case before Matt steamrollers me.

"Firstly, I don't want to return to the City, I want to work from home as much as I can. Secondly, I'm not prepared to work long hours on the case, which I know this case will involve."

"What's the problem – I thought you had some serious reservations," blurts out Matt.

"I've just said lawyers are two-a-dime, and that I've got plenty of money to buy an army of them. I'm not looking for you to do the donkey work, just to direct them. And, what the heck, I think working from home is a good idea. The jungle drums in your area work quite well, don't they?"

"Yes, they do."

"Well, there we have it – you get a fistful of dollars, work from your farmhouse for only a few hours a day, which will give you plenty of time to grow the grass or milk the cows; whatever you country folk like doing. Okay – as I was saying earlier, I've got a helicopter flight booked for half eight. The flight will take about an hour, so I'll see you at half nine. Tell Fiona I'm looking forward to those lovely oat biscuits she makes. Cheers, James," and with that he hung up.

Fiona, my wife, is standing behind me in our main reception room, where I took the call.

"That was rather brief," she said. "Did you tell that irritating man you were not interested?"

"No," I said, collapsing into a chair. "I've told him I want to work from home and only on a part-time basis."

"Did he agree?"

"Yes, but I have a feeling I will regret this decision."

She walks over to me and pats my shoulder, and with a gentle smile, turns away and walks out the room.

"He'll be here in about an hour and a half and is expecting your famous oat biscuits."

"He's out of luck, I haven't baked those in years and if I had, he wouldn't get a crumb."

The helicopter looked so incongruous against the backdrop of the beautiful Brendon Hills, our lovely old manor house and the tranquil countryside with animals grazing peacefully in the fields. All remaining leaves are torn from the trees and every leaf within a hundred-metre radius of the helicopter are swirled up into a dancing and writhing tornado; oh, what a price we pay for our modern conveniences.

I usher Matt and his entourage of five PR people into our main reception room where Fiona is waiting to receive them, while Matt and I retire to my study to look at the summons he has received.

The summons has been issued on behalf of Professor Peter Metcalfe, who is the sole complainant. He is the head of the Advanced Business Metrics department at the University of Bristol. However, in this matter, it appears he does not enjoy the tacit backing of the University; otherwise I would have expected them to be co-complainants. The absence of co-complainants presents an interesting situation. First, as an individual, can the Professor afford to bring a case of this magnitude to court. I point this out to Matt, telling him that on this basis alone, I could probably have the case thrown out as an individual would find it difficult raising the securities necessary to pay total costs, which could run into millions should they not win, or even to pay their own legal bill if no definite decision can be reached. Matt goes almost apoplectic.

"Can't you see, James, this case offers the marketing community the best opportunity to present their case to the world in what will be the biggest and most publicised court case of all time. We're gonna win this case and come out of it smelling sweeter than roses. We couldn't have asked for a better opportunity, even if we'd contrived it ourselves. I don't care if I have to underwrite this fellow myself. Don't, for God's sake, make him scared and get him running for the hills!"

"Matt, this is a question that has to be asked. Any half competent Judge is going to ask for adequate securities to be lodged before the case even comes close to court."

"Okay, but your job is to make sure that this case comes to court and my PR gurus, sitting in the room next door, have to make sure it's the most publicised event in business history. Oh… and don't forget you also have to win the case," says Matt calming down.

"I take it that you have already done some preliminary investigations into the Professor's background and that of his department?" I enquire.

"You bet your cotton socks I have – not that it's thorough at this stage."

"The Professor is your typical boring academic. His entire business career has been in a sheltered university environment where he hasn't lit any fires. He's certainly a prolific writer, if nothing else. He's produced hundreds of papers and presentations all based on his hybrid thinking, which combines the ideas of Intellectual Capital and The Balanced Scorecard to produce new management metrics, which I think is a load of baloney. He has been able to build a small but loyal support base, mainly amongst academia. He does enjoy some limited business support. No doubt the department's sponsors count among them."

"How is the department funded?" I enquire.

"The bulk of its funding comes from two fairly substantial businesses, who have both been financing the department for the past three years," continues Matt.

"Do these sponsors, assuming they are backing him in this matter as they would appear to be the most likely candidates, have sufficient substance to foot a multi-million pound legal bill?" I ask Matt.

"You tell me. The first is Earth Energy, a massive ethanol and methanol producer from South Africa providing almost 7% of the globe's supplies, with their head office based in London. The other sponsor is NewMech, a large, privately-funded manufacturer of electronically and pneumatically controlled mechanical devices, with massive MOD contracts. It appears they specialise in military solutions. They're based in Manchester," Matt concludes.

"Sounds like they have very deep pockets. Interesting that neither the University nor anybody else is prepared to be co-complainants? What's in it for his financial backers, assuming there are some, and that this isn't a horrible hoax? Why risk multiple millions on fighting a damage claim of only two million pounds to go to the department, on a messy case that probably won't have any clear cut rulings? Strange – very strange," I remark.

"You're not a marketing man are you, James – free publicity on a scale money can't buy!" says Matt.

"Sure, Matt – publicity and a potential payback for the parties directly involved, but not their sleeping partners."

"What do I care about them – as long as this action comes to court, and we win – that's all that matters."

"I'll need to speak to the Professor once I've read and digested this summons," I say.

"I'm not going to tell you how to do your job, James, but don't let this fellow get cold feet!"

Matt leaves me to join his PR cronies. I start reading through the summons and all the legal jargon to make sure what Matt had told me during our telephone call the day before was correct. In essence, the Professor is bringing a class action, on behalf of the business community, against the marketing profession represented by the Global Marketing Association, for what he claims are 'grossly inadequate and ineffective performance measurement standards, which allow marketers to squander critical resources under their direct and indirect control, to the direct disadvantage of the business and thus the wider business community'. The 'damage' claim of two million pounds is to be paid to the department to help them further their research into solutions which will supposedly address these problems.

I swing my chair around and stare out over the beautiful countryside, hoping to draw inspiration from the lovely scene that lies before me. I have a beautiful study. It was probably what attracted me most to this house in the first place. It has a huge bay window overlooking the sprawling front lawns. Beyond the lawns are fields with grazing cattle and sheep. To the left is a small forest and to the right you can catch a glimpse of the rolling Brendon Hills. You cannot imagine a more beautiful setting! The study itself has a high ceiling and is lined with bookshelves. It has such a warm and welcoming feeling. My large, oak desk and leather chair are placed close to the window, so all I have to do is swivel my chair and gaze out over the countryside to draw on its inspiration; something I felt I had to do right now, as I have a fundamental concern regarding this case which needs answering. This case will deal with highly contentious 'grey areas' within business, and as a consequence, the probabilities of drawing clear cut black-and-white resolutions are extremely remote. I don't think you have to be too astute to realise this, so what's it all about? Matt is probably right when he said it's just the stage for a huge PR campaign. If that's the case, I can understand what's in it for the Professor, but not his backers. If they are so passionate about their cause, you would think that they would want to stand up and be counted. After all, it's their money at risk. Why risk so much for little, or no apparent gain? In my opinion, it would be easier and probably a lot less expensive, if they just gave the department the two million pounds and let the Professor get on with his research. It doesn't make sense, but then perhaps I'm jumping the gun in making some of these assumptions – I need to talk to the Professor first and establish a few facts.

Just then the door bursts open and in storms Fiona in a furious mood.

"That irritating little man is now treating me like a servant. Fiona, my girl, rustle up another pot of coffee and cookies," she says, trying to imitate Matt's American accent. "What's more, I think they are expecting me to prepare lunch for them, which is nonsense as I was given little notice of the arrival of this horde. One or two people maybe, but not nine!"

"Don't worry, my dear, I will chat to Matt and sort this out. I'm certainly not expecting you to wait on these people."

"The worst is still to come," she says. "I think some of them are expecting to stay and work from the house with you."

"Oh, my God, no," I say. "Our little piece of Heaven has now been invaded by Hell!"

"That's the problem with Matt," she says, "he's too sneaky. He tries to get you to do things for him by not telling you all the facts, or conveniently forgetting about them."

"Perhaps you have a point," I say, reflecting on the thoughts I've just had. What if Matt had contrived this whole thing? Let's face it, he hasn't always played straight. People like him bend the rules to suit themselves: play a little dirty. Suppose the marketing community spends a couple of million on a contrived case like this, making sure they win it. They look good on the international stage and returns for them would be astronomical, possibly in the order of multiple billions – most attractive indeed! If this is the case, I'll have no part in this charade, no matter how big my payday may be!

"My dear, would you be so kind as to ask Matt to join me in the study?"

Fiona nods and disappears down the corridor. A few minutes later I'm joined by Matt.

"Well, chum, anything interesting to report?"

"Matt, I need a straight answer to a straight question. Are you in any way connected, no matter how remotely, to the party or parties bringing these charges against the GMA?"

"What! Have you lost your marbles – bringing charges against my own organisation? What the hell got you to ask such a dumb question, James?"

"It's quite simple, Matt, all you have to do is spend five million pounds or so to get international publicity worth hundreds of millions, and then manipulate the results to achieve a positive outcome worth billions to marketers worldwide," I say.

"And how am I supposed to manipulate the results of a proceeding conducted in an open and fair court?" asks Matt.

"Our legal system is based on the principle of adversarial parties, so it doesn't function effectively when a party's interests are represented on both sides; hardly fair and definitely not open," I remark.

"Well, let me give you my categorical assurance, I'm in no way whatsoever linked or associated with the Professor and the action he has bought against the GMA. Is that good enough for you?" he replies.

"I also give you my categorical assurance that if at any stage I learn that you or any of your associates are involved in any way, I will withdraw from the case immediately."

"Why's the suspicion fallen on me and my associates?" asks Matt.

"Until the motives of the complainant's backers are known, we remain in the dark and consequently, our case is the weaker for it," I reply.

"But we do know their objective – it's to get two million bucks from us by proving marketing squanders resources under their control," replies Matt in a frustrated manner.

"Sure, we know the charges we have to disprove, but had, for example, you been the backer, the motives would have been entirely different and the case would have taken different and unexpected turns," I explained.

"Aren't you making a mountain out of a molehill, James? Your job is to make sure we disprove the charges irrespective of the backer's motives, assuming the Professor has financial backers; perhaps he is a man of financial substance?"

"You are right, but I like to know as much about my adversaries as possible, to help minimise the unexpected," I reply. "Moving on, Matt, there are a few other issues we need to address…"

"Yeah sure, James, I had meant to discuss your package with you first thing but got swept away with other issues. I would like to offer you double your daily rate, beginning from today until the case is concluded, based on a five-day week, irrespective of how many hours you work a day. Therefore, you get paid if you don't work any particular day or only a few hours in that day. In addition to this, I'm offering you a minimum bonus of one million pounds for a favourable outcome. I'm not looking for a clear cut win, as I know that may be difficult, but what I want is for marketing to come out looking good. In fact, depending on how good you make us look, your bonus could easily be doubled!"

"Your offer is most generous Matt, but I had wanted to speak to you about more mundane issues."

"Oh – about what?" he enquires.

"Catering and accommodation facilities," I reply.

"What about them?" he responds.

"I don't provide either of them in this house. You may not be aware of the fact that we don't employ any servants, apart from a young lass who comes in once a week in the morning to help Fiona with certain household chores. I don't expect Fiona to play servant to colleagues of mine, so our ability to cater and accommodate is extremely limited, despite the apparent size of the house. You also know how house proud Fiona is; everything has to be spick-and-span and nothing out of place, or woe betide the person who upsets her universe," I explain.

"So what you're saying is we ain't getting any lunch," jokes Matt.

"You may use the house as an office, as we have four reception rooms ideal for purpose, but nothing else. Your team will have to feed and accommodate themselves. What's more, the house is out-of-bounds after office hours. I don't want our privacy invaded; that would be worse than returning to the office," I explain, laying down the law.

"Fair enough," says Matt, "just point us in the right direction. I'm sure there must be local pubs and B&Bs that will only be too pleased for our business."

"I'm not that well-connected with our local community, but Fiona is – she will be able to put you in contact with the right people, or better still, she can arrange things for you; she's a great organiser. I will have a chat with her right now," I say, rising to my feet and making my way to the 'Morning Room'. The 'Morning Room', so named by my Fiona, is a beautiful little room on the ground floor that catches the morning sun, which she has turned into her studio and sanctuary where she paints and writes.

I meet her in the corridor. "I've made lunch for everybody," she says.

"You shouldn't have done that. I've just told Matt that he and his colleagues will have to fend for themselves," I say.

"In future they will have to, but I can't let guests starve in my house," she says. "I haven't prepared much, just a few open sandwiches with cheese and biscuits."

"Sounds delightful," I say, "I will let Matt know. Can you please do me a favour? After lunch, can you discuss their accommodation and catering requirements for the next few days, and if possible, arrange that these be met by local people? I'm sure the local village pub will be only too pleased to deliver cooked lunches here daily?"

Fiona agrees to make the arrangements, pleased in the knowledge that she's getting rid of Matt. I inform everybody that lunch is being served.

After lunch, I return to my study to phone the Professor.

It takes me numerous attempts and considerable time to get eventually through.

"Hello, is that Professor Peter Metcalfe of the Advanced Business Metrics Department?" I ask.

"Yes, it is," he replies.

"Good afternoon, Professor, my name is James Barton-Marshall, I'm a solicitor representing the legal interests of the Global Marketing Association."

"Oh, I see," replies the Professor, "and what can I do for you?"

"I wish to inform you that my client intends to defend the action brought by you against them. I will notify you and the court officially of our intention to do so. However, part of legal council's duty is to see if the matter can be amicably settled out-of-court," I say.

"I have no interest in going to court; I'm only interested in the outcome. So, if your client is prepared to admit publicly to the charges and to donate two million pounds to the department, I guess I won't see you in Court. But if, on the other hand, they aren't, then I suppose I will see you there," responds the Professor in a self-assured manner.

Not wishing to rise to the bait and his pompous attitude, I move on, "Professor, I note that you are the only complainant."

"That's correct," he replies.

"The likelihood of this being a costly and drawn out affair is particularly high, with costs easily running into multiple millions. As an individual, will you be in a position to post adequate securities to cover these potential costs, because, if you can't, we won't meet in court," I explain.

"Mr. ah…" says the Professor struggling to remember my name.

"James Barton-Marshall," I reply rather coolly.

"Ah, yes," he says continuing, "please don't try to patronise me, I'm not some absent-minded Professor unwise to the realities of the real world. I would hardly institute such proceedings without adequate funding."

"The issue is not so much about whether you have funds to meet your expenses, but rather ours as well. I will call for adequate securities to be lodged with the court as a pre-condition to us entering a defence," I assure the Professor.

"Don't worry, Mr. Barton-Marshall, I have sufficient financial resources to pay your salary in the most unlikely event that this action goes pear-shape, for me," he reassures me.

"I'm pleased to hear that, Professor Metcalfe. You are most fortunate in having backers with such deep pockets, particularly as the University is not backing you in this action."

"Universities are generally very conservative and don't want to become embroiled in contentious, controversial and possibly expensive lawsuits," responds the Professor.

"I understand that, Professor, but for the same reasons why should anybody else want to back your cause?" I enquire.

"Simple – a strong belief in what I'm doing," responds the Professor.

"If this is the case, why don't they publicly back you by being co-complainants?" I enquire further.

"No business wants to be seen to be taking sides on controversial business issues; it's bad PR. However, these businesses want to see the boundaries of business expanded. They want us to drop the legacy of our outdated and antiquated measuring standards, which served the Industrial Age adequately, but are totally inappropriate in our modern world," remarks the Professor becoming most animated. Now was probably the best time to get him to open up and reveal as much about his backers as possible.

"You make a good point, Professor, but it must have taken a lot of effort on your part to get them to place such vast amounts of money at risk for no direct gain?"

"These are big companies, so a few million is small change to help a cause that will ultimately benefit mankind," he responds.

"Having dealt with many large corporations over my long career, I know very few to be that philanthropic, so I don't under-estimate your obvious efforts in getting them to underwrite this action."

"As you know, in the academic world it's a matter of 'publish or perish', and I've published and published. I've also done my fair share of presentations around the world at all major conventions, but to what avail? I've had little or no impact on changing the business mindset. Therefore, about a year ago, I approached the chair's sponsors to fund this legal action which I'm now bringing against the GMA. The idea was initially not well received by either sponsor. However, about a month ago and almost within weeks of one another, both sponsors had a complete change of heart and have actively encouraged me to pursue the matter to its full conclusion. I have their full and unfettered financial support."

"Are you referring to Earth Energy and NewMech as your sponsors?" I enquire.

"I am," he says, "not that they want to be publicly associated with this action and will deny any such involvement."

Having got what I wanted from the call I decided to end it.

"Thank you, Professor, for your time, I have found our chat to be most informative, and I look forward to meeting you in court shortly."

"It's not a meeting you will relish, Sir. I have made this subject my life's work and if anybody can make these charges stick it's me, with the support of a good legal team," he says most confidently, "and may the best arguments win. Good day to you, Sir."

I put the receiver down and turn to look out the window. It's just after three o'clock, yet the autumn shadows stretch far across the front lawn. Each day seems to be getting rapidly shorter.

I'm pleased I had a chat with the Professor, as it has given me a lot more confidence in knowing how I will handle this case and what to expect from the competition. Not that the task ahead will be easy or pleasant; I will have to plough through every one of the Professor's papers and presentations to know where he will be coming from. Fortunately, time will be on my side as this case will take many months, perhaps years before coming to court. I will quickly brief Matt on the outcome of my telephone conversation with the Professor, so that hopefully he and his team will leave us for the evening. It's been a long day and I will certainly be pleased to see the back of Matt and his party.

The main reception room where Matt and his PR team have set themselves up is a hive of activity. Everybody appears to be on their mobile phone, chatting away at the top of their voices while simultaneously tapping away on their laptops. Bedlam probably describes the scene better. Each of these PR executives represents a different company and are apparently top dogs of their respective businesses, or very senior members of staff. Why so many experts and from different businesses escapes me. I would have to put it down to how Matt operates; everything has to be done on a bigger-than-life scale for him.

I catch Matt's eye as he paces in front of the window chatting on his mobile.

"Hello, James," he says ending his conversation and walking across to talk to me, "we've had a busy but successful day. We've got some phenomenal international coverage for this case, which has exceeded my wildest expectations. The guys here have done an exceptional job; worth a good celebration in the pub tonight."

"I'm pleased to hear that, Matt. I just wanted to brief you on the outcome of my conversation with the Professor." While briefing him, I get the distinct impression he's only listening with one ear as he tries to eavesdrop the conversation of his PR team.

"Good," he says when I had finished. "I'm pleased to hear the Professor can pay his own way; one less thing to worry about."

"I should have sufficient time to prepare for this case," I say confidently.

"Don't know about that," replies Matt.

"What do you mean?" I demand.

"Well, I have been able to pull a few strings and call in a few favours, and as a result, our case will be heard in a month or so," he replies, rather full of himself.

I suppose I should be angry and annoyed with him as he doesn't bother to hear the outcome of my conversation with the Professor before arranging to jump the queue and get our case heard before others, who have probably been waiting a year or more. What's the point – this is Matt through and through.

Sensing my annoyance, Matt responds by saying, "We must strike while the iron's hot for maximum effect. People lose interest when things drag on. I have to do whatever I can to move things forward as quickly as possible – you understand, James?"

I nod.

"Now, you're not going to have a lot of time on your hands to prepare for this case, so what I have done is arranged for a top-class young lawyer to assist you. The person I have in mind is an up and coming young man I met about a month or so ago. He's bright and as sharp as a razor; he reminds me of a younger version of you, except he's probably a lot smarter and definitely a lot better looking," he says jokingly. "His name is Richard Petrada," he says continuing, "and he will be here first thing tomorrow morning."

"So I have no choice in deciding who will assist me," I query, becoming annoyed at his exceedingly dictatorial manner.

"No… no," protests Matt, "you have free rein in deciding who you want on your team. All I'm asking is that you consider this guy because I think he will be a huge asset."

"I'll give him a try," I say, dreading having to deal with a bumptious, up-and-coming Whiz Kid – the type that generally appeals to Matt.

"We'll be finishing here shortly," says Matt. "Fiona has organised accommodation for us at the local pub in Wiveliscombe. We're being picked up within the next twenty minutes or so. Why don't you and Fiona join us for dinner tonight?"

"Thanks, but no thanks," I say, knowing how Fiona would never forgive me if I accepted. Anyway, I'm feeling tired and want some time to myself to reflect on the days proceedings.

"You're probably right," remarks Matt, "we all need an early bed. It's been a successful day but the next few days and weeks are going to be hectic. I'm going to Exeter first thing in the morning. I may call in on my way back to London."

Early next morning while it was still dark, I was woken by somebody knocking on the front door. I quickly slipped on my dressing gown and slippers, and made my way downstairs to our reception hall.

Standing in front of me was a young man in his late twenties or early thirties. If there is a 'tall, dark and handsome' stereotype, I couldn't think of a better candidate. This young man had a broad smile on his face as he came to attention, bowed slightly and extended his hand in greeting.

"Good morning, Sir, are you Mr. James Barton-Marshall?" he enquires.

"Yes, I am," I reply.

"Apologies for waking you so early, Sir. My name is Richard Petrada and I have been instructed by Mr. Matt Todd to make my services available to you first thing this morning."

"Please come in, Richard. Would you like something warm to drink?"

"Thank you, Sir that would be much appreciated. May I first collect my briefcase from the car?" he enquires.

I nod approvingly and he returns to his car parked in the driveway. I was struck by the modest car he drove – a late model two-door Vauxhall Astra. Normally, youngsters in his position would be driving the latest, biggest and fastest BMW. So far, he seems to be the complete opposite of what I had expected. I believe first impressions are important and this young man has impressed me. He comes across as a friendly and likeable person. On his return, I lead him through the house to our large kitchen. A few minutes later, Fiona joined us. When she entered the room Richard jumped to his feet, came to attention and bowed slightly.

"Good morning, ma'am," he says before I have had the opportunity to introduce him.

"Fiona, this is Richard Petrada, the young man that comes highly recommended by Matt, possibly to assist me on the GMA case."

"I see," she says sounding rather cool; being suspicious of any of Matt's recommendations. "Where have you travelled from this morning?" she enquires of him.

"From London, ma'am," he says still standing to attention.

"You must have left rather early?" Fiona remarks.

"I left at four, ma'am."

"You're probably a little hungry then? Would you like some breakfast?" she enquires.

"I do not wish to be an imposition, ma'am," he says.

"Nonsense," she says, "James and I haven't eaten and one more mouth to feed is hardly an imposition."

"Thank you, ma'am, you are most kind."

"It's nothing," she says, "sit down and continue your conversation with James."

I wanted to find out a little more about Richard. For one thing, he had the hint of an American accent, an unusual surname and certainly rather pedantic and outdated manners, no matter how flattering and charming they are.

"Can you tell me a little about yourself, Richard?"

"Yes, certainly, Sir," he replies. "I attended the Johnston Military Academy in New York for six years, where I completed my schooling. In my final year, I was fortunate enough to be awarded the Dr Charles Levinson bursary, which enabled me to study a course of my choosing at a university of my choice, anywhere in the world. I chose to read for a business degree at Oxford University with the intention of furthering my studies in law. On completing my Bachelor's degree in Economics and Management, I was awarded the Dr Charles Levinson bursary for post-graduate study. I then read for a Bachelor of Civil Law degree at Oxford, which I was fortunate to be awarded. I then left full-time university education to become a freelance solicitor, while studying part-time for my MBA at the London Business School, for which I was awarded my degree three years ago. Over this period, I remained a freelance solicitor specialising in business matters. This is how I came in contact with Mr. Todd."

"What academic results did you achieve?" enquires Fiona.

"I was fortunate enough to be awarded summa cum laude for both my Economics and Law degree and cum laude for my MBA."

Fiona raises her eyebrows. "Those are impressive results," she remarks.

"Achieved through hard work, not through intellect," Richard responds in a friendly, joking manner.

"Oh, I don't think so. My many years as a lecturer tell me that such results are only achieved through a healthy combination of the two," she replies. I nod in full agreement with Fiona's sentiment on the matter.

"What family do you have, Richard?" I enquire, continuing my interrogation.

"My parents, together with my brother and sister, live in New York. We are a very close-knit family but not particularly well-off. Consequently, I am paying for both my brother and sister's university education."

"That's a heavy burden for a sibling to carry," interrupts Fiona.

"No burden," replies Richard, "it's a privilege to be able to help bring up siblings. Few people get given the opportunity to help bring up two families in their life, as I hope to do. I was fortunate enough to be given bursaries to further my education, which neither my brother nor sister have been given; so the least I can do is give them the opportunity of a decent education."

"That's most admirable," remarks Fiona. "Are you married?" she enquires further.

"No, ma'am, but I am courting a young lady who one day, when I'm in a financial position to do so, I would like to marry."

"Does your young lady know you are financing your brother and sister?" enquires Fiona.

"Yes, she understands my position and fully supports me."

"She sounds like a young lady of exceptional moral standing," said Fiona.

"Yes – she is somebody rather special," says Richard.

Fiona started serving breakfast, which gave me a few minutes to reflect on this young man, and what he had said so far. It appears that he has the appropriate academic qualifications together with a few years practical experience under his belt, but Matt wants him to be my right-hand man. I know of a few people I could rely on, so why take any chances? Perhaps he is extraordinarily good, in which case I mustn't miss the opportunity. Eventually, in making this decision, there has to be a leap of faith; faith in one individual over another. Choosing the known is playing it 'safe'. Business today is about pushing the boundaries, about going beyond what is 'safe'; trying new ideas, concepts, individuals and approaches. Every facet of business needs to embrace this approach if it is to excel; the legal department and its advisors are not precluded from this process. Therefore, perhaps, I'm morally bound to my client to give Richard a chance? It would certainly be the ideal opportunity for an up-and-coming young solicitor to make a name for himself. Furthermore, my career is almost at an end, so if things don't go that well, I haven't a lot to lose! I can afford to be riskier.

When we finished breakfast, Richard jumped to his feet and started clearing away the plates to Fiona's protestation.

"What do you think you are doing?" she demands in a rather indignant manner.

"I'm helping to clear and wash up," he replies in a surprised manner, as if it was the expected thing to do.

"Don't worry, Richard," replies Fiona, sensing his genuine willingness to help, "I have a dishwasher."

"Can I help by stacking it?" he enquires.

"You may certainly do that if you wish, but please don't feel obliged," says Fiona.

"No, ma'am, I'm used to doing household chores and don't find them that much of a drudgery."

Richard busies himself clearing away the plates. When he was out of earshot, Fiona leaned over towards me and whispered, "James, please pinch me – I must be in a dream, this young man seems too good to be true."

I smiled; what if he was everything he appeared to be? What a boon he would be to me.

"Richard, before I make any decisions regarding your position on my team, I would need to evaluate your work and ascertain how well we might work together. I'm sure Matt has already offered you a role and an attractive remuneration package, but I must make you aware that his offer is subject to my approval. Matt may pay the bills, but on this team I call the shots; my decisions are final."

"I understand this relationship perfectly," replies Richard.

"Good! In which case we should waste no further time," I reply. "What I suggest is that you take the Professor's first and last published papers, summarise their salient points, noting any changes in thinking or anything else that you may think will be useful in this case. I will do the same and compare notes, to see just how closely aligned our thinking is."

"I already have copies of all the Professor's published work, including all presentations he has given," Richard said. "I have also started summarising his early published papers and have completed several of them."

"Excellent," I remark. "Let me show you to one of our studies which you may use as your office. You may as well get stuck in straight away, as I can tell you are not one to sit around."

Richard's analysis of the Professor's work was both incisive and insightful. This young man is clearly very bright. He also works at breakneck speed and appears to be extremely well organised. I had no doubts about confirming his appointment with Matt that afternoon on Matt's return from

Exeter. Matt was probably right when he said Richard would prove an invaluable member of the team. What also impressed me was how well he handled Matt. Matt's high energy and demanding personality can often fluster people, yet Richard had the knack of calming him down.

Fortunately, Matt only popped in for a few minutes on his way back to London, much to the delight of Fiona.

Fiona had also offered to accommodate Richard for the duration of the case, which was rather an unusual turn up for the books; our house has seldom, if ever, been made available to business acquaintances. She was obviously very impressed with him and believed he would be no imposition. That's the way I felt anyway. I was feeling confident and upbeat that Richard and I would work well as a team, that he would take a lot of pressure off me, and as a consequence, I would enjoy this case.

Chapter Two

The past month seems to have flown by. Richard has lived up to my high expectations; no, he has well exceeded them. His organisational skills are exceptional. He and his team have produced excellent results, freeing me to consider the wider issues of the case. This has probably been one of the least stressful cases I have ever had to prepare for, thanks in no small part to Richard.

Richard has lived with us over this period and has almost been adopted by Fiona. She thinks the world of him, and I can understand why. He is extremely polite and respectful to everybody; so much so that I have to keep reminding myself that we are living in the twenty-first century. He's also the perfect guest. He gets up at some god forsaken hour every morning and starts work, but doesn't make a sound. In the evenings, he joins us for dinner and always tidies up afterwards. Shortly thereafter, he retires to his bedroom not to be seen or heard until the following day. In fact, he is annoyingly perfect as he keeps highlighting my shortcomings, which Fiona is quick to pick up on. If only I could keep the bedroom and bathroom as tidy as Richard. If only I would pick up things after me like Richard does. If only... I don't know how she has put up with all my shortcomings for so long - she's obviously a saint!

On most weekends, we had the pleasure of Richard's young lady-friend, Felicity Marchant, joining us. She is a petit and most attractive young lady. Well educated, articulate and graceful. She and Fiona just seemed to click from the moment they met. They would sit together for hours, often into the wee hours of the morning, engrossed in 'woman's talk' – whatever that is. I had to reprimand Fiona on a few occasions for monopolising Felicity, reminding her who Felicity had come to visit. Felicity's arrival each weekend was awaited with much anticipation by Fiona. I think Felicity enjoyed her stay with us just as much. I must admit, she did bring a sense of fun with her, livening things up and making weekends feel like a great family event. Every Saturday evening, she had us dining in our large and gracious dining room, using Fiona's finest silver and cut glass, which we never did before, preferring to eat at a table in the kitchen for convenience sake. However, as Felicity put it, "If you have it – flaunt it." Certainly, they were very pleasant evenings and something I looked forward to. She also had us taking long walks through the beautiful countryside together; walks you always promised yourself to do but never got around to doing. She was a breath of fresh air; a delight to have around. Fiona often remarked that she felt Felicity was the daughter she never had. I certainly felt a strong sense of family and enjoyment on the weekends when Felicity joined us.

Matt and his team of PR gurus appear to have been equally busy in drumming up international interest in this case. I have already given numerous telephone and personal interviews, including a couple of TV interviews, which seem to have been shown around the world an inordinate number of times. Fiona has been quick to pick up on my new found 'celebrity' status, pointing out how it opened a whole new world of career opportunities for me. With a smirk on her face and twinkle in her eye, she gleefully regales friends and family with stories of how I am eagerly awaiting my invitation to attend the next round of puerile TV celebrity shows. She tells them how well I would do in one of those survival events, knowing how much I hate camping and going without my creature comforts; particularly, my daily hot bath. She also tells them how well I would do in the cooking and dancing pageants. My culinary knowledge and abilities extend no further than switching on the toaster, and as a dancer I can assure you, I will never step on my partner's toes as I'm always stepping on my own. With great mirth and laughter, she explains how she can see many exciting opportunities opening up for me when all my awe-inspiring, latent talents are exposed in the public spotlight.

"Oh," she sighs, "now he is a celebrity he can bore the nation with less-than-competent performances in activities he is ill qualified to do, but at least he'll earn a fortune!" Never a truer word said in jest.

My opposite number in this case, Sir Michael Rifkin, has been receiving equally high media coverage. I know of Sir Michael, but not personally. According to all reports, he is one of the UK's top paid barristers. Finally, it appears, I'm moving in the right circles. Fiona muses on whether he's a good cook, dancer or survivalist. On a more serious note, the retention of Sir Michael's services certainly shows the complainant's backers are putting their money where their mouth is. We are under no illusion as to the difficulties we face from this case and the complainant's legal team, but I feel confident that we are as ready as we will ever be.

I decided that over the trial period, Richard and I would stay in Bristol rather than make the one and a half hour journey each way everyday. Richard organised a beautiful five-bedroom, Georgian house in Clifton for us. Felicity had offered to accommodate Fiona in her London apartment over this period. She had promised to take some time off from her high-powered executive job as a financial advisor in a major investment company so she and Fiona could go shopping, go to the theatre and generally enjoy the highlights of the city. Fiona was so excited about the prospect of spending so much time with Felicity that she couldn't wait for us to leave. It was arranged that on the weekends we would all meet back at our house in Somerset.

To ensure that no last minute hitches delay us, we decided to leave for Bristol the day before the trial.

Fiona came with us and we dropped her off at the railway station. From there she was to catch a train to London, and then the tube to Wimbledon where Felicity lived. After dropping off a rather excited Fiona, we made our way to Clifton, passing the courthouse on our way. I was taken aback when I saw the media activity outside. Huge scaffolding had been rigged outside the court, which extended partially down the road. There were five or six large, white, external broadcasting vans outside, with technicians swarming all over the place. Even Richard, who normally takes everything in his stride, was struck by the extent of activities, remarking on whether they were expecting a Royal wedding and had perhaps got their dates and venues mixed up. Matt was expecting favourable coverage, but this must exceed even his expectations.

When we got to the house I phoned Matt, which was part of my daily ritual. He didn't seem to be at all impressed by the extent of media activity; perhaps it was what he was expecting. He explained how there was going to be daily interviews given on the steps of the court, and that all the paraphernalia we saw was for that purpose. He had lined up numerous experts to come and discuss the case's progress on a daily basis, using the courthouse as a backdrop, in his attempt to drum up as much publicity as he could.

"James," he said, "this brings me to a very important consideration," and without pausing, he continued. "The public, and business world for that matter, have very short attention spans. Consequently, I need this case to be concluded as quickly as possible, otherwise people will lose interest in it. We need to have it all wrapped-up before Christmas because, if it drags on over the Christmas break, we will lose more than half our audience, and I don't want that to happen."

"You are such a reasonable man aren't you, Matt," I say rather sarcastically.

"Hey, James, I didn't design the human being with its short attention span; that's the fault of some higher authority. I, like you, have to live with the problem. The reality is, you've got three weeks to wrap things up!"

"May I remind you who had the case leapfrogged to the front of the queue which has now placed us in this predicament? What's more, as you are probably aware, there are two parties involved in this case. While you may pull the strings of one, the other may be a little less obliging," I remark rather angrily.

"Relax, James," he says in an irritatingly patronising way, "I have had the foresight to identify this problem and have had a chat with the other party, pointing out it is in our mutual interests to have this matter concluded before Christmas."

"What!" I bellow. "You have been colluding with the complainants?"

"That's a bit melodramatic, James," responds Matt. "All I did was get a go-between to suggest to them that it would be in our mutual PR interests to have a speedy resolution – nothing more."

"I don't agree with any form of collusion," I said.

"Oh, lighten up, James, we aren't living in the age of chivalry; today, people do whatever they have to to get results."

"I know that only too well and I think we are the worse off for it. It's really a silent form of anarchy when people think they don't have to conform to the rules, or act in an acceptable manner. This erodes the social fabric that binds us together and it ultimately leads to anarchy."

"Yeah, yeah… whatever, Professor. In the meantime, I have to make sure I'm acting in the best interests of the Association."

There was clearly no benefit in flogging this dead horse with Matt. Moral issues were never that high on his agenda. Like so many businessmen, Matt places short-term objectives above all else.

Matt and I continued our daily update. He explained who has to prepare and do the regular press updates. This is a PR campaign on a huge scale. Although the cameras are not allowed into court, Matt is planning on feeding the media an almost blow-by-blow account of proceedings. He has everything planned and choreographed to the very last detail.

That evening, I decided to retire early and ponder the major issues of the case, as I have done with every major case I have ever handled. It gives me the opportunity to refresh my mind and focus on the key issues.

Over the past two decades, marketing's influence has been on the wane. This has, to a large extent, been due to their apparent lack of financial accountability, which has resulted in their marginalisation as a discipline. One of the key issues is to determine whether this is a business or marketing problem. Business believes it's a marketing problem, hence this court action, while marketing flounders without any direction on the matter. The other important issue is to determine whether the functions of marketing are becoming less relevant in the eyes of the business community and if so, whether this is a marketing problem or are there other, deeper-rooted problems facing business? The Global Marketing Association, or GMA, stands accused of being 'irrelevant and a squanderer of critical resources' by the business community. The primary claim is that of being 'irrelevant', and the second claim is for being 'a squanderer of critical resources'.

The outcome of this action will have a profound influence on business, resulting in fundamental change. Matt hopes that it will elevate the role of marketing and believes that this action is the best thing that could possibly happen to marketing. Now they can appear in a court of law, where under critical scrutiny, they can restore their good name and return to the boardroom to fulfil their rightful role in business. I can certainly sympathise with Matt because before they were officially charged, marketing was being marginalised, excluded from the decision-making process and generally scoffed at for 'not pulling their weight'. Their stature and good standing have rapidly declined. It's best that it's been brought to a head so that marketing can stand up, in front of all, and set the record straight. I believe this to be in the best interests of all.

The big day has finally arrived. Richard and I decide to leave early, in the hope of avoiding city traffic and possible congestion outside the courthouse. Our assessment proved correct. The crowd was enormous. I never imagined that this matter would catch the general public's interest on a scale capable of generating a crowd of this magnitude. I can only assume that they are associated with the media in some way or another. If this is the case, Matt and his PR team appears to have been very successful in their endeavours.

We met Matt in the foyer of the courthouse after passing through some rather strict security measures. He was busy marshalling his minions.

"Hello, James and Richard!" he bellows. "Welcome to the big event."

"That's no exaggeration," I reply.

"Yes, I am particularly pleased with the support we have received. All the major news networks and specialised media are represented here today. We are now relying on you two guys to produce the goodies – don't let me down," and with that he rushed off, waving his hand in farewell.

The courtroom is abuzz with the crowd anxiously awaiting the arrival of Judge William Harris and the commencement of this historic case. The door behind the judge's bench in this modest, fairly modern courtroom bursts open and in strides Judge Harris with a face like thunder. All I know about the man is that he has been a High Court Judge in the Chancery Division for many years and during his illustrious career, has presided over some very important cases and been responsible for numerous landmark rulings. He's a bright cookie, very astute but rather ill-tempered and cantankerous. He's a non-conformist and does things his own way, 'taking no bull from anybody'. He's an old man, big-framed and rather rotund. His size and mannerisms make him a little intimidating.

In civil litigation cases, it is common that they are only heard and judged by the presiding Judge, without any jury. In this instance, even although the damages claim is large, it has been decided that Judge Harris, due to his experience, will be the sole judge and jury.

After a few court formalities where the case is read out, Judge Harris gestures towards me and in a most informal manner mumbles, "Okay, man, get on with it."

I stand up and start addressing the court with my opening argument.

"My Lord, my client stands falsely accused of being irrelevant and a squanderer of critical resources. They stand before you today not because of any failings on their part, but rather because of the failings of the business community. My client is the victim and not the perpetrator of this crime. And, yes – it's a crime that they are seen, by some, as being irrelevant and a squanderer of critical resources.

"My case rests on the fact that the business community is using an entirely inappropriate measurement standard namely, the Accounting Model, to evaluate my client's actions and performance, and that it's this measurement standard that should be on trial and not my client. I will prove this to you, beyond a shadow of doubt!

"If I may draw a simple analogy between sport and business to demonstrate my point. Business is made up of different disciplines, such as Production, Distribution, Marketing, etcetera, just as sport has many different disciplines. However, when you play football, for example, you don't use the rules of cricket to play and referee the game. If you did, this would raise the question, are the footballers poor football players or are the rules totally inappropriate? The answer to that question is obvious; in a similar way, so too are the rules governing Marketing inappropriate."

On sitting down, Sir Michael Rifkin rises to his feet to address the court with his opening argument.

"I'm confused, as no doubt you are, My Lord. I think our Honourable colleague of the Defence is trying to mislead us with his sports analogy. A business is a single unit, or team, playing the sport of 'making a profit' against its competitors in the market. The rules that govern this game are the measurement of profit. It would be absurd, using his sports analogy, to have a different set of rules for say a football winger than the rest of the team. My learned friend would have us put a business institution – the Accounting Model – on trial. Surely not? It's the cornerstone of what we know and do in business. The whole purpose of business is to make a profit. Everything we do in business is geared around this objective. Does Defence counsel want Marketing to be treated differently? Not to be held financially accountable – how absurd! My case rests on the simple premise that all disciplines are financially accountable and responsible for generating profits, and that Marketing, in particular, is not rising to the occasion," and with that he sat down.

"The Claimants council has just highlighted one of the major problems we face and that is, we accept the Accounting Model unquestioningly, irrespective of whether or not it is an appropriate measurement standard," I replied, standing. "I will show you, over the course of these proceedings, that you don't have to follow the Accounting Model blindly to achieve the profit objective. There are other, more appropriate methods for achieving this objective, but few, if any, question the validity of our Accounting Model, believing it to be the only solution. This goes to the very heart of the claim my client faces and that is, our current measurement standards are inappropriate for measuring my client's and other disciplines performance."

"I would now like to call my first witness, Professor Walters, Head of the Accounting department at Dewberry College, and a renowned expert on accounting practice," I announce.

"Professor, can every business process be measured in financial terms?"

"No, certainly not!" asserts the Professor.

"As a rule of thumb, could you perhaps tell me how many processes can be measured?" I ask.

"That would be difficult to say. It would depend on each business," replies the Professor.

"I agree, but I asked for an average or rule of thumb."

"No such thing," smirks the Professor.

"In recent research conducted by Arthur Andersen of some 3,500 businesses, it was found that Book Value, that is, the value ascribed to the business by our Accounting Model, represented less than 20% of Market Value, that is, the value ascribed to the business by its shareholders. Using this research, could we not infer that our Accounting Model only measures a similar number of business processes?" I asked the Professor.

"Well, I don't know. You could probably use it as a rough guide, but it has no more value than that," he replies.

"We'll do just that and use it as a rough guide," I said. "So, as a rough guide, we only measure and manage a small percentage of our business processes using the Accounting Model."

"Professor, do you accept that the processes we cannot measure add significant value to the business?"

"Yes! We in the accounting profession have for a long time stated that financial results only show part of the picture," he replies.

"Only a very small part, it would appear," I remark. "And why is this true? I will argue that it is because financial profit is not the common denominator of business."

"Professor, is financial profit a value creation process? In other words, is it about adding value to what we already have?" I ask.

"Yes, in a sense that profit is the value you add to your financial capital," he replies.

"Right – so profit is a value creation process. Could we then not argue that businesses are only successful when they add value to what they already have?"

Professor replies, "I only specialise in the field of accounting so I don't think I'm qualified to answer this question except to say that it makes sense, because profit is generated through the underlying value of the business and if that's weakened, then profit is in jeopardy."

"So if businesses are only successful when they add value to what they already have, that means each business process needs to add value to be successful. Value creation is therefore the common purpose of all business processes, so value creation is the common denominator of business. Would you agree with this, Professor?"

"Objection!" shouts Sir Michael. "I'm not sure where this is leading, but you cannot just draw unsubstantiated conclusions and ask the Professor's opinion, because he has already stated he's not qualified in fields other than accounting."

"Sustained," mumbles the Judge, gesturing with his hands.

"I'm not asking for the Professor's professional opinion, I'm asking for his personal opinion. I accept the Professor may not be an expert, but he certainly qualifies in terms of providing an informed, personal opinion," I explain.

"Continue," mumbles the Judge.

"Erh, yes, I can see the logic of your argument. Value creation could be seen as the common denominator of business," replies the Professor.

"Professor, I know you are not an expert witness, but in your opinion, as value creation appears to be the common denominator of business, wouldn't it make sense that we attempt to measure our business processes in accordance with a value creation measure?"

"Well, yes, but I'm not sure how practical that would be," he replies hesitantly.

"Professor, I will call witnesses that disagree with your opinion and think that measuring and managing the value creation process is entirely practical and feasible, but that it does require an entirely different mindset and a complete paradigm-shift in our thinking," I reply.

"I would now like to move on to another line of questioning," I announce.

"Professor, is it at all possible that business can make a financial profit yet destroy underlying value?"

"Umhh, yes, that is possible," he replies.

"And, Professor, would it be possible for business to create underlying value yet show a financial loss?"

"Yes, that could also be possible," he replies.

"So, from your comments I can conclude that there is no correlation between financial profit and value creation."

"Yes, that would be correct," the Professor replies.

"Earlier you agreed that businesses are only successful when they add value to what they already have, and that by inference, value creation is the primary objective of business, yet you have just confirmed that there is no correlation between financial measures and value creation. That means, we have no way of telling if we're successful or not in adding value because the Accounting Model masks reality."

"No, the generation of profit is the most important aspect of business," retorts the Professor.

"That's correct, Professor, the generation of profit is the most important aspect of business, but as you agreed earlier, profit is a value creation process. I'm not challenging the fundamental premise of business, all I'm asking is how best do we achieve the profit objective; through a financial or value creation perspective? You yourself have already admitted that our financial model is exclusive, whereas value creation is fully inclusive, and therefore more representative of business performance. It would therefore appear to me that we should adopt a value creation perspective rather than a financial perspective in measuring and managing our profit objective," I reply.

"Yes," replies the Professor, "but I did say value creation measurements would be difficult if not impossible!"

"That's your opinion, Professor, with which I strongly differ and will call witnesses to back up my contention."

"Thank you for your time, Professor. I will summarise what we have agreed with you. First, our financial measures only measure a small portion of business activity. As a result, it gives us a poor reflection of true market value. The processes that are not measured can, and do add value, as evidenced in the chasm that exists between Book and Market value. Second, financial measures are not the common denominator of business and therefore, cannot be used to measure value creation. Yet, we agreed that businesses are only successful when they add value to what they already have, meaning we have to measure all business processes to evaluate value, but we cannot use the Accounting Model for this purpose. Third, there is no correlation between financial measures and value creation. That means financial measures mask value creation activities, so we could impede or even destroy value without knowing it, thereby destroying or limiting underlying value, which sustains future wealth creation. Thank you, Professor, no more questions."

"Professor," said Sir Michael rising to his feet, "what you're saying is that the financial model, or our Accounting Model, is our only universally-recognised measurement standard, and that it is on this standard and nothing else business performance is evaluated. Yes or no?"

"Yes, but…" replies the Professor before he is interrupted by Sir Michael.

"I only asked for a yes or no. Thank you, Professor, that's all."

Over the next days and weeks, Richard and I present what we believe to be a strong case, supporting our supposition regarding the declining relevance of the Accounting Model; presenting research and comments made by eminent people and organisations within the accounting and financial sectors on the subject. I include a summarised version of these submissions so that you may judge for yourself how the Accounting Model is becoming less and less relevant as a measurement standard for business.

- Research by Arthur Andersen of 3,500 companies revealed that the balance sheet explained 95% of market value in 1978. However, by 1998, it only explained 28% of market value and by 2001, this had fallen to only 15%.

- "There are going to be a lot of problems in the future as accounting is not tracking investments in knowledge assets." – *Alan Greenspan, Federal Reserve Board Chairman.*

- "As intangible assets grow in size and scope, more and more people are questioning whether the true value – and the drivers of that value – are being reflected in a timely manner, in publicly available disclosure." – *Arthur Levitt, Former SEC Chairman*

- "The GAAP system has, for all its faults, served business and the public well, like an octogenarian butler. At the same time, there's increasing evidence that the faithful, old servant isn't just misplacing a spoon here or there, but has lost track of some valuable jewels, paid no attention to the furnace and the water heater, and put the place at risk. Investors simply don't value what accountants count." – *Thomas Stewart, Fortune.*

- "The income statement, balance sheet and statements of cash flow are about as useful as an 80-year-old road map." – *Robert A Howell, Professor, Tuck School, Dartmouth University.*

- "Today, substantially all of a company's profitability depends on intangible assets, so the accounting problems associated with intangibles becomes quite serious." – *Peter J Wallison, Resident Fellow, American Enterprise Institute.*

- "The Value Measurement and Reporting Collaborative (VMRC) believes business value is defined not only in monetary units but also in objects, ideas, events or processes. The VMRC, in which the American Institute of Certified Public Accountants (AICPA) participates, is a global effort of the accounting profession to help boards of directors, senior management, investors and other stakeholders make better strategic decisions using value measurement and reporting. Its members' say a company's worth exists not only in its present operational value as accounted for historically in its financial statements, but also in its potential to create future value." – *Journal of Accountancy, Dec, 2004*

- "Since the applicability of the traditional accounting framework is constantly declining, there is no point in trying to include intangible assets on the balance sheet. Instead, a whole new framework for measurement will eventually have to be developed." – *Silvia Wompa, American Management Association.*

Over the past weeks we had concentrated on the Accounting Model, attempting to prove its inadequacies as a universal measurement standard. It was now time for us to turn our attention to Marketing, and for me to call my first Marketing expert to give evidence. For this purpose, we had enlisted the support of Mr. Charles Jones of the Greystone Manufacturing Company plc.

As soon as Mr. Jones had been called, I asked him, "What is your position in the company and how big is your company?"

"I'm the Chief Marketing Officer and the business is the biggest supplier of washing powders in the world, employing over 20,000 people worldwide," he replies most confidently.

"Mr. Jones, I would like to ask you about the use of Marketing Metrics. Firstly, I would like you to explain to the court what it is, and then for you to explain if you believe it is the right approach for Marketers to follow, and why?"

"Right," he says, feeling quite full of himself, "Marketing Metrics is the practice of attempting to measure marketing performance in terms of financial measures, and yes, I am a strong believer in Marketing Metrics because as Marketers, we need to be able to measure accurately our performance."

"So you want to measure your performance to show how you are contributing to the company's financial performance?" I query.

"Well, not only contributing to the company's performance but for our own benefit, to show us areas where we could possibly improve our performance."

"Mr. Jones, how many business processes under your direct control can you apply these Marketing Metrics to?" I asked.

"Not that many!"

"So, Mr. Jones, do the processes you cannot measure with your Marketing Metrics add any value to the business?"

"Oh, unquestionably, yes," he replies.

"Why can't you measure them?" I ask.

"Well, its difficult – no, impossible, to measure these processes in financial terms," he replied.

"So you'd like to measure them but you can't, and you know they add value to your business."

"That's correct," he asserts.

"So in your opinion, the problem stems from an inadequate measurement standard?"

"Yes, but I'm trying to address the problem by introducing Marketing Metrics wherever I can."

"Mr. Jones, we've already heard that, as well as the fact that you haven't been particularly successful in this endeavour as the Accounting Model, on which you base your Marketing Metrics cannot measure most of your business processes and that these processes, by your own admission, add substantial value to the business," I remarked.

"Why then have you based your Marketing Metrics on the Accounting Model when you know it's inadequate, and only provides a partial solution?" I queried further.

"Well, what else is there? Everybody is judged according to financial measures and I think it's better to be doing something rather than nothing," he replied in a more subdued manner.

"So, Mr. Jones, you know the Accounting Model cannot provide the solution, yet you persist in using it because you believe there are no other alternatives?" I ask.

"I suppose that would be correct," he replies.

"Mr. Jones, hasn't Marketing faced this problem since its inception, where much of what it does cannot be measured in financial terms?"

"Yes, I would agree and even go a little further to say it's getting worse," he responds.

"What impact does this have on your profession generally?" I asked.

"Well, as you can imagine, if you can't measure effectively it's difficult to make people accountable and if you aren't accountable, you're not responsible. Because we cannot accurately account for what we do, our credibility is brought into question and as a consequence, our standing in the business community has slipped considerably, and in my opinion, getting worse. For this reason, I want to make my department more accountable. It's like going to work every day, working hard, but only being credited with a small fraction of what you do. However, if we weren't there, then we'd be sorely missed!"

"Thank you, Mr. Jones, no more questions."

Sir Michael rises to ask Mr. Jones a question, "Mr. Jones, by your own admission you're saying that Marketing should not be held responsible?"

"No, I'm saying it's difficult to hold us responsible because it's difficult to measure our performance," he replies.

"Mr. Jones, if we cannot measure accurately, doesn't that leave the business processes over which you preside open to abuse, perhaps not by individuals of integrity such as you, but by less honourable practitioners in other businesses?"

"Yes, that's a possibility," he replies.

"So therefore, because we cannot measure performance, we could assume that some or all the activities undertaken by Marketing may be irrelevant, self-serving, or in some way unproductively employed. Would that be correct?" queries Sir Michael.

"It may be correct, but I don't think it represents the reality of what's going on within marketing departments today," replies Mr. Jones.

"Well, Mr. Jones, that's only your opinion and you have just admitted that it is possible that some or all Marketing's activities could be irrelevant or squander resources, and that's what Marketing is charged with."

"Yes, but that's..." Mr. Jones attempts to reply before he is interrupted by Sir Michael.

"That's all, thank you, Mr. Jones."

Over the next week, I lead arguments presenting how concerned Marketing is at measuring their performance. For this purpose, I used respected resources from within the industry. I include a small sample of this evidence for your consideration.

- "Today's top marketing executives admit that their group's performance is not up-to-par, and that's causing a lack of influence and credibility within the corporate hierarchy." – *Chief Marketing Officer (CMO) Council – "Renovate To Innovate" study.*

- "The heat is still on to prove marketing's value: 81% of CMOs said they feel high or very high pressure to prove their value to the CEO." – *The Red Herring Second Annual CMO Survey.*

- "A scant 7% of senior-level financial executives surveyed report being satisfied with their company's ability to measure marketing ROI, according to a study published in March 2007 by Marketing Management Analytics, a unit of Carat, and Financial Executives International, an association of senior corporate financial executives." *Management Analytics and Financial Executives International.*

- "The number one priority of marketers is to 'Quantify and measure the value of marketing programs and investments' according to the Chief Marketing Officer (CMO) Council's 2007 Marketing Outlook Survey." – *Chief Marketing Officer (CMO) Council.*

In fighting this case we have used a three pronged attack. The first was to prove that the Accounting Model was inadequate. The second was to prove that marketers themselves acknowledged the need for improved evaluation, but that the solution did not lie with the Accounting Model. The third and final stage is to show the court that there is an alternative measurement and management model available which serves the profit objective more effectively than our old and antiquated Accounting Model. Who best to introduce the argument than Dr. James Witherspoon of the University of Southampton's School of Management, who specialises in Modern Value Management.

"Dr. Witherspoon, you specialise in a field called Modern Value Management. Can you, as succinctly as possible, describe to the court what Modern Value Management is?" I asked him.

"Yes, certainly," he replies. "Modern Value Management is all about optimising the profit objective on a sustained basis through adopting a value creation perspective, rather than a financial perspective. Financial measures are important, but they can no longer remain our sole and dominant measurement standard."

"Why do you say that, Doctor?" I query.

"The Accounting Model only measures a small percentage of what is going on in business because it only measures financial transactions, and is therefore classified as an exclusive measurement model. However, there are many other activities undertaken by businesses which cannot be expressed in financial terms, but which add significant value to the business. If we are to get an accurate picture of business performance, we have to adopt an inclusive measurement model such as Modern Value Management. The reason for this is that it measures the lowest common denominator within business, namely 'value added'. Businesses are only successful when they add value to what they already have. Therefore, every process within business should add value, otherwise it is destroying value."

"Does Modern Value Management provide a management and measurement standard?" I query further.

"Modern Value Management is applicable to all businesses and provides us with a universal set of rules to value creation, and thus the basis to achieve optimum and sustained wealth creation. It also provides the foundations for a new measurement standard, which will give us the first comprehensive and accurate business evaluation model."

"Let me understand you correctly. Are you saying that this management and measurement model would enable us to measure Marketing's performance more accurately?"

"Absolutely," replies Dr. Witherspoon. "Not only Marketing but all business disciplines."

"Thank you, Doctor, no more questions."

"Fascinating, absolutely fascinating," says Sir Michael in his customary, sarcastic manner. "We have heard, at some length, Marketing experts explain how difficult it is to ascribe value to what they do, and to some extent I can see their point, yet you are now telling me you can measure these activities accurately? How do you do this, with smoke and mirrors?"

"No, Sir, with more conventional techniques called Artificial Intelligence Technologies," replies Dr. Witherspoon, clearly irritated by Sir Michael's attitude.

"What is this, something you've learnt from ET?" Sir Michael says trying to rile the Doctor and put him off his stride.

"No, fortunately we have an extensive body of research to back these technologies up, although I would have loved to have met ET," says Dr. Witherspoon responding with a broad smile on his face, realising what Sir Michael was up to.

"Perhaps that can be arranged, but before that, can you elaborate, in layman's terms, what Artificial Intelligence Technologies enables us to do?" responds Sir Michael in a friendly manner, realising his ploy had backfired on him.

"Artificial Intelligence is a sub-field of computer science that focuses on the development of intelligent software and hardware systems that emulate human reasoning techniques and capabilities. In the case of Modern Value Management, it utilises three technologies, namely, Decision Trees, Ruled Based Systems and Fuzzy Logic, to provide accurate evaluations of business performance where mathematical models are totally inappropriate," explains Dr. Witherspoon.

"Fuzzy Logic, doesn't that sum it all up in a nutshell?" says Sir Michael. "We don't have a clue apart from some fuzzy notion of the outcome; hardly useful I would say."

"Whenever I mention Fuzzy Logic to laymen, I always get the same response; they think you are using fuzzy reasoning or logic and thus the outcome has to be illogical or fuzzy. Nothing could be further from the truth. What's critical to realise about Fuzzy Logic is that it provides logic to fuzzy circumstances and is not logic which is fuzzy; just as the laws of probability are not random, so the laws of fuzziness are not vague. Fuzzy Logic provides a way of arriving at a definite conclusion based upon vague, ambiguous, imprecise or missing information. Fuzzy Logics mimics how people make decisions and is based on a simple, rule-based approach to solving problems rather than attempting to model a system mathematically. The Fuzzy Logic model is empirically-based, relying on experience rather than a technical understanding of the problem or system. In business there are many things that are difficult to measure because either they are too complex, or we may not be able to identify all inputs; yet we are still able to measure and make sense of them using the principles of Fuzzy Logic. Fuzzy Logic suggests we focus on solving the problem rather than attempting to model the system mathematically, if this is even possible. So, a proven solution to measuring complex situations is definitely available to us," states Dr. Witherspoon rather emphatically!

Further witnesses are produced to corroborate the measurement techniques used by Modern Value Management. One expert described how they flew a helicopter with a severely damaged rotary blade, which no human pilot would have been able to control, using Ruled Based Systems and Fuzzy Logic; all mimicking the human thought process, but reacting a lot quicker and more effectively.

The case had finally come to an end after just over three weeks. Today, both the Claimant and I are to address the court with our closing argument before the Judge retires to consider his verdict. This could take weeks, which would mean Matt misses his Christmas deadline unless, in true Matt style, 'he's had a chat with the Judge'.

Sir Michael is to present his closing argument first.

"My Lord, Marketing is the Defendant, nobody else, so while Defence counsel may wish to cloud the issue, we must remain clear on what Marketing has been charged with, and that is of being irrelevant and, or of, squandering critical resources.

"Mr. Jones, the expert Marketing witness introduced by the Defence, agreed that critical resources could be squandered and, or utilised on irrelevant tasks because of what he thinks are inadequate measurement standards. Defence council also explained that this measurement problem has evidently been present since the inception of Marketing. Therefore Marketing, knowing it's got a problem and knowing the problems are getting worse, according to Mr. Jones, have done nothing about it! This makes them negligently culpable at the very least.

"What shocked and amazed me was Mr. Jones' revelation that he intended to pursue his current thinking on Marketing Metrics when he told us it only addresses a small portion of what he needs to measure. What's going to happen with all the unmeasured processes? Who's going to wave a magic wand and fix Marketing's problems – the accountants? What an indictment – you know you have a problem, and you wait for others to solve it, or just claim it's somebody else's problem and do nothing about it. Doesn't this make Marketing irrelevant and a squander of resources?

If you cannot find the Defendant guilty of being irrelevant, then you must find them guilty of squandering resources, as they have done nothing to solve a problem they claim to have.

"Thank you."

The Judge turns and nods towards me; I stand and walk towards the bench.

"During this trial we have learned several things.

"Firstly, we have learnt how non-representative the Accounting Model is of business, or as the experts put it, 'an exclusive management model'. How it can only be used to measure a small number of business processes and as a consequence, only reflects a small portion of underlying business value. We have also learnt that there's no correlation between financial measures and value creation, meaning our financial measures mask value creation activities. Yet, we have heard that businesses are only successful when they add value to what they already have, but we have no way of measuring and managing this value.

"We have also learned that value creation is the common denominator of business. This means that every business process can be measured in terms of value creation criteria. It could therefore be argued that our primary business model should be based on the principles of value creation, as it's a fully inclusive model, unlike the Accounting Model which is highly exclusive.

"We have also witnessed one of the biggest problems associated with the Accounting Model and that is, most people think it's exclusively and inextricably linked with the profit objective. This could not be further from the truth! You don't have to adopt a financial perspective to achieve the profit objective. In fact, how can a highly exclusive model be representative of all business processes, and thus wealth creation? Numerous witnesses attested to significant value being added by business processes not measured by the Accounting Model. Our financial perspective provides an exclusive and therefore restrictive view of business, so it should not be used as our primary model. I'm not suggesting we get rid of our financial measures, far from it, just that it can no longer remain our primary model.

"We have also learnt that financial profit is a value creation process, so we can achieve the same results, if not better, using a value creation perspective, as after all, a value creation perspective is fully inclusive and representative. Until all business disciplines and processes are incorporated into the mainstream of business measurement and management, we will not get a true reflection of business performance and value.

"So, from what we've heard, it appears that our measurement standard is at fault and not Marketing.

"The Accounting Model not only excludes most Marketing processes from measurement, but many other disciplines as well, so this is not a Marketing, but rather a business problem. So, we can't hold Marketing exclusively responsible for the failings of our measurement model. We have also heard from many leading marketers how Marketers themselves desperately want to accept responsibility and accountability, but have been thwarted in this endeavour through our inadequate measurement standards.

"Yes, perhaps Marketing have foolishly attempted to base their Marketing Metrics on the Accounting Model when they knew, or should have appreciated that their problems stem from an inappropriate measurement standard, namely the Accounting Model. Consequently, they should be looking for, and working on, a suitable value creation model and not wasting their time and efforts pursuing a dead-end cause. I think, we've proved that the Accounting Model cannot provide the solution they seek! However, like all other business disciplines which have unquestionably accepted the Accounting Model as a given, not to be queried or challenged, but to be accepted as a fact of life, they are no guiltier than others. I therefore call upon this court, having been presented with the evidence, to reject both claims against my client.

"I'm sure that Marketing and the business community have learnt a valuable lesson from this trial and will immediately go about addressing the identified problems, namely the inadequacies of our financial measures in measuring and managing the value creation process, thereby allowing Marketing to return to its rightful role in business and to continue contributing to the strategic direction and well-being of business.

"I thank you, My Lord."

The Judge then stood and announced that the case was closed and that he would retire to consider his verdict, which would be announced in due course.

That evening, we all met at our Bristol residence to celebrate with a party hosted by Matt.

Matt was in extremely high spirits. It looked and sounded like he had invited all of Bristol to celebrate with us. As usual, he had the TV cameras present. When Richard and I arrived at the house, Matt pulled us aside and shook our hands vigorously, proclaiming we were the best team ever and that he was extremely pleased with our performance, and looked forward to a favourable outcome. According to him, the positive international coverage Marketing had received had exceeded his wildest expectations.

"Guys, this has been one heck of a good outcome for Marketing – you showed the world it's not a Marketing problem but a business one, and that Marketing has been victimised by business's short-sighted fixation with their stupid Accounting Model. We've made the international business world sit up and take notice."

Not long after arriving at the house, Richard received a call from the Clerk of the Court informing him that the Judge would announce his verdict shortly, and that it was probably in our interest to stay in the Bristol area. It was unusual for a verdict to be reached so quickly, but then I persuaded myself that we had presented such a convincing case that the decision was easy to make. Matt was over the moon with the news. Getting a verdict so quickly helped maintain public interest in the case, and meant he didn't have to worry about the dreaded Christmas break interfering with his PR campaign.

On the third day after the trial, we received a message from the Clerk of the Court informing us that the verdict would be delivered that afternoon.

The courtroom is hushed as the Judge delivers his verdict.

"I have had little problem in arriving at my verdict as I found the issues to be rather clear cut.

"On the claim that the Defendant's services to the business community are irrelevant, I reject this claim completely."

A loud scream of jubilation goes up from Marketing's supporters.

The judge calls the courtroom to order.

"Clearly Marketing has a role to play in adding value to what a business does, but I do find that the Claimant has proved quite adequately that Marketing has squandered critical resources."

A mixed reaction of loud noises fills the courtroom. The Judge once again calls the courtroom to order and continues the reading of his verdict.

"I think current measurement standards are inadequate and, until this problem is addressed, the potential to misappropriate resources is a distinct possibility. The excuse that the Defendant is no guiltier than any other disciplines for not taking action earlier in solving this problem is no excuse, as they were aware of the problem but did little to address it, despite alternate solutions being available. Marketing is the most affected by our inadequate measurement standards and consequently, should have taken a leading role in finding a suitable solution. Through them showing no apparent initiate in this regard, has made finding against them considerably easier. This is a serious situation and, unless business can effectively measure performance, resources are bound to be misappropriated. Nobody knows precisely how serious the problem is and can only surmise; but one thing is certain, it's significant to say the very least," he continues.

"I believe Marketing does have an important role to play, which it's currently not fulfilling. Marketing not only has a duty to themselves, but also to the wider business community to sort this problem out. Had they responded earlier to this problem, this case would never have come before the courts, and it's a pity it has, except that hopefully it has provided the much needed stimulus. One thing is very clear to me, Marketing needs to step forward and live up to their responsibilities. They must stop hiding behind excuses and deliver to the business community an understanding of what our new management and measurement model should entail. They are the most affected, and therefore, it impacts more urgently on them. Their careers are on the line, not ours! Their discipline is being marginalised, not ours! While other disciplines may appreciate the need for change, their sense of urgency cannot be as profound as that of Marketing's," says the Judge, continuing his verdict.

"I understand that Marketing has a lot on their plate; rapidly changing markets, fiercer competition, more competition. Amongst all this tumultuous change, what stands out as the single most important factor that will affect theirs and the business community's long-term prosperity? I'm no Marketing expert but neither am I a fool, and the answer is as clear to me as day and night! Until you can measure what you are doing, you are working in the dark, and as business is about optimising returns on resources, we can't have a big, black hole in business consuming resources without any accountability! No wonder you've been ostracised. I think people generally believe marketing works and want to invest in it, but they do so reluctantly, as they feel they are 'sending good money after bad'. As Lord Leverhulme once remarked, 'I know marketing works, I just don't know which part!'

"I get a sense that Marketing has lost their way. Perhaps they've been bombarded with too much change and upheaval. As a business discipline, they've certainly had more than their fair share and perhaps as a result, they can no longer see the wood for the trees. Therefore, my message to them is a simple one, intended to put them back on the straight and narrow – sort out this measurement problem and do it quickly!

"This claim has been brought by Professor Peter Metcalf on behalf of the business community, with the claim to be spent on improving business measurement standards. However, evidence has been given in court which makes me seriously doubt the direction Professor Metcalfe will follow in solving this problem. Professor Metcalfe, over his career, has adopted a hybrid approach to this problem, using two disciplines which I think are entirely inappropriate for the task, namely Intellectual Capital and The Balanced Scorecard. Intellectual Capital attempts to measure 'intangibles' without considering the underlying value creation processes. Accounting 'intangibles' will remain intangible and unfathomable, unless you understand the 'rules' of wealth creation. You only unlock value by managing the value creation process, not by introducing another set of almost meaningless measures which, in essence, is what Intellectual Capital does. In my opinion, it provides a distorted picture of business which, in some instances, is more misleading than the Accounting Model's data. Regarding The Balanced Scorecard, all this model does is provide structure in proposing questions. It in no way attempts to provide solutions based on any understanding of the universal structure to the value creation process and until we do that, we will go around in circles. Dr. Witherspoon, on the other hand, seems to have a very firm grip on the problem and has made substantial progress in addressing the problem through his Modern Value Management approach. Consequently, what I have decided to do is award Professor Metcalfe costs for this case, but the claim is to be awarded to Dr. Witherspoon. I'm entitled to do this as the claim was brought on behalf of the business community and in my opinion, the business community's interests will be best served through Dr. Witherspoon. With regard to the extent of compensation, I would not be doing Marketing or the business community any favour by not imposing harsh compensation. Therefore, the compensation amount I'm awarding is considerably higher than that claimed. I think the problem is sufficiently large and urgent that considerable resources need to be thrown at the problem. While Marketing, through the Global Marketing Association, will have to pick up the tab, its membership internationally comprises all major corporations, as well as large and small companies, in other words, virtually the entire business community; so, indirectly, the business community will pick up the tab. I think this is correct because it's a joint Marketing and business issue. The claim to be awarded is twelve and a half million pounds."

There were some loud gasps in the courtroom.

"You have the right to appeal against this verdict; however, you Marketers know you have a problem and the quicker you fix it, the better for all. It's not as if you've lost money, its money that will be wisely invested in researching and developing solutions for your benefit. In fact, I err on the side of leniency. You, the Marketing community, in your own good faith, should donate further to the research and development Dr. Witherspoon will undertake on your behalf."

And so ended this historic trial…

Chapter Three

I have decided to go into full retirement.

Leaving one's profession on a high cannot be beaten. It gives you an incredible sense of achievement and worth. I certainly don't need to work anymore. I have no debts, my house is fully paid for, and I have a tidy retirement fund helped by the generous bonus of just over two million pounds paid by Matt at the conclusion of the case.

Despite having had a huge claim awarded against The Global Marketing Association, I, like Matt, am pleased with the outcome. The important role Marketing plays was fully acknowledged, as well as the fact that our measurement standards and not Marketing inefficiencies lie at the heart of the problem, was effectively exposed. It's not as if Marketing has lost anything – far from it! They have gained hugely; their reputation has been partially restored, and a significant amount invested in research and development that will directly benefit them. In my opinion, the claim of twelve and a half million pounds is only a drop in the ocean for big business. To you or I this may appear to be an astronomical figure, but if put in context, it's very small. For example, one well-known cosmetic marketing company pays a skinny, little girl, whose name I have forgotten, over twelve million pounds per annum to advertise their products. Judge Harris was correct when he said he erred on the side of leniency in awarding this claim, and why he encouraged businesses voluntarily to support the research effort.

It is late January and we have just had a light dusting of snow on the hills above the house. The possibility of further heavy snow is likely. I decide to take the dog for a walk as she loves playing and rolling in the snow. I enjoy the bracing air and the scenery is absolutely out of this world, just like the postcards depicting an English country scene in winter, with snow resting on top of bleak branches, snow-capped stone walls, narrow winding lanes and a blanket of snow on rolling fields.

Fiona has decided to pop into the village to do some shopping. Not that we appear to need anything. I'm convinced women are genetically programmed to gather things, which is manifest in their innate desire to shop at every opportunity.

Lilly, our much loved dog, and I returned to the house late that morning to be met in the foyer by Lucy, the young lass who helps Fiona with the housework on a part-time basis.

"Hello, Lucy, how are you today?" I enquire of her.

"I'm fine, thank you, Sir," she replies in a broad, West Country accent.

"Good. Has your dad recovered from his asthma attack?" I enquire further.

"Yes, he's much better, thanks." Her father is one of the local farmers who rents part of the estate from me.

I let them rent the land at ridiculously low rates so that the land is productive, and we get the benefits of living on a working farm without the hassles of running it.

"A Mr. Todd phoned earlier, Sir. He said it was urgent, and you were to phone him as soon as you returned."

"Thank you, Lucy."

"Would you like a cup of tea to warm you up, Sir?"

"That would be splendid, thanks, Lucy. I shall be in my study phoning Mr. Todd."

What on earth does he want me for so urgently?

The snow is falling heavily now, covering the front lawn in a thick, white blanket. The view from my study is that of a winter wonderland. It's incredibly quiet and peaceful. The only noise is the crackling of the log fire in my study. Lucy, bless her good soul, must have lit it earlier knowing how much I enjoy sitting in front of it reading a book. So tranquil and beautiful is the scene that I find it difficult to pick up the phone and call Matt.

I finally muster enough will-power and give him a call.

"Hello, James, I thought I'd let you know that the American Marketing Association has just been served papers similar to the claim we faced."

"That doesn't make any sense," I remark. "Our international showcase trial made the point and got the desired action on behalf of the international community, so why pursue this matter further? Nothing else can possibly come of it."

"Well, somebody thinks differently," comments Matt. "In fact, I have heard rumours that similar cases are to be brought in Canada and Australia shortly, but it's only a rumour at this stage."

"Who is behind this?" I ask.

"What do you mean? There's nobody behind these claims. These claims all appear to emanate from local universities, just like ours did," replies Matt.

I have a great unease with these developments; they are too coincidental. I remember when Matt was first served papers, how the Professor's backers involvement concerned me. I couldn't understand why they were prepared to risk multiple millions on a cause they did not benefit from directly. They were fortunate, they got their money back, but they haven't benefited directly from this case because to this day, the general public don't know who underwrote the Professor. In fact, if they felt strongly about the Professor's work, which he claimed they did, they must be extremely upset with the outcome because he got nothing out of it and could not continue the work they were supposed to believe in so strongly. Initially, this relationship worried me, but over time my concerns dissipated. With these new developments, my concern regarding backers motives has returned tenfold.

"Anyway, the reason for the call was to let you know of developments, and to tell you that I told the Americans you are the man to speak to if they need any help," continued Matt.

"Tell them to contact Richard as I'm not coming out of retirement for anything, but do please keep me informed of developments as they intrigue and concern me."

"Sure thing, buddy," and with that he hung up.

I'm not going to dwell on this matter, intriguing as it may be, because Fiona has an eagle eye and ear and can spot Matt Todd involvement at a distance of over five hundred miles. My solemn promise of full retirement, made to her at the conclusion of the case, will sound a little hollow if she gets the slightest scent of me dealing with Matt again.

Later that afternoon, Fiona returned from her shopping trip in high spirits.

"I've done it," she said, "I've done it!"

"Well done. Now may I enquire as to what you have done?"

"I have booked a holiday for the entire family this summer. We are going on an African Safari," she proclaims. "We are going to the exclusive, private game lodge of Timbavati, next to the famous Kruger National Game Park in South Africa, for three glorious weeks," she says rather excitedly. "The boys and girls are going to absolutely love it; just as much as you and I will. We've always dreamt and talked about going to Africa and seeing its spectacular scenery and wildlife," she continues.

"You do, of course, realise our summer is their winter," I remark.

"Well, of course I do," she replies rather indignantly. "The lovely lady at the Travel Agent recommended we go over in their winter otherwise the heat is evidently unbearable in summer. By all accounts, it gets cold at night, but during the day their winter temperatures soar as high as 30 degrees centigrade," she continues excitedly.

"Everything from game sightseeing drives, tours to the local African village – everything is laid on for us. It really looks a lovely place. I'm so excited, I just can't wait to tell the boys how their magnanimous father has booked a luxury, three week holiday in Africa for them. Do you know, we haven't had a long, family holiday together for over 20 years?"

In an excited tiz, she leaves the room to phone the boys. It makes me feel so good to see her so happy.

That evening after dinner we retired to one of our small reception rooms, as we do every evening, because it's such a cosy room with a lovely, old fireplace. We've also had the latest flat screen television and surround sound system installed, which gives one the experience of being in a cinema. Fiona has decorated the room most tastefully, as she has done for the entire house. I particularly enjoy the large and comfortable leather chairs she has chosen for this room. Just flop into them and within seconds you are whisked off to the land of nod. Tonight was an exception as I kept thinking of my conversation with Matt, even though I had attempted to put it out of my mind completely. Something didn't make sense and it bugged me.

"James," I hear Fiona calling in the distance as I mulled over ideas, snapping into a conscious state quickly.

"What's the matter with you?" she enquires.

"Nothing! Why do you ask?"

"You haven't heard a word of what I was saying about today's shopping trip with Jane. You seem to be in a complete daydream."

"I must have drifted off," I reply.

"No, you hadn't, you were looking straight ahead but your mind was elsewhere. You have been acting rather strangely this evening, as if there is something on your mind."

"Nothings bothering me," I reassure her.

"You're not worried about the holiday are you?"

"No, certainly not. I'm looking forward to it as much as you are."

"Good," she says, continuing to recount her shopping trip to Exeter.

About ten days later, Fiona takes a call from Matt.

"Hello, Fiona, my love. How's that beautiful country girl doing?" he says, trying to rile her?.

"Did you speak to James about a week or so ago?" she enquires of him in an unfriendly manner.

"Well, let me think. Um… ah. Well, now you mention it, I think I did."

"That explains it," she said. "Hold on and I will transfer you to his study."

I pick up the receiver in my study and Fiona blurts out, "That horrible, little man you spoke to about a week ago and didn't tell me about, and have been worrying about ever since, is on the line."

"Hello, James, aren't I allowed to speak to you anymore?" enquires Matt.

"It's no secret you don't count among her favourites," I reply.

"Now you've really upset me, James. Couldn't you have broken that news a little more gently? Anyway, let's get down to business. The Canadians and Australians have confirmed that papers have been served on them as well."

"I'm convinced something is behind this," I remark.

"Well, I would have to agree that there is possibly something in your conspiracy theory, particularly when you consider that I have received rumours of possible further cases being brought in Germany, Brazil, Italy and a few other countries," says Matt.

"That confirms it! This is no longer a debate. There is undoubtedly a master plan behind these events," I state most emphatically!

"If there is, it's certainly not apparent, and it's got me totally flummoxed. Have you got any ideas?" says Matt.

"I have been giving the matter some thought over the past week and have arrived at what I think is a possible scenario. It isn't a particularly attractive one," I reply.

"Well, spill the beans, man," says Matt.

"I'd rather not until I've had the opportunity to go over my thinking again and perhaps to bounce it off another person who could possibly spot any flaws in it, as it is a fairly, scary scenario and I don't want to become a fear-munga for the sake of not thinking something through carefully."

"What are you waiting for, use me?" says Matt.

"As I said, I need to think it through thoroughly and with due respect to you Matt, I would prefer to use somebody like Richard to discuss it with first."

"That's okay by me," he says, "but let's not drag our heels on this".

"I won't, but it's not going to make me popular with Fiona."

"Hey, pal, I've been there – it's not pleasant, but what the heck, you're a tough guy with broad shoulders. Speak to you soon."

These are unwelcome developments. I had desperately hoped that Matt would tell me that the Canadian and Australian cases had not materialised. To hear that there are possibly further cases being brought was all I needed to confirm my worst fears. If my hypothesis is correct, or has a slim chance of being correct, I cannot walk away from this matter as it is a lot bigger and more sinister than I could ever have imagined. I have a moral obligation to follow this through.

I turn my chair and stare out over the countryside. I wonder how many previous owners of this house have done the same as I'm doing now, drawing on the beauty of the surroundings for inspiration or to uplift the spirit. I wonder who they were, and what they were thinking about?

I'm startled as a hand is placed on my shoulder. It's Fiona, standing behind me with a cup of tea in her hand.

"I thought you may like a cup of tea," she said.

"Thank you. I must have been deep in thought," I said.

"That's right," she said, "like you have been over the past week or so."

"There have been some developments associated with the case that have been worrying me," I admit and without pausing, continued. "I would like to invite Richard and Felicity to come and stay with us over the weekend as I would like to discuss some ideas with Richard."

"You think that by inviting my favourites for the weekend will soften me to your cause?" she said.

"No, that's not my motive. I need to get Richard's advice to help determine our next course of action."

"May I remind you that you have retired," she said quite sternly.

"This isn't a legal matter and about me returning to work, but rather about what I perceive to be a plot brewing which could potentially destabilise our international economy."

"Haven't you been watching too many conspiracy theories on your silly History channel to make you think there's a master plan behind all innocent events?" she enquires.

"You could be correct," I say, "but I would be remiss if I did not check them out first. That's why I want Richard's incisive thinking to confirm or deny the possibilities. If there is nothing to my theory, then that's the end of it," I reassure her.

"Okay," she says, "invite them for the weekend. I look forward to seeing them anyway. At least Felicity and I can catch up on things, but remember, if Richard doesn't think much of your theory then you are to drop it."

"Fair enough. I will give Richard a call now to see if he can make it for this weekend," I said.

During the trial, I tried to promote Richard as much as possible, allowing him to present most arguments and to do most of the daily press conferences, with the express intention of promoting him. My career was coming to an end whereas his was just beginning. This has proved invaluable for Richard. He has received job offers from virtually all the prestigious legal practices around the world, offering him partnerships and astronomical salaries. So far, he has decided to remain on his own and has already attracted considerable work of a prestigious nature, which should enhance his reputation even further. Whatever direction he takes, he is on the path to becoming an extremely wealthy and successful lawyer. For these reasons, I doubt whether his diary would accommodate our request to spend the weekend with us at such short notice. Only one way to find out and that is to ask.

He has taken up Chambers in central London, sharing facilities with another legal practice. On getting through to his office, I'm questioned as to who I am and what I want, before being told that he is in consultation and will return my call when he can. About two hours later, Richard returned my call. I explained to him all the developments surrounding the case and that I had developed a theory as to who may be behind them, and for what purpose. I also explained that I thought we best consider it in a quiet, uninterrupted environment, such as my study over the coming weekend, where we could give it due and thoughtful consideration. It isn't something you discuss briefly over the phone in a pressured environment. He fully agreed and said that he and Felicity had made other arrangements for the weekend, but would cancel them and see us late Friday evening. In typical Richard Petrada courtesy, he asked me to convey his 'regards and respects to Mrs Barton-Marshall and thank her for offering to have Felicity and I over the weekend'. I think Richard is so successful because his manners and courtesies sweep opposition from his path. In modern society this is a lost art; where businesses have to spend billions per annum training personnel on the absolute basics of respect and courtesy towards their customers, through the use of simple words such as "please" and "thank you". Richard, on the other extreme, gets his respectful behaviour and courtesies to work wonders for him.

Fiona is very pleased with the news of Richard and Felicity accepting our invitation. She immediately set about making preparations, even though it's only Wednesday.

Fiona prepared a rather tasty dinner for us on Friday evening, which we ate soon after their arrival at about nine-thirty. Richard requested that he retire early as he was feeling tired after a busy week. Felicity joked that he was tired due to having driven all the way from London in his old, dilapidated car which required great concentration and effort to get it remotely close to the speed limit. Richard just shrugged his shoulders saying he didn't require anything better as he relied heavily on public transport. Felicity won't let him off lightly, regaling us with stories where recently, due to his new-found fame, has been invited to several high society functions where his old Vauxhall Astra stands out as a source of embarrassment. Some of the stories were admittedly rather funny and embarrassing. Felicity requested that I convince Richard to buy a new car as she had failed in this endeavour, and he looked up to me as a father figure. I was rather flattered and proud that this capable and successful young man thought of me in this manner. I did suggest that he considers buying a more modern and prestigious car but not to be too ostentatious, as he had nothing to prove through the car he drove. The ladies totally disagreed with me, suggesting he buys the biggest and flashiest model, naming the models, which amazed me. I thought women didn't know much about cars – how wrong you can be. Richard didn't have much to say on the subject, which means he's made up his mind and won't be budged.

After Richard retired, the ladies became engrossed in their own discussions, so I thought it the ideal opportunity to beat a hasty retreat. Perhaps I could watch the History channel in the bedroom as Fiona doesn't enjoy it at all.

The next morning after breakfast, the ladies set off on a long walk destined for the Brendon Hills overlooking the house. Richard and I headed off in the opposite direction, towards the outbuildings, discussing my conspiracy theory as we walk.

"From the very outset, I questioned the motives of Professor Metcalfe's backers. Why were they prepared to back a cause they did not benefit from directly? Initially, they were not keen to back the Professor and yet within two weeks of one another, these apparently independent businesses stumped up the money to get the highest paid lawyers in the country to fight their cause. At the time, the explanation that they believed in the Professor's cause seemed plausible. However, in the light of current events, their motives need to be revisited. What if these businesses, which backed the law suit, are fronts for organisations with wider, more sinister objectives? Assuming they are, and the timing is right to start implementing their master plan, whatever that maybe, they instruct the businesses they own to back the Professor fully and to do it immediately. This explains why two supposedly independent businesses acted almost in unison in backing the Professor. The timing of their decision, and the fact that they both made U-turns on their previous decision, are more than coincidental. It also explains why they have kept a low profile, as they don't want anybody to trace their association with the organisation they front."

Richard listens intently to my explanation. "Carry on, James," he said, "it sounds plausible, but I'm sure there is a lot more to your theory than this?"

"You are right, there is a lot more to the theory. All these actions being brought worldwide against Marketing associations have a similar modus operandi to our case. This is what alerted me to an orchestrated plot."

"Fair enough," says Richard, "but what is the plot, and who's orchestrating it?"

"If you consider the fundamentals of our case revolved around the inadequacies of the Accounting Model in measuring business performance, and that Marketing was the most vulnerable to its short comings," I explain further.

"Yes," says Richard, "but what of it?"

"These shortcomings have been inherent in Marketing since its inception. To an astute individual, it would have been apparent that the situation would worsen over the years, and that they could use this to their advantage. Consequently, they infiltrate the universities by sponsoring departments. This is a long-term process, perhaps occurring over the past decade or so. They bide their time, waiting for the right moment to initiate their plans, which we see unfolding now."

"Yes, but what is their plan?" queries Richard with a slight hint of frustration to his voice.

"What we have seen so far is only the start of a series of court cases. The first case has been brought against the body that represents marketing globally. Their objective was to get the Court to accept the fact that because of poor or non-existent measurement standards, the Marketing community has in all probabilities squandered critical resources. Armed with this damming ruling, they institute similar court cases around the world. The likelihood of them obtaining a similar ruling in their country is high."

"Yes, but for what purpose?" queries Richard further.

"The Global Marketing Association only represents marketing associations and institutes, not corporations directly, whereas local associations and institutes will represent them directly. Going global on these court cases should mean they have bagged every publicly listed company in the world."

"I think I know where you are going with this line of thought," says Richard and after a small pause, continues. "If a Court can draw a direct relationship between the company and the association to which they belong, which they can do through its membership of the association, and if there is no evidence that the company disagreed with the direction the association was taking, then by inference you can conclude the company supported the association's direction. If the association is found guilty of being aware of practices that knowingly squander resources and have done little to address the problem, then the company, through its association, is equally guilty as they should have been equally aware of the problem."

"Precisely," I say. "This then leaves the road open for individual shareholders to bring class actions against these companies for knowingly squandering shareholder funds. Such claims could amount to multiple millions per claim."

Richard nods his head in agreement. He then continues the narrative on my behalf. "Only one or two cases need to be brought anywhere in the world and every major corporation knows it faces the same fate. This sets off a chain reaction on the global stock markets, where investors rush to divest funds in businesses likely to be affected. Problem is, every major corporation will be affected, so we see a crash in global markets like we've never seen before."

"Exactly," I say. "The organisation behind this plot has identified the other critical weakness in our economic system and is using it for their own ends. Investors on the Stock Exchange aren't really investors, like their true investment counterparts in small business. True investors put their money in for the long-term, where they experience the ups and downs with the business because they believe in it, and are involved with it.

"On the Stock Exchange, where money is so volatile and can be moved around the world in a blink of any eye, fortunes are made or lost through only small movements in share prices. Investors on the Stock Exchange are not really investors in the true sense of the word, they are speculators or gamblers, swapping bets regularly to make money. If these people, who make up a significant portion of share owners, take fright through these events, which they definitely will, they will run for the hills, setting of a self-perpetuating, downward spiral on the international Stock Exchange."

"Who would gain by such an action?" queries Richard.

"I'm not sure, but think about this. If you were an enemy of the West, where would you strike the most devastating blow? Bring its economy to its knees – that will affect every one of us! Isolated terrorist attacks shock us, but life continues with hardly a hiccup for most of us. Such attacks do little if anything to advance the fanatical group's cause. In fact, they are possibly counterproductive because it strengthens our resolve to bring the perpetrators to book. However, if they can seriously disrupt the 'engine' of the West, namely our economy, they will hurt all of us. If a stake could be driven through the heart of our economy – they win."

Richard remains silent, staring ahead.

I continued, "What if simultaneously to the attack on the economy, they also launch a major terrorist attack on communications infrastructure? This will drive the Stock Exchange down even further and faster, possibly leading to its complete collapse."

"So what organisation do you think is behind this?" asks Richard.

"I surmise, but it's probably Al-Qaeda, funded by rogue states. What if their earlier terrorist strikes were only practice runs for a larger, more coordinated strike?" I suggest.

"This will have required a lot of forethought by an astute mastermind," concludes Richard.

"Without doubt," I concur, "but then we always tend to underestimate our enemies, don't we?"

"Well, what do you think of this as a possible scenario?" I ask Richard.

"It's all supposition obviously, and as such it could be true, but then it could equally be untrue. Pedalling these ideas will quickly brand you as a conspiracy theorist and diminish your credibility," remarks Richard.

"I accept that, but I'm not concerned about my credibility as I'm retired and don't need to worry what effect it will have on my career. I'm of the opinion that if there is a glimmer of truth to my hypothesis, it must be investigated before it's too late."

"I would wait a little," says Richard, "to see what other developments take place."

His comments struck me as being a little odd for Richard, who is normally very decisive. Perhaps my ideas were a little too fanciful. It certainly took the wind out of my sails when considering the possibilities.

"You say you are not concerned about your credibility, but you have also told me how pleased you are to have retired on such a high note. Why risk this excellent reputation to be branded a conspiracy theorist, which will tarnish your good name and respect in the profession, and the wider community, taking the top off the pinnacle of your career?"

It had started to sleet quite heavily and Richard suggested we return to the house.

We walked back in silence, with me mulling over everything that had been said, considering the options again and again. I could not believe that Richard had not identified the possibilities as I had done. If there is a glimmer of truth, action must be taken to investigate further, otherwise we are doing a great injustice to our fellow citizens. On nearing the house, Richard suggested that we not discuss the matter any further as we could possibly dampen the spirits of what would otherwise be a lovely weekend together. I agreed completely with him.

That evening Fiona and Felicity organised dinner for us, which we had in our dining room. This has become a Saturday evening tradition whenever Felicity joins us for the weekend. During dinner, Fiona enquired of Richard in a joking manner, "What is your verdict regarding James's sinister hypothesis?"

"I have recommended that James drop the whole affair as it could possibly tarnish his excellent reputation, to no avail to him or others," he responds.

"Well there you have it," said Fiona, "you said that if Richard didn't see anything in your hypothesis you would drop the whole affair."

I just smiled and carried on eating. I have no intention of dropping this matter, I cannot! I'm disappointed that Richard and I do not see eye-to-eye on the matter, but then neither did he shoot it down, and if doubt exists, it must be followed up – surely he can see that? Anyway, I'm putting the subject out of my mind for the weekend at least. I would hate it to spoil what has always proved to be a happy event.

I cannot believe how quickly the weekend has come and gone.

Certainly Fiona and I enjoyed ourselves, as much as I hope Richard and Felicity did.

Chapter Four

Early Monday morning I gave Matt a call, as promised, and explained my hypothesis to him.

After listening intently to what I had to say, he said, "It's not a very pretty picture is it? What did Richard think of it?"

"He felt my argument was plausible but suggest I wait and see what develops, otherwise I may be labelled a conspiracy theorist which could potentially damage my 'respected' reputation," I replied.

"Nonsense," says Matt jokingly, "you don't have a respected reputation!" Becoming a little more serious, he comments, "That doesn't sound like Richard, he's normally very decisive. It's usually a matter of 'go' or 'stop' with him, no waiting around for better days."

"I agree, it wasn't like Richard at all, but irrespective of what he thinks, I believe we can't afford to wait and see as time is not on our side. We need to get this theory checked by the authorities as soon as possible."

"I can't agree more," says Matt. "I'll have a chat to a few pals and see if they can put us in contact with the right authorities. Well done, James! I can always rely on that sharp brain of yours to come up with the answers."

"I don't know that I have the right answer, just an idea that needs checking out."

"Well, it makes a lot of sense to me, and in the absence of any other logical explanation, we have to go with your idea and move fast," says Matt.

Later that day, just after lunch, Matt phoned me back.

"Hello, pal," he says, "I've got an appointment for you to see Sir Andrew Sweetman tomorrow afternoon at two o' clock. I told Sir Andrew about your theory as best I could. He sounded very interested and keen to help. He and I felt it best that you and he meet first, before he takes the matter any further. He can then ask you pertinent questions, which he in turn may be asked."

"That makes sense," I reply, "but why Sir Andrew, he's only a businessman? I had hoped that with all your connections you would have arranged a meeting with some high-ranking government official."

"Let me tell you, pal, Sir Andrew has the ear of the Chancellor and the Prime Minister. So, if you can convince him, he will convince them on your behalf. And I'm sorry, I thought getting the ear of the Prime Minister at such short notice not too shabby, but what the heck, next time give me a couple of days and maybe I'll get you an audience with God," he jokes.

"Thanks, Matt. Let's hope something positive comes of this meeting."

Now to the difficult task of telling Fiona I am going to London tomorrow, particularly as I had told her I would drop the whole affair. Perhaps she could be persuaded to agree if I invited her to join me, and to arrange for her and Felicity to have lunch together at one of London's finest restaurants. Bribery has a knack of working on women, provided you dangle the finest and most expensive trinkets in front of them.

The ploy worked. She didn't even ask why I was meeting Sir Andrew. She did, however, make a few stipulations. The first was that the restaurant had to be of her choice. Secondly, she had to be allowed three hours shopping after lunch. It's despicable what women will do when they know they have you over a barrel.

For convenience sake, we decided to drive to Bristol Airport and catch the bus from there to London, as I don't enjoy driving in London at all. The bus is a most convenient option as it drops one off at Victoria Station only minutes from the City centre.

On arriving at Victoria Station, Fiona and I parted company. She took a cab and made her way to her luncheon appointment. I decided to walk to my appointment as I had considerable time to spare, and I enjoy walking in London as, in my opinion, it is a most charming city. I didn't enjoy living and working there; it soon loses its charm and becomes just another large, hustling, bustling city. However, seen through the eyes of a tourist, which I was today, it oozes charm.

Sir Andrew has a suite of offices in a modern tower block overlooking the Thames. Sir Andrew is almost a carbon copy of Matt Todd, except Sir Andrew is the English version. Sir Andrew is a self-made multi-millionaire who, from humble East End beginnings, is today purported to be worth over three hundred million pounds. Over his chequered career, he has had his fingers in many pies, but today I think his major interests lie in property development. I believe he owns the office block that houses his office, and the new office block next to it. At one stage in his career, not that long ago, his entire empire almost came crashing down, but in true, gritty, survivalist manner, he pulled it from the brink and breathed new life into it. I recall this quite well as I represented some major creditors trying to get money from one of his ailing businesses. I remember how, in a relatively short period, he miraculously turned the business around and we all got paid. Like Matt and many of the *de novo rich* from humble backgrounds, he lacks essential social graces and is rather a rough diamond, calling a spade 'a bloody shovel, mate'.

I arrived at my appointment about ten minutes early. Sir Andrew's offices occupy the penthouse suite and are modern and plush; in keeping with the overall image of the building. At precisely two o'clock I'm ushered into his office, which is cavernous. In the centre of the office is a huge, black desk with three black-and-chrome chairs in front of it. Facing the window is a large U-shaped, black leather sofa looking out over a panoramic view of London and the Thames. Sir Andrew comes towards me, hand outstretched and a broad smile on his face. "Hello, James," he says in a rather loud voice. He shakes my hand very firmly and beckons me towards the sofa. "You've made rather a name for yourself recently," he says, obviously referring to the recent GMA case.

"Yes, Sir Andrew, I was pleased with the outcome."

"None of that 'Sir' bullshit," he says, "my friends call me Andy. I only use this title thing to get me a good seat in a restaurant," he laughs aloud.

I just smiled.

"Matt thinks highly of you. I personally don't have much time for lawyers. Firstly, they charge far too much money and when they get to Court, they dance around with one another running up huge bills for their clients. It sickens me. Quite frankly, legal processes and procedures need a big shake-up, making things easier and simpler, just like the massive shake-up you have proposed for the measurement and management of business. I fully endorse your argument and the Judge's ruling that our Accounting Model needs to be replaced by a more appropriate, fully inclusive value management system. How can a five hundred year old accounting system serve the needs of modern business? The answer is, it doesn't. Until you highlighted the work done by that Doctor on Modern Value Management, I didn't know anything about it. Subsequently, I have read an interesting book on the subject and am convinced this represents our future measurement and management standard. Changing how we view, measure and manage business is the most fundamental change we can make. It's therefore going to have a profound affect on everybody and every business, and I'm not going to be caught with my pants down. I've already made changes in my business where we have started managing our profit objective from a value creation, rather than a financial, perspective. I'm convinced it will produce positive results. It makes so much sense; manage the value in your business and profits will follow. Modern Value Management actually provides the rules to value creation, irrespective of the size or type of business you are in."

I had started to wonder if I would be able to get a word in edgeways, so I thought I had better interrupt him before I got the full lecture on Modern Value Management, no matter how fascinating that may be. "Andy, what has Matt told you about my concerns regarding recent developments pertaining to the GMA case? "

"Yeah, I've been a little sidetracked talking about my pet interest, Modern Value Management, but if your theories are correct about these recent developments, it sounds like I could be back on the street corner selling flowers again."

"Let's hope it doesn't come to that," I remark.

"So your whole idea is that Al-Qaeda is behind these court cases?"

"I don't know that, all I can do is surmise. Given the circumstantial evidence before me, it would appear that somebody is manipulating events with potentially disastrous circumstances for the world economy. Destroying the international economy holds no benefit for the international community, apart from those radical groups who despise what they see as the pillar of Western decadence, namely its economy. To them, they see the West pursuing money at the cost of all else. Given these circumstances, I can only conclude that a group like Al-Qaeda fits the bill perfectly."

"Makes sense," he said.

"I don't believe we can sit around doing nothing, waiting to see what develops; we have to move now, and quickly."

"I agree with you completely, but what needs to be done immediately, apart from alerting the authorities?" he asks

"MI6, or whoever is the appropriate body, must check the financial backers of these cases to see if they have any affiliations with known terrorist groups. These affiliations are going to be well hidden so it will need the considerable resources of MI6 to investigate these thoroughly and quickly. Only when we can find the true identity of the backers will their motives become clear. We don't have time because, as soon as they can create panic on the stock market, it's all over for us. At that point they are in command, but right now, we are still in command."

"You're a convincing man. I can see why Matt likes you and why you are such a good lawyer. Maybe you've changed my mind about liking lawyers," he says jokingly.

He gets up and walks over to his big, black desk where he picks up the phone, "Get me the Chancellor," he says.

I get up and walk over to the window to enjoy the panoramic scene stretching out before me.

He was on the phone for some time before he returned to the sofa and flopped onto it, stretching out his arms and putting them on the back of the sofa.

"I'm seeing the Chancellor tomorrow at 10:00, so by this time tomorrow, the Prime Minister will know about your theory," he says in a self-important manner.

"That's good," I say "and thank you for your help."

"We're all in this together, and we can be thankful that your astute brain has picked up the danger before it's too late. So tell me, you think they're going to use the Stock Exchange to bring us to our knees?" he says.

"I think we are dealing with some very clever, far-sighted people who identified enormous weaknesses in our financial systems, and set in motion plans many years ago to fully exploit them. They have used the inappropriateness and ineffectiveness of the Accounting Model as the catalyst to their master plan. They will then use the inherent weakness in our stock market trading procedures to deliver the *coup de grâce*."

"How's that?" enquires Sir Andrew further.

"So called investors on the Stock Exchange are not real investors, they are commodity traders who deal in shares. They buy and sell shares based on minor price variations. Fortunes can be made or lost through only minor changes in share values. Consequently, they are continuously looking for opportunities to buy low and sell high. Because they trade on a short-term basis, they have a fixation with short-term business results, yet we all know that short-term financial results belie the truth of most businesses. They know this as well as you and I, but they don't care as they have no allegiance to their current investment portfolio, only to their own investors, so they flit their money from one good bet to another. These trading practices benefit only a few at the expense of the wider community. This was never what the Stock Exchange was conceived to do. Its primary objective was to allow people to invest and to develop an investment culture. However, we've lost our direction somewhere along the way and should get back to the fundamentals of investment as being the key to making profit and not trading in share. If investors could become what they are supposed to be, namely owners of the business, then they will play a more important and constructive role in creating greater wealth. Because of the Stock Exchange's fixation with short-term, quarterly financial results, many Chief Executive Officers produce good financial results at the expense of the underlying value in their business. If investors were in for the long haul, they would work with the business to help create long-term value and drop their ridiculous and distracting interest in almost meaningless, short-term financial results."

"I agree whole-heartedly with your sentiments," asserts Sir Andrew.

"Investments should be made on a long-term basis. This would ensure investors look into their investments thoroughly before buying as well as becoming deeply involved in these businesses, helping them to create long-term value. This is where their reward lies, not in buying and selling shares willy-nilly. This will create greater wealth for all and stop potential runs on Stock Exchanges'. Because we have a trader and not an investor mentality, we are extremely vulnerable to runs on the Stock Exchange which can potentially destroy our economy. We have seen it many times before where panic selling destroys otherwise viable and successful businesses."

"Again, I agree with you, but the problem is it's difficult for potential investors to determine the true value of a business because our only evaluation tool is the Accounting Model," says Sir Andrew.

"You are correct, the investment community requires the right measurement tools to be able to determine the true value within the business, which the Accounting Model distorts or even hides," I said.

"And that's the role of Modern Value Management," says Sir Andrew, "which can show investors the true value in a business and how much value has been added to the business over a period of time. It is this underlying value that ultimately creates greater wealth or profit."

"Yes, precisely," I said.

"For a lawyer you have your feet firmly stuck to the ground – I like that, I like you," he said, nodding his head in approval.

"I'm pleased I've been able to help in some small way," he said continuing, "and would like to see how events unfold, so please keep me abreast of developments and if I can be of any further assistance, don't hesitate in giving me a call. And now, can I offer you something to drink?"

"I would enjoy a cup of coffee, thank you."

He gets up and goes over to his desk where he barks out some instructions.

On returning to the sofa, he enquired, "You don't live in London anymore, do you?"

"That's correct; I have retired to the Somerset countryside."

"Did you drive up today?" he enquires further.

"No, I caught the bus from Bristol Airport."

"What!" he said in an indignant manner, "you caught the bus?"

"That's correct, it's a convenient way of travelling," I said rather emphatically!

"As a general rule, no friend of mine travels on the bus when I'm able to offer them a more convenient means of travel," he said jumping to his feet and returning to his desk.

"Get Jack urgently for me," I overhear him say.

He waits at his desk for a few minutes before a call is put through to him. He chats for a few minutes and then returns to me.

"I've organised for my personal helicopter to fly you back to Bristol," he said, with a broad smile.

"Thank you, Andy, you are most generous."

"Nonsense, it's the least I can do for somebody who's just saved the world, and is a friend to boot," he said jokingly. "I have a helipad on the top of this building where the helicopter will pick you up at around five-thirty."

"Thank you once again," I said.

We finished our coffee over a few pleasantries and he asked that I excuse him as he had a few other appointments scheduled for the afternoon. I was ushered into a large function room next to his office where I made myself comfortable in a chair placed next to the full-length window, with equally spectacular views of London. I phoned Fiona and told her to meet me at Sir Andrew's office as I had managed to hitch a ride home on a helicopter. Having a long wait ahead of me of over two hours, I decide to take forty winks.

I'm roused from what must have been a deep sleep as Fiona burst into the room carrying numerous parcels and boxes, ably assisted by a young lady carrying an equally large number of parcels. She smiled politely, deposited the parcels at my feet and left. She evidently worked at reception for Sir Andrew. How on earth Fiona had managed carrying all these parcels on her own through the busy streets of London escapes me entirely. Shopping is an art form Fiona has mastered to a tee, including the art of carrying great quantities of booty from stores single-handedly.

"Hello, my dear," I said, "looks like you've had a successful and enjoyable day – leave much for anybody else?"

"Yes, thank you, dear," she replies in a calm, unflustered manner, "I left a few crumbs behind."

Just after five o'clock, I saw a huge, black helicopter approach the building, hover above us and then slowly descend. It was amazingly quiet in the building. I don't think I could hear a sound. At about five-twenty, a smartly-dressed, young lady entered the room, introduced herself as Sir Andrew's PR Manager who was to escort us to the helicopter and see we were comfortable. Gathering up all Fiona's parcels, I was pleased they had sent a large helicopter.

I have never flown in a helicopter before. What amazed me was just how large and comfortable it was inside. The cockpit was completely separate from the cabin, like that of an aeroplane. It was also a lot quieter than I had expected, with little engine noise apart from when the engines started up. The flight back to Bristol took little under an hour and during that time, I definitely acquired a taste for helicopter flight; or rather a taste for expensive, executive helicopter flight.

Almost a week after meeting Sir Andrew, I received the much-anticipated telephone call from MI6. I had almost given up on them, believing they didn't think it necessary to speak to me. Initially, I thought I would receive a call from them the same day Sir Andrew met the Chancellor, or the following day at the latest, expressing the urgency I felt the case deserved. I now have mixed feelings towards this call; I am pleased they have called because I think it is important for them to speak directly to the person raising the concern, rather than relying on hearsay information three or more times in the telling. On the other hand, I didn't feel happy that they have taken so long to take action; but then, of course, they may have been working on the case and just want to let me know of progress, or want me to clarify an issue or two.

"Phillip Stopford of MI6, Sir," he announces. "We have received a request from the Prime Minister's Office to investigate possible Al-Qaeda involvement in recent civil cases brought here, and in other countries."

"With regard to this matter," he continues, "as MI6 is now officially investigating these claims, they fall under the Official Secrets Act and you are therefore prohibited from discussing or making known any information you may have regarding this matter to anybody for any reason. Do you understand what has been said?"

"I do," I replied.

"Good. You will receive a letter in the post shortly stating the terms and conditions of the Official Secrets Act to which you have agreed. I must apologise for having gone through this rigmarole with you first, Sir, but you need to know where you stand on this matter."

"No, I understand, you can't have any loose cannons blabbing away while you conduct a sensitive investigation."

"That is correct, Sir. I must also let you know that we are under no obligation to keep you abreast of developments, or to disclose our conclusions or discuss any outcomes with you. Furthermore, you are not to work on this matter any further or to attempt to contact us. If we require your assistance, we will contact you, you are not to contact us directly or indirectly."

It felt like I had just been run over by a steamroller. It left me speechless, which is most unusual for me. I can understand the need for most of these requirements, but how they were presented to me leaves much to be desired. I felt belittled and annoyed.

With hardly a pause, he continues. "We require a written statement from you stating the nature of the threat and how you came to this conclusion. You must then post this as a 'registered signed for item' to an address I will give you; nothing is to be emailed over unsecured lines."

It felt like I was a criminal making a statement to the police, not a person trying to help the Government avert a potentially catastrophic event. I was fuming.

"Why have you people dragged your heels in setting this matter in motion when even faintly intelligent people could see the urgency? Furthermore, I will expect to hear of the outcome of your investigations, otherwise I will go straight back to the Chancellor and demand one," I said breathing fire and smoke from my nostrils.

Sensing my anger, he attempted to explain his actions. "As I mentioned earlier, Sir, you need to know where you stand in terms of our procedures."

"Listen, my good man, its not the procedures I have a problem with, it's the way you have come across presenting them. I can understand that legally you don't have to keep me informed of your findings, but this is open to your discretion. As and when your findings are available, you would assess whether or not to inform me. If you decided not to inform me and I kicked up a fuss, then you would refer me to the fact that legally, you have no obligation to do so. I'm just a citizen trying to do my civil duty, yet you heap procedures and rules on me rather than showing some appreciation and gratitude for somebody who has made the effort."

"I apologise if I have offended you Sir, it's just that you are a lawyer and I thought you would like the ground rules made clear up-front."

"I'm a human being first and foremost and because of my legal background, I don't need all the T's crossed, and I's dotted, thank you. Just give me the address to which I am to send this letter."

He gives me the address for which I thank him and hang up. What a buffoon. I do hope he's not in charge of this investigation. I think he would be better suited to work in the Receiver's office checking Tax Returns. Mind you, upon reflection, that's exactly what this chap is – he's an accountant. Obviously, this case needs to be investigated by financial buffs who can unravel a tangled investment web. This chap is a stereotypical accountant who thinks the facts and figures are more important than the people involved. I tend to do things the other way around. I consider the people issues first, and then the facts and figures. It normally produces more favourable results, which this buffoon should learn.

I have done my bit, and the Government has told me in no uncertain terms that I am to do nothing more. Like the good citizen I am, I will obey them explicitly and get on and enjoy my retirement to its full.

Three weeks have passed since hearing from MI6, during which time Fiona and I have been getting out a lot more; taking day trips to discover the beautiful area in which we live. I think it is because we are carefree, enjoying everything for what it is without having the nagging worry about work or financial issues, that we can enjoy ourselves more thoroughly. I admit, in the past to carrying my work around with me no matter where I went, even if only in my head. Perhaps I'm just too intense in how I approach things, but I can assure you I have never felt better having shed these burdens. This has brought Fiona and I a lot closer. I have always thought of ourselves as soul mates, which in a way is strange because I would never have thought the two of us could grow any closer. I am indeed a fortunate man.

One of the rituals we have got into, and one I look forward to, is our regular Thursday morning trip to the village to do the shopping and to visit a quaint old coffee shop which serves an excellent cappuccino and custard slice, for which I have a rather strong penchant.

It was on one of these shopping trips that I received a call from Phillip Stopford of MI6 asking if he could call in and see me tomorrow at ten o'clock; to which I agreed.

The next day at ten o'clock sharp, Mr. Stopford and a colleague arrived at the house, both being ordinary, nondescript individuals. Although I was introduced to the second man, I cannot recall his name. I lead the two gentlemen through to my study where Fiona kindly provided us with tea and coffee. After a few simple pleasantries, Mr. Stopford cleared his throat and announced, "I would like to get to the point of this meeting directly. Our investigation has been concluded and its findings delivered to the Office of the Prime Minister, who in turn instructed us to inform you of our findings. A forty-eight page, detailed report has been submitted, of which we are permitted to disclose the conclusions only. After extensive investigation by a twelve man team of specialist investigators, we were unable to establish any commonality whatsoever between claimants and, or their backers. Consequently, we conclude that there is no threat of a plot to disrupt stock markets here or anywhere else in the world. We have strongly recommended that no further action be taken and this matter be closed."

I was dumbstruck. It's amazing how wrong you can be even when you get a strong premonition that things aren't right. I felt quite stupid; my great theories have been shot down in front of the highest authorities in the land. I have also cost the Government a considerable amount of money through my alarmist theory, but then I console myself through the fact that they willingly undertook the investigation.

"Although we consider this matter to be closed," continues Mr. Stopford, "I must caution you that it still remains an official secret and as such, all information you have on this matter cannot be discussed with, or disclosed to, anybody for any reason whatsoever."

I nod my head in approval.

In unison, the two men stand.

"I would like to say it has been a pleasure meeting you, but quite frankly I don't enjoy having to redirect critical departmental resources to go on wild goose chases simply because somebody has the ear of the Prime Minister and fills it with ridiculous, unsubstantiated conspiracy theories. Good day to you, Sir. We shall find our own way out, thank you." Both men turned on their heels and marched out the room.

The man is out of order. What I did, I did in the belief of helping fellow citizens, not in furthering my own objectives. No matter how misguided my beliefs, I acted honourably and did what I still believe was the right thing to do. What an ignorant and obnoxious individual.

I turn my chair and look out the window. I'm missing something! If there is no common backer and therefore no common purpose, then there must be one or more shared objectives or many individual objectives at play. And yet, I can't think of one that makes any sense. I'm probably overlooking the most obvious. Often something in plain view is overlooked, like the salt cellar you can't find in the cupboard, and yet it's right in front of you all the time. I'm going to put this matter into the back of my mind and let my subconscious work away at it. In a day or so I will probably have a clearer understanding. This is a technique I've used throughout my life, fairly successfully. It was taught to me by my father who, whenever faced with a difficult problem, would walk away from it for a day or so, but when he returned, he invariably resolved the problem or fully understood all the issues.

I'm upset and annoyed but I'm going to let the whole matter go away for now. I'm certainly pleased there is no sinister plot behind these events, but I would still like to understand the motives of the claimants in these new cases. If I get an insight – great, but if I don't, it won't worry me.

Chapter Five

'Time flies when you're having fun' goes the old adage. If it can be believed, then I must be having the time of my life because it's already Thursday and Fiona and I are driving to the village to do our weekly shopping. It's a cold, grey day with intermittent rain and I'm looking forward to our regular visit to the coffee shop. It's on days like this that the coffee shop is greatly appreciated. The warm shelter it offers from the bitter wind is most welcome and the aroma of coffee is simply irresistible, not to forget the allure of the custard slice either.

Our routine dictates we visit the library first then the coffee shop, and then we do our shopping. Never shop on an empty stomach is a throwback to our struggling student days and bringing up a family on a shoestring.

I hustle Fiona along after visiting the library; the warmth of the coffee shop and my custard slice beckoning.

The coffee shop is a quaint little place with no more than five double tables. It has a little bell over the bright, green front door that jingles when you enter. We have become friendly with the proprietor who has got to know us and our tastes well.

"Good morning, Fiona. Good morning, James," says Joan as we enter. She then beckons us closer and starts whispering.

"I'm sorry, James, but that gentleman over there," she says nodding her head in the direction of a dishevelled, middle-aged man sitting in the corner, "has eaten all my custard slices. He's been here for the past hour scribbling away on his notepad. Don't know who he is. He's not from around here."

"Not to worry, Joan," says Fiona smiling, "James needs to cut down on his sugar intake so the cheese and biscuit platter will suit him perfectly."

"No, Joan," I protest, "do you have any of your lovely, homemade apple pie with thick, clotted cream?"

She nods her head with a big smile.

"Good," I say walking towards our table, "plus the normal, thanks, Joan."

Once seated, I glanced across at the man who had devoured my custard slice. He was a skinny, middle-aged man wearing very thick glasses. He wore a black suit, but looked distinctly dishevelled with his tie askew and uncombed hair. He didn't look up when we came in; he just continued scribbling on his notepad.

There was another couple in the shop who Fiona knew and got chatting to. I wish she hadn't as I wanted to have a look at one of my library books which I'd had on order for a couple of weeks.

Fiona's friends finally leave and I get to enjoy my second cup of coffee, while glancing through my books.

When we finished, we were the last couple in the shop, apart from this man who appeared to be drinking endless cups of black coffee which I overheard him ordering. As we rose to leave, he came over to speak to us. Fiona beats a hasty retreat to the counter to pay, no doubt expecting to hear some hard luck story and a request for money.

"Um, erh, erh, are you Mr. James Barton-Marshall?" he enquires.

I was taken aback. How does he know my name? Who is he?

"Yes," I reply.

"Good… um, um, good," he stutters and stammers.

"My name is Dr. John Abromovitz of MI6 and... and I need to speak to you urgently about the matter you raised with the department recently."

"The matter has been closed," I told him.

"Far from it," he replies. "I... I need your help, but... but we can't talk about it here. Please meet me briefly in the car park behind the shop."

"Come to my house and discuss it," I said.

"Can't do that," he says, "your house has been bugged. We can't be seen together. We are probably being watched now. It is extremely urgent that we meet briefly so I can tell you a few things. What you stumbled on is a lot bigger than you thought. I need to explain some things to you, but not here. Please meet me in the car park in five minutes time. Don't go there directly, walk around the block. Please... please it is very, very urgent! There is a lot more at stake than you ever thought."

I stood at my table in a stunned state, while he shuffled off to the counter and paid.

I must have been standing there for a few moments as Joan came over to me and enquired, "Is everything alright, James? You're not sick are you, you look a little pale, I'll call Fiona."

"No, don't do that, Joan, I'm fine, thank you."

I'm dumbfounded. I'm being followed and my house has been bugged. What on earth is going on? I'm interested to hear what he's got to say, but then equally, a little afraid. According to this man, the threat is a lot bigger than Al-Qaeda; how much bigger could it possibly be?

Fiona is waiting outside for me.

"Who was that man?" she enquires. "He shuffled past me, head bent, not looking left or right."

"He claims to be from MI6," I reply.

"Oh, yes, and I'm Father Christmas. What did James Bond want with you then?" she enquires rather sarcastically.

"He says he has some information about the case and he needs my help. He asked me to meet him in the car park." I didn't want to give her any further information, otherwise she would stop me meeting this character.

"Please, James, leave this matter be. This is not your problem. Let that creepy man sort out his own problems."

"I would like to hear what he has to say. By hearing him out doesn't mean I will become involved, does it?"

"Sure, but I know you a lot better than that. If it sounds interesting you will become involved. Please yourself, but I beseech you not to become involved, remember you have retired and work for me now," she said with a hint of a smile. With that, she turned and headed off in the direction of the shops. I followed Dr. Abromovitz's instructions and walked around the block, entering the car park from the rear. Standing in the corner, in a half crouched position with his head barely visible above the car roofs, was Dr. Abromovitz. This all seemed quite surreal. As I approached him, he stood up.

"Um, erh... thanks for coming," he says, fishing something out of his jacket pocket and thrusting it towards me. It was his wallet with an identification card. I had a careful look at it. It appeared to validate who he said he was.

"I've got to be quick," he said, "as you and I can't risk being seen together."

I attempt to speak but he puts his finger to his lips to indicate I should remain silent.

"You were correct when you identified the nature of the plot, but only partially correct in identifying its full scope. You were wrong in identifying the perpetrators, but I will explain all this to you later. Right now, I need your help. I need someone I can trust and by you raising the alarm, I assume you are clean."

"What do you mean 'clean'?" I enquire.

"MI6 has been infiltrated, that is why this case has been closed down and that is why my research spanning over twenty years on the matter has been lost or destroyed; or so they think. In the coming months, we are going to see the collapse of our economy and a lot worse. Right now, I am the only person standing between these events unfolding and some effective action. The final elements in our enemy's strategy were set in motion with your court hearing and will escalate rapidly over the next few months. There is not much time left now, so I implore you to help me, in the interests of the free world, to stop these events unfolding. It really is that serious, even though it may sound melodramatic and you may be a little overwhelmed by me approaching you as I have; I desperately need your help."

I nod my head, not because I agree but because he was correct, I was totally overwhelmed. Is this man for real or completely whacky?

"Thank you," he says, assuming my nod indicated acceptance. "I must tell you the stakes are not high, they are astronomical. Our lives and those of our families are worth less than a second thought to these people. We cannot be seen together from now on. We are probably being watched right now. Your house has been bugged and your every move followed. They probably know everything about you, down to the most intimate detail. I must leave now. I will contact you this afternoon. The woods to the left of your study window is a safe place to meet. Your outbuildings are probably riddled with listening devices as well. Don't talk to anybody about this and don't discuss these matters in your house, otherwise you, and I will be compromised. Watch the woods for a signal. When you see it, come alone. Thank you, I will see you later."

He picked up his briefcase and scurried off in a semi-crouched position. This can't be real? In fact, I hope to wake from this horrible nightmare shortly. International plots, corrupt MI6, nutty professors and my life threatened – what more? It definitely sounds too crazy to be true, but what if he's telling the truth; what am I letting myself in for? I can't do this to my loving and trusting wife. I can't do this to myself. I feel quite nauseous. I'm not a brave man. I don't have the makeup or constitution to be involved in espionage, if it's anything like its depiction in books and films.

While walking back to the shops to find Fiona, I mull over some statements made by Dr. Abromovitz which could possibly corroborate his story. Firstly, he knew the layout of my house, knowing where the woods were in relation to my study, and that they were easily seen from the study. This would indicate he, or others, had been in my house. If they have been in my house, unbeknown to me, they could easily have bugged it. Secondly, he knew my regular movements, knowing where I would be on a Thursday morning. Clearly, somebody could only do that if they had been following me for some time. Furthermore, I still can't come up with any logical explanation for these mass international court actions; a cover-up would explain the MI6 actions. Admittedly, an MI6 cover-up sounds fanciful, but nonetheless, conceivable. I'm going to phone Matt when I get back to find out what developments have taken place on this front. If there are any new cases, the more convinced I'll be of an orchestrated plot.

It's a strange feeling, I have always felt my home is my sanctuary yet, while turning our car into our long, tree-lined driveway and catching a glimpse of the house, I get a cold feeling, as if it's hiding secrets from me. A house is where you hide secrets from the world, not the other way around. As soon as this happens, one's home becomes a bleak and unhappy place. My house spies on me for the benefit of others. What a chilling thought.

I haven't told Fiona what Dr. Abromovitz said, apart from endorsing my theory and continuing the investigation on his own. It's a little white lie, which I'm not partial to, but it will satisfy her curiosity for the time being. I know she's not entirely happy with my explanation, or these new developments.

After helping unload the car, I went to my study and phoned Matt. It wasn't good news, but entirely anticipated. Several new cases had been filed around the world. A further interesting development has been that the American claim has been leapfrogged to the front of the Court queue. This is rather reminiscent of our case, and I wonder if Matt was as influential in getting our case leapfrogged as he thought he was? Whoever it is that's orchestrating events is certainly turning up the heat. These are frightening developments. What if one person, namely Dr. Abromovitz, is the only person standing between us and a catastrophe, as he predicts? We certainly don't have the support of MI6. Who else knows of these events? What can be done to tell others? I swing my chair and look out over the rainy scene before me as fearful thoughts engulf me.

I must have nodded off as I was startled when Fiona placed her hand on my shoulder.

"I brought you a cup of tea," she said.

"Thank you. I must have been dreaming."

She smiled, patted my shoulder and turned to leave. As she got to the window she stopped and looked out.

"I'm sure I saw a light flashing over there in the woods," she said.

I jumped to my feet. I didn't want her seeing that. I pretended to look, but quickly turned her around and headed her towards the door. "The only flashing you saw was the stars in your eyes when you saw me," I said.

"You are certainly an accomplished comedian," she replies, leaving the room.

As soon as she left, I returned to the window to see if I could see the flashing light. It would be dark in little over an hour so I should be able to see it easily, even though it's misty and raining fairly heavily. I peer through the mist, which is not that thick, towards the woods but cannot see anything. I decide to go and investigate anyway. I open my desk draw and rummage through it looking for a torch which I had left there a few days earlier. I then hurriedly made my way to the foyer, where my galoshes and coat are hung, in the hope of escaping Fiona's inquisition.

I'm halfway out the door when I hear her calling, "And where are you going at this time and in this weather?"

I step back inside, "I thought I would check out the flashing lights as we have established conclusively it's not stars in your eyes."

"Oh, don't be silly," she chides me, "the weather's appalling and it will be dark soon."

"Not to worry, I need to get out and stretch my legs."

"Nonsense, you had a long walk in the village today. In fact, you complained about how much we walked."

"I feel invigorated now," I say, "I will see you shortly, my darling." I turned and closed the door quickly behind me. Time was slipping by, I didn't want to get into a debate on whether I should stay or go. She would soon be volunteering to come with me, which would be more difficult to wriggle out of. I hurried down towards the outbuildings, which are some distance away from the house. The outbuildings comprise several sheds, which I rent to a local farmer. As I passed them, I wondered why we have to meet in the cold, wet woods when there are adequate, warm and secure sheds available. Come to think of it, he did mention the sheds may also be bugged – how amazing. After leaving the sheds behind me, I cross a small field and entered the woods. The woods are quite extensive, with a frontage of nearly one mile, extending equidistance on both sides of me and descending into a small valley in front of me for another mile or more. I start moving to my right, to a position that would be visible from my study. I hadn't gone far when I saw a small light flashing not far ahead of me. It appeared to be one of those new, white lights with a blue hue used on bicycles. I headed for the light. There I found Dr. Abromovitz sitting on a stump of wood. He looked terrible. He appeared to be completely drenched. His hair was plastered to his head and water streamed down his face. His raincoat, or what appeared to be his raincoat, was saturated. His trouser legs had mud on them and his shoes were completely caked in mud. He didn't look much like a saviour of the world to me; it looked more like he needed saving.

"Thank you for coming. I wasn't sure if you had seen the light or not," he said, taking off his glasses and wiping his face.

I looked at this skinny, little man in front of me. Protruding check bones, hollowed cheeks; almost emaciated. I felt sorry for him.

"You are probably wondering why we are meeting here and not in the outbuildings?" he said, replacing his glasses and looking at me.

I nodded.

"The listening and recording devices we have today are extremely sophisticated. Putting them up in sheds is easy and quick, and they work well; knowing the people we are dealing with, this is exactly what they would do. The same cannot be said for woods; too much external interference from wind, rain and light."

I nod my head again.

"This is an ideal place to meet and conceal our secrets," he said.

What a strange way to describe this meeting, but then Dr. Abromovitz is a strange bird.

He continues, "I'm a forensic accountant with over thirty years experience in the field of money laundering. My doctoral thesis was on the subject. I have presented numerous papers, written many articles and two books on the subject, one of which is used worldwide as a reference. I feel justified in referring to myself as an expert in this field. Please check my credentials and my website. My entire career has been devoted to working for British Intelligence on matters of money laundering. Almost twenty years ago, I noticed an interesting change in money laundering procedures from an emerging Underworld boss, one Manuel Alvarez. He is a highly intelligent, ruthless and far-sighted Underworld boss who, twenty years ago, was a rising star. His empire was expanding rapidly and yet their money laundering activities, utilising known practices, were in rapid decline, to the extent that about ten years ago they stopped completely. I tracked these trends for a few years before realising that he had adopted new laundering techniques and started investigating what he was up to. As you can imagine, money laundering is a highly risky business, so those who 'wash' the money take the lion's share of the proceeds. For most, this arrangement is acceptable; criminals pay a high price for having their ill-gotten money 'washed' but in return, they get their money quickly. Then along comes Manuel Alvarez who's not prepared to lose a penny on laundering money; in fact, he expects every penny of his money to grow substantially, like any good investment. So he adopts an entirely new approach to money laundering. He takes the long-term approach. He's very shrewd and like any wise businessman, he knows the long-term options pay best. There are several ways he has done this, but as I don't have time to tell you all of them, I will explain the pertinent ones," says Dr. Abromovitz, taking off his glasses and wiping his face again.

He shudders from the cold, continuing, "The concept of social networking is a fairly recent phenomenon and yet almost twenty years ago, Alvarez identified it as an important tool he could use to manipulate society for his own ends, while using it as a conduit to launder money on a highly profitable basis. Networks work by sharing knowledge and information, and utilising the influence they can bring to bear. He realised he could 'own' a network if he provided 'soft loans' to ambitious and unscrupulous individuals within the network, of which there is never a dearth. A soft loan is similar to those you may have heard about in films such as *The Godfather*, where the Mafia may help you with a loan at very favourable rates and repayment terms, but once you've accepted, they may call on you to perform services for them. Failure to comply is no option. Once you're caught in the web, Alvarez can manipulate you. He could ask you to favour certain people or businesses over others, or to promote a certain idea or concept; he has power over you and therefore, over your network. Once ensnared, he encourages you to promote his 'easy money', or the influence the network can offer, to other unsuspecting 'prospects'. You soon realise that by getting others to join your network and to support you makes your life a lot easier, so you start actively promoting these soft loans and benefits. Your new master judges you on your ability to recruit new prospects and to extend your influence within the network. They take kindly to people who promote their involvement and who toe-the-line, but deal ruthlessly with those that don't. Consequently, Alvarez's influence within the network grows quickly and spreads to other networks, until his control and influence is omnipresent."

He stops as a coughing spasm takes hold of him. I wouldn't be surprised if he has pneumonia, the way he's coughing. When he stopped, I suggested I get him some warm clothes and something warm to drink. He refused, saying we couldn't stay here too long and that he was alright. He doesn't look alright to me.

He continued, "You have seen inexplicable events occur where individuals are promoted over better, more qualified colleagues, or where contracts are awarded to second or third contenders, or even non-runners?"

I nod in agreement.

"These are often as a result of Alvarez-controlled networks influencing decisions in their favour. It might be that by getting the decision to go their way, the person favoured becomes indebted to the Alvarez clan." He pauses for a few seconds and then continues.

"If your business desperately needs to win a contract to survive and this is generally well known, you may receive a call from somebody telling you they can possibly swing the deal, but in return you are to scratch their back one day. It's that easy to ensnare an innocent victim, but once they are caught in this web, their loyalty is ruthlessly enforced. You don't forget your commitments to Alvarez easily, that is if you value your life and that of your loved ones."

We were interrupted by a further coughing bout. When he recovered, he took a few deep breaths and continued. "Rather than laundering money traditionally, Alvarez makes his 'dirty' cash and influence in these networks readily available to all.

Playing on the human weakness of greed, his networks grow quickly and over time have infiltrated every conceivable walk of life. Alvarez keeps pumping more and more money into these social and business networks, and keeps growing his influence daily. He gets his money back with interest, but more importantly, the power he can exert anywhere and everywhere in the world increases phenomenally. While other criminal enterprises saw money laundering as an end to a process, Alvarez saw it as the start of a new, highly profitable and influential venture. He gets all his money back plus interest, but more importantly, he now manipulates millions of highly influential people around the world to do his bidding."

"How can he possibly control what you are intimating could be many millions of people, each with a unique relationship with the Alvarez mob? It sounds almost inconceivable to me," I remark.

"Inconceivable!" says Dr. Abromovitz, with an annoyed tone to his voice and a frown on his face.

"Large international banks record millions of transactions daily. Alvarez's organisation doesn't need to record the same volumes, but believe me they are a technology-savvy organisation. They are early technology adaptors, spending multiple millions on developing their own effective systems. They invest more in technology than many small countries. He has more money to invest in technology than the largest international bank. Alvarez knew he had to embrace technology as an integral part of his wider strategy, and he has done this very successfully. He also has an extensive organisational infrastructure managing these networks, like bank managers, so to speak."

He paused for a moment, drew a deep breath and continued. "Remember, they aren't interested in micro-managing these networks. They are only interested in manipulating them in terms of their objectives. Consequently, they only activate cells within the network when they are to carry out their bidding. Some cells may never be activated; others may be utilised extensively. It's like switching a light bulb on or off when you need it. Most of the time they couldn't care what these networks get up to. With effective technology and an effective organisational structure, they can manage vast networks, switching cells on and off at will. Dissenters are dealt with by a specialist, roving hit team that show no mercy."

"Your point is taken. This is extremely disturbing," I said.

He cleared his throat. I expected another bout of coughing, but he managed to contain it and continue. "Alvarez's new money laundering techniques don't stop at this; they actively seek out struggling businesses with potential, but who are facing a cash crisis. Again, they offer soft loans or take up favourable share options, all paid for by 'dirty' cash which the struggling business may not be aware of, and probably don't care as their backs are against the wall; to them, the offer is like manna from heaven. Again, Alvarez gets all his money back plus interest and has these businesses where he wants them. He's clever, devilishly clever. I'm sure, during your career, you have witnessed businesses making miraculous recoveries when on the brink of disaster. You will also have witnessed small businesses gobble up their much bigger competitors. Where do you think the cash comes from? Where do you think most Russian oligarchs found vast sums of money to buy up entire industries at the drop of a hat?"

"I assume the authorities are fully aware of this man's activities? You must have made your findings available to them immediately you were aware of what was going on?" I enquired.

"I certainly did, but learnt early on that the parasitic nature of his networks had spread quicker than could be imagined. In the early days, when I presented findings to my superiors, they went missing or were inexplicably lost and I was told, in no uncertain terms, to drop my investigations. Fortunately, I kept copies of my work and continued building a case of evidence over the years, in secret. Look what happened to your enquiry. It was dead in the water before it started. They probably told you they could find no commonality between backers of these claims, and yet when I glanced through the list, unofficially of course, as understandably they didn't assign me to this case, I immediately recognised a few business names."

Pausing for a few moments, he said, "Let me explain a possible scenario for the case you were involved in recently. Part of Alvarez's strategy is to invest heavily in research and development over a broad front; humanities, religion, business, science, you name it. He gets businesses he owns or manipulates to fund university departments. He favours departments who undertake controversial research, or who are leading-edge thinkers. The reason for this is that if they make a breakthrough he can exploit their work, or even if they produce controversial findings he can use these findings to manipulate markets or attitudes to his benefit, using his control of the communications media for this purpose. He gets his 'front' businesses to invest in these universities, and then he waits for them to produce results, or for events to unfold, where he can exploit their research. The Advanced Business Metrics department at the University of Bristol is a classic example of such a 'fringe' department doing research in a controversial area. He possibly invested in them many years ago, then, as part of his master strategy, when the timing is right, he instructs his front businesses to fully back Professor Metcalfe in bringing a claim against the Global Marketing Association."

"That makes sense," I said. "Professor Metcalfe told me that his backers had shown no interest in his proposals and then, almost a year later and in unison, two supposedly independent businesses back him to the hilt. The backers appear to have little or nothing to gain from the action but carry the financial risk. It was this that had me worried and baffled from the beginning."

"Precisely," said Dr. Abromovitz. "I hadn't come across the names of the backers of Professor Metcalfe before, but given a few weeks research, I would no doubt be able to trace them back to some common denominator within the Alvarez organisation."

"When MI6 was asked to investigate commonality of backers, was it Alvarez's control of networks, one of which had infiltrated MI6, that had the investigation closed down?" I asked Dr. Abromovitz.

"That's correct. Now you can see what started out as a money laundering exercise, has resulted in the domination of our society and economy by Alvarez," says Dr. Abromovitz.

"Good God, man, this is frightening stuff," I comment.

Dr. Abromovitz nods his head a few times.

"I can understand what you have told me so far about how he can manipulate society and our economy, but I'm not clear as to what end. Clearly he must be an extremely wealthy and influential man, so where is this leading to, if anywhere? He must have everything anybody could ever wish for?" I enquire further.

"For this you need to understand the man Alvarez," said Dr. Abromovitz.

He stood, shook the rain from his coat, removed his glasses and wiped the rain from his face.

"We must hurry now; I don't want to arouse any suspicions. We need to meet again. There is a small B&B three and a half miles from here, on the road to Coombe End; it's called Rosewood Cottage. Meet me there tomorrow at two o'clock sharp. Do not use your car. Don't tell anybody about this meeting and don't walk on the road; cut across country. Furthermore, when you leave the house walk in the opposite direction until you are out of view of the house, then cut back inland. This will reduce the risk of them knowing where you are going."

He picked up his briefcase and extended his hand to me.

"I'm sure you will have a lot of questions for me. See you tomorrow," he said, turning and walking down the valley. It was dark and within seconds he had disappeared, although I could hear him coughing in the distance.

I make my way back to the house. It's pitch black and raining. I thought it best not to use the torch. I stumbled a few times. On one occasion, I fell to my knees and my trousers were covered in mud. Eventually, with some relief, I caught sight of the outbuildings lights and the small field between them and the woods. With a sense of relief, I leave the woods and cross the field. On reaching the outbuildings, I stopped to catch my breath. It was then that I noticed what I thought was a figure standing in the shadows at the far end of the building. I fumbled for my torch; I didn't want to slink back into the shadows as this would arouse suspicions as to why I'm here, although I instinctively felt like doing so. I shone my torch in the direction of the person, but if there was anybody there, they were long gone. I don't know if it was my imagination, poor visibility, or whether there was somebody there. A little shaken, I quickly made my way to the house.

As I approached the house it is in complete darkness. I find this strange as I have a timed light over the front door which is scheduled to come on when it gets dark, and switches off at midnight. Normally, by this time, there would be a few other lights switched on which would be visible from outside. I'm filled with apprehension as I quicken my pace.

"Fiona... Fiona?" I shout as I enter the house. I wait for a response. Nothing is forthcoming so I start running up the stairs. Then I hear her voice.

"I'm here, James." I see a flickering light at the end of the passage. Fiona approaches carrying a candle. "Where have you been?" she demands.

"What's happened to the lights?" I ask,

"I don't know. They went off soon after dark," she replied.

"Did you check the mains box?" I asked.

"Well, of course I did. Nothing has tripped; it all looks fine to me," she replied with an indignant tone to her voice.

"That's a bit strange," I said. "The lights are on at the sheds."

"Yes, but they are on a totally different circuit," remarks Fiona.

"I know that, but it does show that it's not a supply problem but rather a problem with our electrics," I comment.

"That's just charming," she said. "I haven't prepared any dinner and there won't be any hot water for a bath tonight. Look at you! You're covered in mud. Where on earth have you been?"

"It was dark and I tripped," I explained.

"Where were you – in the woods?" she asked.

Not wishing to draw any attention to the fact that I was, due to the possibility of being eavesdropped, I ignored the question. "I'm feeling cold and wouldn't mind a bite to eat, my dear. Let's go and make ourselves a sandwich; the stove will keep us warm," I said, putting my arms around her and leading her off to the kitchen.

"I was quite scared when the lights went off," said Fiona hugging me tightly. "I went straight to the bedroom, closed the door and lay on the bed."

I kissed her forehead. I do hope there's no ominous explanation to our electricity failure. And what of the figure lurking in the shadows? Could this be that I'm being warned off, or is it all coincidence? Whatever the explanation, I will double check that windows and doors are tightly secured for the night.

Chapter Six

The next day dawns sunny and bright. Fortunately the electricity is back on, much to my relief. Fiona has her monthly Woman's Institute meeting in the village and will be gone most of the day. That will give me the opportunity to slip out and meet Dr. Abromovitz without her knowing. I have to get to the bottom of his story. I have many unanswered questions, and until they are answered to my satisfaction, I don't know what to believe. So far, Dr. Abromovitz's story is a compelling one, although the scope and far-sightedness of the scenario he paints borders the unbelievable. I anxiously wait to learn more about Manuel Alvarez, which will hopefully shed more light on the subject.

I'm perplexed as to why the infiltration of networks has never been raised or discussed publicly before? The nature and extent of the parasitic invasion of networks has frightened and appalled me. I suppose the whole affair has never surfaced publicly because, if you are a corrupt member of a network, you are not going to advertise the fact, and if anybody starts sniffing around, the corrupt elements within the network will ensure the investigating is closed down and doesn't see the light of day to protect their own interests. If the extent of network infiltration is high, then the likelihood of any media leakage is minimised. So if I've never heard about this until yesterday, it would show extensive and effective infiltration.

I suppose if you are not a corrupt member of a network, you wouldn't be any wiser to the goings on of others. Also, each different network is totally independent of others, so although you may be a member of one or more networks, the existence of a multitude of other networks will be unknown to you. Their goings on will also be unknown to you, so you wouldn't see the bigger picture of network domination, and therefore it wouldn't worry you. Essentially networks are low profile, isolated units, perhaps touching other networks periodically, but remaining independent around their specific cause or goal. The insular nature of networks and the presence of corrupting money within them, ensures they retain their secrets.

There are other possible reasons this issue has never been raised before, and that is; to what ends would anybody want to control these vast networks, which know no territorial boundaries extending across the world? Who would have the money, ability and desire to control such vast networks? The scale of the operation would make most people think the whole affair is just too fanciful to contemplate.

I suppose I may have answered my own concerns on this matter, but what of Alvarez's strategy regarding his attack on our stock markets? It wouldn't make sense for him to bring the economy to its knees, as I had predicted, so what does he have planned for us? When I first met Dr. Abromovitz, he said the scope of the strategy was much bigger than I had envisaged, but what's bigger than crippling the economy? Criminal activities generally prosper in strong economies, so why weaken the economy, unless Alvarez's astute criminal mind has found a new opportunity. This wouldn't surprise me as he appears to be most ingenious, if Dr. Abromovitz's stories can be believed.

Soon after Fiona left, I decided to set out. I would have ample time to reach Rosewood Cottage, even following the devious route suggested by Dr. Abromovitz. I would take a slow and leisurely walk, enjoying the hills and vales of the area. I knew where Rosewood Cottage was; I had driven past it on numerous occasions. I had never walked there before, and certainly not across country. I was looking forward to the walk in the bright sun and brisk air.

I followed Dr. Abromovitz's instructions to the letter, heading in the opposite direction until out of sight of the house and then doubling back across country. Before I knew it, I was on top of the hill overlooking Rosewood Cottage. Below me, stretching for as far as the eye could see, was a patchwork of agricultural land. Large scale commercial farming has destroyed many of the small fields, but in this area we are fortunate that most have survived. The hedgerow and stone walls of the area are beautiful and help support a diversity of life.

Rosewood Cottage is a small, old, white-washed building with a thatched roof and neatly laid out garden; what you would call a typical old, English, country cottage. In summer when the flowers are out, it is spectacularly beautiful. Fiona loves little cottages like this, and I'm sure she would swap our home for this without a second thought. I wish she could be with me now to enjoy the scene.

I found a small rock to sit on and enjoy the scenery. I had some time to kill before my meeting.

Small whiffs of smoke drift from the cottage's two small chimneys. It is very beautiful and tranquil. I could imagine myself being transported back two hundred years in time. Nothing much has changed apart from the tarred road, electricity and telephone poles. I could just imagine an old horse and cart trot pass the cottage on a muddy road.

It's almost two o'clock so I start making my way down to the cottage. There's a stile opposite the cottage, which I head for. As I stepped into the road having just climbed off the stile, a small car came hurtling around the bend. I flung myself back against the stile as the car narrowly missed me and continued at high speed up the road. The occupants appeared to be two young men who were gesticulating wildly towards me as if it were my fault they had almost run me over. This certainly brought me back to the twenty-first century with a resounding thump. I can't imagine how any intelligent, thinking being can drive at high speed on narrow, country roads. This is, of course, a rhetorical question. It saddens me when I see just how many wild animals are killed on our country roads through excessive speed by individuals of this ilk.

A little shaken, I knocked on the cottage door. I hear the latch being undone and the door flung open. In front of me stood a little, old, grey-haired lady with the biggest smile that I have ever seen.

"Hello… hello, Mr. Barton-Marshall, I'm very pleased to see you," she announced.

I was taken aback by this greeting. Firstly, I don't know who this woman is and secondly, I thought security was an issue; Dr. Abromovitz and I couldn't be seen together.

Sensing I had no idea who she was, the little, old lady attempted to explain. "I'm Elizabeth Morgan, your wife and I are members of the local Book Club. I've been to your house on a few occasions; it's a beautiful place and so tastefully decorated. I haven't met you before, but I immediately recognised you from all your TV appearances concerning that very important case you were on. It's so nice to have such an important person living in our area. I don't think we have ever had such an important person live here before."

"Thank you for your kind words, Mrs. Morgan. Fortunately, I'm not an important person. I'm just a retired lawyer who was lucky enough to work on some interesting cases."

"You are too modest, Mr. Barton-Marshall," she says with a girlish giggle to her voice. "Your, friend Mr. Edwards, is waiting for you in the lounge," she said pointing to a room on her left. "He has asked that you not be disturbed, but I will bring you a cup of tea and a teacake. It looks like you could do with a nice, strong cup of tea, my dear," she said.

"Thank you, Mrs. Morgan, you are most kind."

She smiled, turned around and scurried off in what I assumed was the direction of the kitchen. I entered the lounge, which led directly off the entrance passage. It's a very small lounge, with four, large, wingback chairs and a small coffee table in the centre. There is barely enough room for the four chairs. Sitting in a chair furthest away from the door is Dr. Abromovitz. He rises to his feet as I enter the room and extends his hand in greeting.

"Hello… ah, hello, I'm pleased to see you again," he says in his typical nervous manner.

Dr. Abromovitz looks considerably better than when last I saw him. His hair is combed and he's wearing a cream-coloured, polo-necked jersey and tweed jacket, with dark, brown trousers. Although a lot better, he still looks scruffy. His jacket looks like it has been taken from a small suitcase, where it has been successfully crushed.

He gestures towards one of the chairs.

"I'm a little confused about the security arrangements, which you say are so important. You told me we must not be seen together, yet we meet in a house where we can both be easily identified. Last night we had to meet under a veil of secrecy in a ridiculous place under appalling conditions – why?"

"I… I can understand your concerns and will explain all," he said. "Firstly, did you follow my instructions on getting here?" he enquires.

"Yes, I did," I replied.

"And nobody saw you?"

"Not that I'm aware of, apart from the two youngsters who almost ran me down outside the cottage a few minutes ago," I said.

"Did they see you enter the house, or knock on the door?" he asked.

"Definitely not, by the time I knocked on the door they must have been miles away and had probably run over a few pedestrians in the process," I reply.

"Good," he says. "I'm sure they know I'm in the area, even if they haven't seen me yet. I'm sure they would have figured out that you are the reason I'm here. As long as they don't know where I am right now, that's okay. I have to remain one step ahead of them, always," he replied.

"What about me?" I ask. "They know exactly where to find me."

"You're okay, for the time being, as they will think you have nothing to harm them with. They may try to frighten you off, but I don't think your life is in any danger yet. I, on the other hand, have extensive incriminating evidence which they may or may not suspect I have, and consequently, more at risk."

"You keep referring to 'them'. Who precisely are they?" I enquire.

"Primarily Alvarez's henchmen, who in turn may have the assistance of MI6 and even the local police," he replies.

"My God," I say in total despondency. "You're on your own, with all the odds stacked up against you."

"That about sums it up," he says. "Nobody has seen the threat so nothing has been done about it. People don't realise the dire straights we are in and that we are fighting the final battle to retain the democracies of the free world."

"Oh, come on, Doctor, I'm not some naïve, comic-reading child that sucks in some far-fetched story of some evil empire about to overthrow us and install an Orwellian, totalitarian State!"

"Do me the courtesy of hearing me out before condemning what I have to say. I'm equally no idiot. However I have facts to back me up, which you don't in so freely condemning me. I can tell you, I wish I had never stumbled on these events because now, morally, I have to carry the burden. I wish this were all fantasy and I am Don Quixote titling at a windmill, but unfortunately, I am not. Hear me out and then tell me I am wrong," he says indignantly.

"Returning to your earlier security queries," he said. "We will need to meet again. When that meeting will take place and where I don't know as we cannot risk meeting in the same place twice. Therefore, I need to have a common point where we can communicate with one another to set up future meetings, as we cannot use traditional communication methods. The woods are the ideal area for us to meet quickly and to make such arrangements, as we have done for this one. You need to look for a signal everyday at about the same time, around the appointed date. I know this is a little inconvenient and a bit like Biggles, but I don't know of any other way."

I nod my head.

"By the time Alvarez can piece together the fact that you and I met here, I'll be long gone. As long as they don't follow you to our meeting points, I should be okay. I have scanned this house for bugs and it's okay, and it's certainly a lot more comfortable than the woods."

There's a knock on the lounge door as Mrs Morgan enters carrying a large tea tray.

"I have brought you a lovely pot of tea and some homemade teacakes, my dears," she says, placing the tray on the coffee table.

I get to my feet and thank her for her generosity.

"I won't disturb you any further, I know you must have important matters to discuss," she says, leaving the room and closing the door behind her.

After pouring the tea and enjoying Mrs Morgan's teacakes, Dr. Abromovitz resumed his story.

"When I first noticed changes in Alvarez's money laundering activities, I was totally flummoxed. I could make little sense of what was going on. His practices in no way conformed to any known procedures and yet whatever he was up to, he was perusing more aggressively year-by-year. I realised that the only way for me to understand what was going on was to understand the man more thoroughly. I only had very scant information on him and assumed he was just another drug baron; how wrong I was. As in many things in life, be it business, sport or war, you need to know your adversary. You need to understand their psyche. Only when I did this did the pieces of the jigsaw start fitting together. Right now, you can't make much sense of the plot facing us, even though you have identified most of the threats and know who is behind them; that is because you know nothing about your enemy. That is his greatest strength; anonymity. His parasitic invasion of society has gone undetected for reasons we have discussed earlier. When you understand more about this megalomaniac, his master plan will become clear to you and the threat very real." He paused for a moment, as if gathering his thoughts.

"Had you heard of Manuel Alvarez before I told you about him?" he asked.

I shook my head.

"Of course, you've heard of Bill Gates and Warren Buffet?" he enquires further.

I nod my head.

"Manuel Alvarez is worth considerably more than the combined wealth of both these men. It is difficult to estimate his true wealth, but conservative estimates have put it close to, or just over, six hundred billion pounds Sterling. Such wealth is almost inconceivable, particularly when you consider the short period over which it has been amassed. When rich lists are compiled, his name is never on them. The man in the street has never heard about him, and yet he may be the very person who 'bought' them and is pulling their strings today. Alvarez's association with the business and social networks he owns follows a very torturous route, and it's difficult to associate him directly with them, yet he most certainly pulls their strings." He cleared this throat; fortunately no coughing bout followed.

"Manuel Alvarez was born in the Colombian city of Bogotá in 1961 to middle-class parents of Spanish origin. He is the third of five children. He had one brother, who was ten years older than him and the oldest child. He had a loving and supportive family, with both parents working. His father was a successful bank manager and his mother a teacher. From an early age, Manuel showed great academic talent and was exceptionally bright. His brother, on the other hand, was a complete dropout who became embroiled in the drugs trade and was shot and killed when Manuel was only twelve-years-old. This had a devastating effect on Manuel who was very close to his brother. His brother's killing tore the family apart. His mother had a nervous breakdown as she partially blames herself for his death. This incapacitates her and forces her to lose her job. This, in turn, worsens her condition and she becomes virtually an invalid, requiring full-time attention from Manuel's father. This places huge pressure on him, which results in him losing his job. This all happens by the time Manuel is only thirteen. Manuel's father finds part-time work, but the family is in financial difficulties. They lose their house in a middle-to-upper class suburb and have to move to a small apartment in a disreputable part of the city. The family battles to survive, yet Manuel's father does everything to give Manuel and his two younger sisters a good education. His eldest sister turns to prostitution to help support the family. This almost kills Manuel's father, who can hardly live with the shame but is forced to accept her charity. She has not entered this profession through choice and has essentially sacrificed herself to help keep the family alive. By the time Manuel finishes his schooling at the age of seventeen, one year ahead of his peers and with excellent results, he is extremely bitter and revengeful. He is driven by one objective and that is to protect and provide for his family, and to seek revenge from those who he believed abused or took advantage of his family. His father, who he loved and adored, did everything he could to get Manuel to go to university through bursaries he had managed to arrange. Manuel would have none of it. He knew the fast-track to achieve his objective lay in the drugs trade; a university education would take years to acquire and then many years thereafter before it bore any fruits, and then not on a scale this ambitious youngster expected. So on leaving school, this bright, ambitious, young man with the stamp of a great leader all over him, became involved in the drugs trade. His father is bitterly disappointed, believing this would just add to the misery and tragedy of the family who are essentially good, god-fearing people.

"Manuel Alvarez, however, is no normal recruit to the Underworld. He is highly intelligent, far-sighted and driven by a burning passion to rise to the top, so he can fulfil his ambition. He also proves to be totally ruthless. He is credited with having killed, in cold blood, several of his older sister's 'clients' who he felt had defiled her. He is also credited with having hunted down and summarily executed those who he thought were responsible for, or implicated in, the killing of his brother. His ruthlessness, drive and intellect helped him rise through the ranks very quickly. In little after two years of joining the organisation, at the age of only nineteen, he is sent to Florida in the USA to oversee their expanding American operation. There, he quickly builds a strong infrastructure through cleverly outmanoeuvring and, or ruthlessly eliminating, competition.

"Soon he becomes restless and frustrated by the limited thinking of his bosses. He has big ambitions for the organisation. He wants to grow it into an international crime syndicate. His bosses are happy to be very, very rich – nothing more. Consequently, when he was only twenty-three-years-old, he masterminded a coup to take over complete control of his organisation. In the process, he not only achieved this objective but by carefully manipulating events, was able to eliminate a large portion of his Colombian competition, showing him as a strategic mastermind. He now turns his attention into growing a worldwide crime syndicate. Rather than muscle in on other syndicates, he devises a plan whereby he forges strong relationships with other crime syndicates around the world, planting 'sleepers' in their midst."

"What is a 'sleeper'?" I interrupt him.

"A 'sleeper' is an individual identified for future leadership that is planted into an organisation, or who may already be in the organisation and is won over to the Alvarez camp on the promise of being the future leader of their syndicate. 'Sleepers' then wait until the moment is right to rise and destroy the current leadership. Alvarez forges strong ties with other syndicates under the pretext of co-operation, but his real objective is to identify potential 'sleepers' or plant 'sleepers', and to get closer to his enemy to know when the time is right to strike the fatal blow and take over the syndicate."

He continued, "Once Alvarez was in control of his own organisation, he set about developing and expanding it rapidly. Over the next few years he also aggressively stepped up his campaign to infiltrate other crime syndicates through his 'sleepers', waiting for when the time was right for them to take over the local organisation for him. This is done through a meticulously planned coup using Alvarez's 'imported troops', much like a military coup d'état where foreign troops are used to prop up the new regime. The uprising would be quick, brutal and always successful for Alvarez. In this manner, in only five years after the bloody takeover of his own organisation, he headed the largest crime syndicate in the World, operating in every major city around the World. By 1989 Manuel Alvarez, at the age of only twenty-eight, is the head of the world's largest crime syndicate, with an annual income well in excess of the combined GDPs of many small countries."

"He doesn't sound like a particularly savoury character," I commented.

"Had his brother not been killed and had he not had to endure the terrible conditions of his adolescence, his brilliance and drive might have been channelled for the good of all. Unfortunately, his upbringing resulted in him having a rather twisted perception of how he can benefit mankind. As strange as it might sound, he is driven by his own weird notion of helping. Like many megalomaniacs before him, such as Adolph Hitler, they too had some weird notion which they believed in passionately, and which they thought would help mankind," responds Dr. Abromovitz.

"How does his story continue?" I enquired.

"Alvarez became embroiled in the Underworld for the main purpose of protecting and providing for his family; this was his driving ambition. After only six years, when he took over his organisation, he had amassed enough money, to the extent that they would never have to worry about it ever again! However, being the highly motivated and visionary individual he is, he saw the opportunity to achieve much greater heights, so he continued to pursue his objective of building a huge worldwide crime syndicate. In 1989 when his goal was achieved, and he was recognised as being the biggest crime boss in the world, things changed in his life."

He stopped for a few seconds and composed his thoughts, then continued. "At this stage, his original objective of protecting and providing for his family remained as true as it was from the first day, but now the scope of his objective changed. Here was a young man with immense wealth, influence and far-sightedness who now saw his responsibilities for protecting and providing for mankind, as he did for his family. He wishes to protect mankind from their own follies through establishing a new order, where decisions are made for them and standards imposed."

"Establish a totalitarian state?" I interrupted him.

"That is correct," he responds. "He sees weaknesses in our democratic system, which he believes makes us ineffectual in dealing with major issues, such as global warming, degeneration of society and poor economic strategies. He believes hard decisions have to be made on behalf of mankind as our democratic political system hinders us from making them. The masses, in his opinion, need fathering, not given choice. He thinks democracies are reactionary, as they only evolve at the pace of the average person. They are not visionary in anticipating future events and implementing appropriate plans for the benefit of all. Consequently, democracies are always fighting fires because of their short-term approach to problems or opportunities. In a democracy, political power is seldom won through adopting a long-term policy requiring immediate and significant sacrifice by the proletariat. Firstly, terms of office are too short to address, implement and follow through on long-term issues, and secondly, voters, while paying lip service to long-term issues, are seldom keen to pay the price themselves. The masses generally adopt an attitude of 'live today – face the problems tomorrow'."

"Sounds as though you support his ideas," I comment.

"Far from it," he replies. "I had family members who were victims of the Nazi Holocaust. So while I acknowledge there are shortcomings in our democratic principles, the system far outweighs that of a totalitarian State. Why do you think I'm putting my life on the line? I'm doing this to stop this megalomaniac in his tracks and maintain free democracies throughout the world, despite their numerous shortcomings."

I nod my head in agreement.

"I must point out that he hasn't done a particularly good job of looking after his own family," he said.

"Why is that?" I asked.

"In the early 1990s, Alvarez buys a small island somewhere in French Polynesia, I think it was one of the Marquesas Islands, and reputedly builds a fortress on it. He, according to reports I have read, built a network of air raid bunkers, anti-submarine, anti-landing craft and other defences; in fact, you name it, he had it. The island is equipped with the latest, most up-to-date surveillance systems, manned permanently by an elite army of around 100 men. Evidently, you cannot get within miles of the island before being challenged and headed-off by his security team. I know this sounds a bit like Ian Fleming's villains, but evidently it's quite true. He and his family together with support staff and his small 'army', live permanently on this island. Alvarez evidently has an underground bunker which he uses as a war room, where he closets himself and his advisors, day-in and day-out directing his international operations. He is a recluse, never leaving the island. The same applies to his family who all live on the island with him. They cannot want for anything material. He has built them beautiful mansions in idyllic settings, with everything that opens and shuts, but they are prisoners on the island. Consequently, they cannot enjoy life to the full. Their lives are empty; they cannot exercise their free choice. I'm sure Alvarez doesn't see it that way and nobody would dare to challenge him either. He now wishes to impose a similar form of 'caring' on mankind, where we may become better-off materially because of better, long-term planning and action, but the value of life will be stripped from us, as our ability to exercise free choice is seriously curtailed; just like his own family."

He paused and coughed a few times. I offered him another cup of tea and the last remaining teacake, which he accepted; a little to my disappointment as the teacakes are absolutely scrumptious, and I am a little hungry.

"Why the need to keep his family prisoner?" I asked.

He chuckles. "Alvarez doesn't do business through negotiation; he does it through the barrel of a gun. He's not seen as a father figure by any, but rather as a ruthless leader who will stop at nothing. He would have no compunction in killing his adversary and their families in resolving a dispute or gaining an advantage. Consequently, he has many enemies who would gladly see him and his family dead. His family would be a soft target for his enemies, so he keeps them hidden away, under his protection."

"How charming," I say. "This is the calibre of person we have to deal with."

He nods his head as he places his cup on the table.

"Being 'as rich as Croesus' and heading an international crime syndicate leaves him well short of the mark of replacing the free democracies of the world with his own brand of government," I comment.

"That is true," he replies. "It was at this juncture in his life that he starts contemplating possible strategies to implement his plans. The form of government his regime will follow has never been in question; to him, it's very simple – the strong rule the weak. He believes all successful enterprises are run by decisive and strong leaders, and that governments should exemplify this. In most things Alvarez does, he thinks big and he thinks long-term. He sees himself as the modern day Alexander the Great, conquering the world, but on a new and totally different battlefield. His battlefield is not one where two enemies standoff against one another. No, Alvarez has changed the rules completely."

He stopped as a coughing bout took hold. After a few minutes, he composed himself and continued.

"There are two parts to his strategy; own people and own knowledge. He implements his first strategy in a similar way to that used when he so successfully took over control of rival syndicates, where he plants 'sleepers' in networks who can be woken up at anytime to do his bidding. What makes this strategy so different from before is the sheer scale of the operation. In taking over rival syndicates he may have used thirty or forty 'sleepers', whereas now this strategy involves multiple millions. He sinks most of his money into this strategy. Rather than owning shares in businesses, he owns people. This is how it works; a bright, ambitious person seeking financial assistance or favours to advance their career is put in contact with what is euphemistically referred to as a 'helper'. This is one of Alvarez's local 'network administrators' who this person meets and discusses their requirements with. Invariably, they will help by arranging favours or providing funds. The terms and conditions of any loans are explained, which are normally very attractive. It is also explained that as they have scratched your back, you may be expected to do the same for them someday. You are also asked to spread the word that anybody seeking 'support' should contact them.

"Many people fall prey to the allure of easy money and influence, but there is no such thing. People who are ensnared in this web find they are indebted for life. They may have to keep returning favours well beyond the single favour or small loan they received. Once they are in, they never get out; Alvarez owns their soul. For those dissenting individuals, their 'helper' points out that they don't have to kill them or rough them up, they will just smear them by using every dirty trick in the book, and as a consequence, they will face a humiliating future worse than death or physical harm. They can do this very easily, and often do, to set an example to people who think it's easy to dissent when, in reality, it's not.

"Money and influence are an easy social drug to pedal and this is the new drug he pedals so successfully. To administer this programme he has had highly sophisticated software developed, which enables his 'helpers' to administer debts and keep detailed records of each 'client'. For example, what favours they have sought, who provided the support, what favours they have been asked to provide plus much greater detail on the person.

"When asked for help from somebody, these 'network administrators' or 'helpers' have at their fingertips all the necessary information to oblige the person and so ensnare them. These 'helpers' are extremely well paid and well educated people; most of them are multi-millionaires, and he has many of them."

"How prevalent is this activity?" I ask.

"Extremely prevalent," he replies. "It goes totally unnoticed by the average person. It is just like the drugs trade. If you are a user, you know exactly where to get your supply, yet to the outsider, they don't see any drug trading, except of course if you live in a poorer part of a city where drug trading may be conducted more openly, but not in affluent areas where drug abuse may be just as prevalent, but unseen.

"Alvarez realised that it's better to own people than shares in a business. That is why he never appears in any rich lists as most of his money is not held in traditional shares; his money is being circulated among business and social networks, buying up and ensnaring new recruits every day. When you think of the vast sums of money he earns every year, in addition to his already massive fortune, most of which is tied up in his networks, you start to get a glimpse of the size and the influence he can bring to bear on individuals around the world; it's truly frightening. He does, of course, still own a massive investment portfolio by normal standards, which recently, through shrewd investment and market manipulation, managed to double its value while others lost everything. I tell you this story as an aside, it's not part of his master strategy, but it does reinforce the message that we are dealing with a highly intelligent and far-sighted person who reads unfolding events like a book.

"Way before the 2008/2009 slump, he identified that we were heading for a fall. Greed was pushing the boundaries of risk-taking pushing it over the edge – something had to give. Rather than discourage the practice, he indirectly fuelled and tirelessly promoted a culture of excessive bonuses within the banking and investment sector, knowing an unrestrained bonus culture increases risk substantially, and that somewhere, sometime, the pack of cards would come tumbling down. As the old adage goes, when somebody makes a big loss on the financial markets, somebody else makes a killing. He saw this as the opportunity to make a killing. How he goes about achieving this objective is quite remarkable. He had observed, as perhaps other shrewd investors had done, that Goldman Sachs, the giant financial services group, alumni often leave the organisation in their early forties, as by this stage they are extremely rich, and can afford to take up so-called 'public service' jobs in the treasuries, central banks and Stock Exchanges around the world. From these lofty position, they manipulate and coerce the international monetary market to guarantee the wealth of their alumni. Alvarez recognised this strategy and had them manage a massive portfolio of his, using his front organisations. I can confirm this, as I tracked these investments.

"After the 2008/2009 financial crisis, many newspaper articles were written about Goldman Sachs, who like the Phoenix, rose from this crisis, unscathed and extravagantly enriched, where many similar sized organisations perished To many, the story is too incredible. How could a company that played a major role in causing the debacle, and had to be bailed out by the American government, emerge financially stronger than ever before? Alvarez knew his money was safe. He, better than anyone else knows, what can be done when somebody is pulling strings in your favour behind the scene and unbeknown by others. When you consider how successful this small Goldman Sach 'secret society' is, you get an idea of the potential power of Alvarez's network. This is what frightens the hell out of me!"

I sat in my chair numbed by the appalling state that we have got ourselves into. I begin to see what Dr. Abromovitz has been saying about Alvarez, how extremely intelligent and far-sighted he is. How he has capitalised on the basic human trait of greed, and provided the drug to satisfy that need, and in the process got us caught just like any other drug user. The scale of the operation is truly amazing. To think anybody could see the control of these vast networks as feasible and to have the money to make it happen, requires a far-sighted and dedicated visionary.

Dr. Abromovitz could see I was appalled by what he had just told me, so he paused and allowed me to gather my thoughts before continuing. "Alvarez's second strategy involved owning knowledge," he said.

"Hold on, before you continue, I have a question for you, the answer for which I probably already know, but I would like to hear it from you anyway," I ask him. "Why has nothing been done to stop him before it has got to this level?"

Dr. Abromovitz chuckles. "There are probably numerous reasons for this," he said.

"The implementation of his network strategy has been a process which started small, but has grown into a massive infestation. By the time people realise there is an infiltration, it's already too late. This is what happened to me all those years ago when I first presented my findings on Alvarez; my documents went missing or were destroyed and the investigations closed down. Who in the department is involved, I don't know. Perhaps it is Phil Stopford or it may even come from above him. Perhaps Phil is not the guilty party and is as frustrated and concerned as I am, but cannot trust anybody with his thoughts. This demonstrates a classic side-effect of this type of parasitic invasion, where you become mistrustful of colleagues and as a result, the organisation can no longer function effectively. It becomes immobilised through the spread of this parasitic invasion, which will ultimately lead to its demise. In my case, it is a little like 'water, water everywhere but not a drop to drink'. In my job, I'm surrounded by so-called experts who should be fighting this invasion tooth and nail, but I cannot turn to anybody for help for fear of falling foul of Alvarez.

"Only people with a wider vision of events could possibly identify a single source as controlling all networks. If you are seeking help you only meet with your local 'helper' and deal with him only, you don't know anything beyond that, such as who he is associated with or affiliated to. As far as you are concerned, it's just a local network with no sinister undertones apart from helping members make money by 'cooperating with fellow members'. Furthermore, if you were involved you are not going to go around advertising the fact, you want everything hushed up and if there was any likelihood of something coming to the surface, you would help suppress it."

"I surmised as much," I commented. "I suppose if anybody suspected anything, not on the scale you have intimated, but locally that somebody was pedalling easy money and influence, it wouldn't even reach the local media as the network's local influence would stifle it," I commented further.

"That is correct," he replied. "However, for example, assume it did manage to reach a local newspaper, as they don't 'own' everybody; the Alvarez team would start a campaign to discredit the person who raised the concern. They will use every dirty trick they have. They will fabricate lies and get people to corroborate them. They will plant incriminating evidence. They will use the media they own to go on a witch hunt and destroy the person's credibility. In the end, Alvarez's network will remain a secret and the person raising the alarm will be crushed."

"So what you are saying is that it has been easy for them to keep things under wraps while it was growing into this massive parasitic invasion," I said.

"No, it wasn't easy in the beginning, but their ruthless and effective methods of keeping it covered up worked brilliantly. As time passed and their sphere of influence spread, it became considerably easier to conceal their activities. Take your recent brush with MI6 and how they returned a 'don't waste our time verdict'. The Prime Minister and Chancellor are blissfully happy there is no mastermind behind these events, and consequently they trundle towards the precipice. The network quickly and effectively closed down this enquiry at the highest government level. I doubt any work was done on the matter at all, apart from investigating you more thoroughly and putting you under surveillance."

I just sat there in a stunned state shaking my head. I could see how we had allowed ourselves to get into this position; man's greed, vast amounts of money and influence freely available, administered by advanced technology and ruthlessly enforced by a determined man. I can now see how we have allowed the enemy to creep up on us without us even knowing. There are still several unanswered questions, but I'm sure the good Doctor will get around to explain them shortly.

"Are you alright?" queries Dr. Abromovitz. "Do you want to take a short break?"

"Another nice cup of tea would go down very well right now," I suggest.

"I agree," he says, picking up the tray and heading for the door. He opened the door and called Mrs Morgan. She came scurrying from the back of the house.

"Would you like another cup of tea, my dears?" she asks.

"Yes, please, Mrs. Morgan and if there are any more teacakes I would be most grateful. I have never tasted such delightful teacakes before. I will ask Fiona to get the recipe from you," I said.

"I would be delighted to give it to her. It's an old recipe my grandmother taught me many years ago," she said.

"Your grandmother was obviously a most accomplished cook," I remark.

"Indeed she was, Sir," said Mrs Morgan with a girlish giggle.

We returned to the lounge and waited for the tea without speaking, both immersed in our own thoughts.

After tea, Dr. Abromovitz took up his story.

"Returning to the second part of his strategy, namely, owning knowledge. I must point out that it isn't a matter of him attempting to corner all the knowledge, as that would be impossible and impractical, but rather of him owning or being involved in what he has called 'strategic knowledge'. Strategic knowledge is knowledge that would have a major affect on how we run our lives in the future. This involves, amongst other things, our fuel sources of the future, how we measure and manage business, new propulsion technologies, in fact anything that could radically change our lives in the future. He achieves this objective through underwriting university departments involved in this research, using front businesses. Where such technologies reside outside universities, in the hands of private investors, he buys up controlling interests wherever he can. His normal strategy is to buy people as they transcend company boundaries and its people that innovate and lead, not corporate entities. However, if the intellectual property is held by a business entity, he is forced to buy those companies. Naturally, he will try to have his networks infiltrate the business first, but if they fail, be buys the business. Once he owns this knowledge he can decide how it is to be disseminated. He's not so much in it for the money, although that is a nice bonus; he is more concerned about how he can use this knowledge to manipulate events. With most research findings, it is possible to emphasise certain aspects of the research and play down other parts, thereby providing a deliberately manipulated message that favours one view. Alvarez does exactly that to help strengthen his networks at a higher level, such as at a government or corporate level. For example, he may have a research paper released by a reputable university that shows that logging in the Amazon has a limited effect on global warming, and that it has far greater, long-term benefits to mankind than we had previously imagined. Large logging companies and perhaps even the Brazilian government are indebted to him for this report. To the outside world, it appears to be an independent, reputable and researched view. In reality, it is none of these things. I'm sure you have heard of research findings contradicting one another? These events could quite easily be as a consequence of university department sponsors manipulating findings.

"Alvarez works very cleverly in how he entangles research universities in his web of deceit. He becomes involved with them very early on. He does not meddle in their affairs at all for

134

the first five years or so. He constantly increases his investment, making them more and more reliant and trusting of him. Only later may he step in and start meddling, and asking that findings be reworded to favour one opinion over the other. It now becomes difficult for the university to refuse as he will pull the plug on them immediately and they will be in serious trouble, so they concede. Nobody suspects the department's sponsors as being the report's manipulators as they have been with the department for so long and their involvement is purely philanthropic; for the benefit of the discipline. They are certainly not 'Johnny come lately', trying to buy research results, like a tobacco company funding research to show smoking is not harmful. However, they are worse than the tobacco company because their motives are entirely cloaked. They are not there for the benefit of the discipline or mankind; they are there to serve Alvarez's cause."

"I may be jumping the gun a little, but I think I know what you are going to tell me about how he uses these two strategies to implement his master plans," I say.

"By all means, let me hear your thoughts," he replies.

"He will use his control over strategic knowledge to set in motion the major events, and then use his control over the networks to direct proceedings to a successful conclusion," I remark.

"In principle, you are correct," he said. "However, when he set his two strategies in motion, it is highly likely that he had no definite idea on how they would pan out in providing him the means to impose his will over the free democracies of the world, except the clear understanding that something would emerge that he could exploit. In any event, when he set these plans in motion, his first requirement was to make sure his plans worked successfully, as only when he owned the networks and had access to strategic knowledge could the next phase of his plans be implemented. Once he had achieved this control, he waited for events to unfold and for the opportunity to strike to present itself."

"I take it that we have reached that defining moment?" I asked.

"You were the person who highlighted the significance of events surrounding your recent court case. I believe you were correct when you predicted that the objective of the exercise was to attack our stock markets and to cause panic selling, sending the markets into a nosedive. As I mentioned to you before, I believe this will only be the start of much bigger events. Simultaneously, they will launch a terrorist assault worldwide on an unprecedented scale. This will drive the markets down further and faster, particularly if the attacks are sustained. This should bring the markets to their knees. Alvarez will then implement the next phase of his master plan; he starts civil unrest using his crime syndicates to orchestrate and manage these events. They start looting and rioting on a massive scale, causing further unease and panic among the populace. Calls for troops to be used to quell the unrest are thwarted by his control of the networks. The situation escalates out of control and anarchy ensues. Governments appear weak and ineffectual in dealing with the situation; that is because they are. Alvarez's networks have almost paralysed government departments; they wallow in despair as Government orders are counter-commanded by Alvarez. The next phase in the strategy is then unleashed. Alvarez's government 'sleepers', or 'government in waiting' now raise their ugly heads. They make the case, supported by international media, which Alvarez controls, that we need strong leadership and that we need it now. They argue that if action is not taken now, the country will slide into the abyss. They point to the sorry state that the economy is in and the anarchy that exists. They claim this can only get worse, unless they can take over immediately as an interim government. They argue there is no time to hold elections and bold action by bold people is what is required, after all, they are only seeking an interim appointment to sort things out.

"What will happen next is one of the smaller, more fragile democracies will succumb to what appears to be an enticing offer, and an unelected, interim, puppet government installed. Almost miraculous, law and order is returned, the economy

136

rebounds as fickle investors find a haven of hope, in a tumultuous world, to invest. Events in this country are watched closely by the world and its success heralded by the international media as a template for others to follow. Shortly thereafter, the next country follows and enjoys similar success. Immediately after this, an avalanche of countries follows suit. All these new puppet governments show a rapid return to normality, which places the remaining dissenters under enormous pressure to follow suit, which they all do."

"And you have documented proof of this?" I say in a rather scathing manner.

"Well, of course I don't," he said rather indignantly. "I have had to surmise as I am not privy to his master plans. I have surmised as much as you did when you identified a possible Al-Qaeda involvement and took it to the Government. Have you heard any major flaws in what I have said that warrants your scoffing?"

"I apologise," I reply, "I was not scoffing at the content, but rather at how incredible it would be if you have documented evidence of all this," I continued.

"My documented evidence only goes as far as showing his involvement in front organisations, and how he laundered money through networks. There's more than enough documented evidence to tie him directly to current events, but how they will pan out beyond this point is anybody's guess. Knowing him and how he works, I am probably the best person to surmise," he said.

"I understand that," I said. "But given that you are only guessing, there are a few issues I need clarity on. Firstly, you said that simultaneously to the attack on the stock markets, he will launch a terrorist assault worldwide. I must have missed something in between because his association with, or control over-terrorist organisations has never been mentioned. In fact, when I mentioned a possible Al-Qaeda involvement, I was told I was barking up the wrong tree."

"One of the underlying principles of investing in strategic knowledge is that it often provides controversial findings. Controversy is the material Alvarez seeks, as it is often the instrument of change. What better group to invest in than religious organisations, particularly those that are radical and have militant backgrounds or aspirations. I believe that Alvarez became deeply involved with Al-Qaeda not long after their inauguration. I understand that he is their major backer, not only financially but also technically. He gives them access to the latest technology, weaponry, know-how and intelligence. Don't you think it a little strange that with all the resources thrown at capturing Osama bin Laden, he still manages to elude his enemies? I wouldn't be at all surprised to learn that Alvarez has got a senior CIA agent working for him who is feeding back their strategies to Al-Qaeda's top brass, or Osama bin Laden himself."

"So I was right that Al-Qaeda is involved," I said.

"Yes, but only as a pawn in a much bigger game. In fact, I wouldn't be surprised if they didn't become the sacrificial lambs in these unfolding events," says Dr. Abromovitz.

"Why is that?" I ask.

"Wouldn't it be amazing if in the early stages of the new regimes life, they delivered up Al-Qaeda, a feat which our previous international governments have been unable to do over the past decade or so? This would provide the populace with great confidence in their new government's ability, and allay any fears of sinister undertones. After all, their new governments have brought the wicked terrorists, who were entirely responsible for these heinous acts according to the international media, to book quickly. Under the new government, things return to normality very quickly. The civil unrest stops immediately and in fact, things go the other way, where nobody dares step out of line as Alvarez's syndicates dispense their own justice to non-law abiders. The threats to financial markets disappear before their eyes, international terrorist groups are crushed; life looks rosy under the new regime. This buys them enough time to entrench themselves and eradicate democracy entirely. By the time the average man wakes up to the reality that they have lost their democratic rights and freedom, it is far too late; there will be no return to our past.

"I have an old aunt who lives in the Wiltshire town of Shrivenham. Nearby is a large military academy where they train army personnel in many different specialised fields. What saddens me is to think the people within this academy go about their daily chores in an industrious fashion, oblivious to the fact that their enemy has so radically changed the rules of war that their efforts and knowledge are totally irrelevant in this new theatre. In fact, they are so irrelevant that they are a total and unnecessary drain on resources. By changing the rules of warfare, Alvarez has slunk up on us, captured and destroyed our democracy without us even being aware that we were fighting a war; without us even knowing our enemy. Yet, had some foreign power pointed a gun at us and declared their intention of removing our democracy and placing their totalitarian puppet government in its stead, we would have thrown everything we had at them to resist. As long as our enemy plays by the rules, we are okay; but when they radically change them, we are lost."

He paused for a few moments, gathering his thoughts, and then continued. "When I think about it, I want to laugh. No, perhaps I should rephrase that, it makes me want to cry! The government has got its strategy on fighting this silent war, and the so called 'cyber war', so horribly wrong it's frightening. Only a few years ago, the government announced the establishment of a department at GCHQ to combat the threat of cyber warfare. Typical of the government, its lack of imagination and understanding led it to believe that the threat would come in the form of a direct attack, where one computer would infiltrate and, or destroy another computer. Consequently, they hired computer geeks and hackers to counter this threat. The problem is, they have completely misunderstood the threat. We live in an era of creativity which affects all of us; if you are not thinking creatively and differently about the problems facing you, your competitors or enemies will take you out at the knees. We have only started to see how emerging technologies are being used creatively to gain competitive advantage. If governments believe this creativity precludes their enemies, they're sadly wrong. The threat of cyber warfare does not lie so much in a direct attack, but rather in how our enemies will use technology to launch more subtle, but equally dangerous attacks, on us. The government should have employed strategic thinkers, not geeks and hackers. Alvarez has proved my point. He has invested heavily in technology, developing a sophisticated system to manage a vast and complex international network. His networks don't represent a direct threat to our cyber world, yet his networks unquestionably represent a far greater threat to our society than any direct cyber attack will ever be."

"The threat of a direct attack must still be very real," I remarked.

"Obviously, it is, but to think it remains the only, or the most significant, threat puts you in a fool's paradise. Unless you are thinking ahead of the game, considering all possibilities, you will be caught offside. The more entrenched your thinking, the more spectacularly you will be caught offside. And now, because of our lack of understanding and inappropriate action, what stands between us and this horrible fate? Two puny, old men – you and I."

This is just too incredible. If everything he has said is believable, then there are just two of us facing a formidable, organised and determined enemy. I'm sure there must be many others who will help and support us? Before I query him on this and lose my train of thought, there is another comment he made that didn't sound particularly plausible.

"Another point I would like some clarity on is, you said that the networks would be able to counter-command instructions from the highest authorities. I find that a little difficult to swallow. For example, if an instruction came from the Prime Minister to mobilise troops to stop looting and rioting, I can't see that order being ignored," I comment.

"I cannot say with any certainty what will happen in the case of any particular government under these circumstances. However, what I can say with absolute certainty is that there will be no coherent and effective implementation of such an order from any government, anywhere. The reason for this is that there will be individuals in positions of authority who will be instructed by the network not to implement these orders. They may not be able to go against a direct order from the government, but they may be able to question it, delay its implementation, or only partially implement it. At each stage in the hierarchy of implementing this order and orders like it, you will come across network members who will all respond in the same way in hindering its implementation. Eventually, at best, you will end up with a half-hearted, shambolic effort. Remember that at the same time, there, will be a barrage of media coverage discouraging the use of troops against civilians; supported by the networks. Also remember that at this stage the real enemy has not been identified or their strategy known, and therefore the fact that by not deploying troops at this critical stage is not seen by those who disobey the order as a huge betrayal of their country, and the free democracies of the world. To them, it's probably not a big issue. To you and I, who see the big picture unfolding, it's absolutely critical and therefore incomprehensible that people don't do the right thing. They only see their own myopic world. The networks will play a huge role in making current governments look incompetent by acting in a sluggish, indecisive manner; that is the purpose of having developed them. The people causing this problem will be oblivious as to who is really pulling their strings and for what purpose. They would definitely respond differently if they knew the big picture, but they don't. This is a silent war which nobody apart from our enemy knows we are fighting."

Things just seem to go from bad to worse.

"Surely there must be others we can call on to help?" I ask him.

"For my entire working life I have been with British Intelligence; I'm a background boy doing the numbers. I hardly ever came into contact with other people outside the department. If an outsider wanted information, they would approach somebody within the department, who would then approach me to do the work. The results would then be handed back to my department colleague, who would handover the report. My only real contact came when I presented academic papers on money laundering or attended similar events myself. Consequently, I do not have a wide circle of colleagues, even fewer I can trust. Why do you think I'm talking to you? I don't really know you. I did a background check on you, and you appeared to come out clean."

"That's because I am clean," I respond.

"Yes, but I don't know that for sure," he replies. "As much as I'm sure you have nagging doubts about what I have told you; to you this must all sound surreal, but I can assure you it's not. I have no option but to take a risk on you and you in turn have no option but to take a risk on me. If neither is prepared to do that, the fate of the world is sealed. Nobody asked me to become involved. When I saw events unfolding, I knew I had to step up to the mark and take responsibility. I had to act swiftly on behalf of my fellow-freedom loving citizens. I had family in Nazi concentration camps, most of whom never made it. For them and the rest of the people who gave their lives in attempting to stop totalitarian states being foisted upon them around the world, I have no hesitation in offering my life. You know as much as I do now. You now have to make the same choice I made. We are fighting a silent war. Our Allies do not even know they are in a state of war; even less are they aware that the final manoeuvres to strike the fatal blow have been put in motion. As incredible as it may seem, only you and I stand between them and their inevitable success. You probably have more to lose than I, but it pales in insignificance to what the rest of the world will lose."

"God Almighty, I'm not a strong man. I'm just average. I'm more like what you described earlier as a puny, old man. I don't know what I can do to help?" I exclaimed.

"That is exactly what I felt," he said. "However, I took action nonetheless. All I can do is take one step at a time and evaluate what comes of it; at least I'm doing something," he explains.

"So you don't have a plan?" I asked in a worried tone.

"I do know what our next steps should be but much beyond that, I don't know. Clearly, our objective must be to get what we know directly to the highest authority so they can make a pre-emptive strike against Alvarez. If they could obliterate him and his computer systems together, we stand a chance of averting this disaster. The problem is, we have to get what we know to the very highest authority, because anything less could mean we become exposed to Alvarez's networks and our efforts thwarted. My thoughts were that as you have already gained access to the Chancellor and Prime Minister, this avenue may be open to you again."

"That's a little unlikely," I say, "given that MI6 have already trashed my idea in the eyes of the PM and branded me a 'conspiracy theorist'."

"This is probably true, except that this time the documented proof that was not forthcoming from the department will be available, and the case will be argued by an articulate and highly convincing lawyer, not a go-between," he says.

"You have this documented proof?" I asked him.

"I have kept records of all my research into Alvarez, even copies of my early reports that went missing, or were mysteriously destroyed. I have filed them in five tin trunks and stored them in separate locations around the country for security reasons. My next task is to get these trunks and bring them to you. I also have one person who I think I can trust, however, I cannot make contact with him. You, on the other hand, can and that is what I would like you to do while I collect my documents."

"Why can't you contact him?" I ask.

"Because I am AWOL from the department. I asked for leave which was due to me, but it was refused; possibly to hinder me pursuing this matter further. Whatever their reason, I can't afford to wait around as time is not on our side. As soon as you go AWOL from the department, you go onto their security alert list, which means they will le looking for me at every exit point from the country. While you may be under surveillance, they can't stop you leaving the country."

"I take it then that your contact is not a UK resident?" I ask.

"That's correct," he replied. "The man's name is Gonan Mehad; he's a CIA agent working for Mossad, Israel Intelligence."

"What is he – a double agent?" I ask.

"No, he is nothing like that. He was seconded to the CIA from Mossad due to the research he has done on radical Islamic groups. I came in contact with him many years ago when I presented a paper on money laundering practices in Washington DC. He met me afterwards and expressed an interest in exploring the possibility of crime syndicates funding radical Islamic groups. In those early days, the reasons why crime syndicates should bankroll radical groups were unclear, although he and I had picked up activity that they were. We thought they were supporting these groups to help protect and nurture their supply lines of heroine from Afghanistan, but when my research picked up support for other radical groups without direct links to profitable ventures, we had to rethink and review their motives. Gonan has done considerable research into the funding and relationship between Al-Qaeda and the Alvarez organisation. As a result, he can play an important role for us for two reasons. Firstly, he can provide the expert evidence and knowledge to corroborate the role Al-Qaeda will play in Alvarez's master plan, and secondly he may be able to alert the CIA's top brass to this plot without falling foul of the networks."

"What am I supposed to do?" I ask

"You are to contact him and explain everything as I have told you today. You are then to request that he gets this information through to the highest authority. Furthermore, he should make available to you whatever documented proof or research he has on the liaison between Alvarez and Al-Qaeda to make our case easier when we plead it with the authorities. He will probably be most reluctant to give you anything, unless you are convincing enough, and he believes that you and I stand a chance of influencing the authorities to act."

"You said you thought you could trust him. What if we can't?" I ask.

"If we can't trust him our options have more than halved, as now our message won't get through to the CIA and we will have exposed ourselves in the process," he said.

"Yes, and me particularly," I say.

"No, we are both equally exposed," he explains. "Even if we were exposed, I don't think they would go to the extreme of bumping you off straight away; I think they will try to frighten you off first or try to buy you over to their cause. If that fails then, without question, you would simply disappear. I, on the other hand, might be metered out a slightly different fate as they already know I can't be bought, and I'm just a nuisance to them. You, however, may have more value to them, particularly in selling the new regime to the populace in its early days. It would be reassuring to have a respected and widely known lawyer back the new regime in its infancy. People would be more accepting and tolerant of the bold move to install an unelected government if backed by a prominent lawyer."

"Thank you," I say, "how reassuring it is to know that I'll be roughed up before being bumped off."

"I'm just trying to be realistic," he says.

"So where is Gonan Mehad to be found?" I ask.

"He lives and works in Istanbul," he says.

"A CIA agent working for Mossad and living in Istanbul – what a combination," I said.

He then lent forward and handed me a small slip of paper. On it was printed an address in Istanbul.

"That is Gonan's last known address," he said.

"What do you mean – his last known address, don't you know where he lives?" I asked.

"I got a colleague who works in the computer department at MI6 to do some unofficial snooping to find Gonan's address. The address he came up with was last updated eighteen months ago, so whether or not he still lives there, we cannot be sure."

I took the slip of paper, folded it and put it in my jacket pocket.

"We must move quickly now," he said.

"Tomorrow I will start collecting my documents and you must make arrangements to meet Gonan as soon as possible. It is going to take both of us a few days to accomplish these tasks so what I would suggest is that from next Wednesday onwards, you look for my signal from the woods about the same time as before. We can then meet briefly where I will tell you where our next rendezvous will be."

He stood up. "It's getting late," he said, "and I know you would like to get home before it gets dark."

He extended his hand towards me. "Good luck, James," he said, "for everybody's sake, I hope you and I are successful."

I shook his hand and bid him farewell.

Chapter Seven

It was already getting dark when I crossed the road and climbed the stile. It will take me a good hour to get home. Fortunately, there are clear skies and the moon is already high, so I shouldn't have any difficulties finding my way home. The long walk will enable me to gather my thoughts.

What have I got myself into? I wish that I could turn back the clock. If I could, I wouldn't have raised my concerns and left everything alone, as Fiona had asked me to. Too late now, I am involved. The unsettling thing is that I have to take the word of a man I hardly know, and decide whether or not he is telling the truth. For all I know he may be a total charlatan and I am being sucked into his fantasy world. I suppose it's who I am and my profession that has made me a little cynical, and somebody who always wants the facts before making a decision. Now I must make a decision on gut feel alone. The facts and evidence may be available, as claimed by Dr. John, but then I don't have them to hand or the time to evaluate them. He has made a most plausible case; it is just the audacity, far-sightedness and scale of the plot which remains a source of doubt. However, if he's right and I think he is, then I'm in over my head.

What a time in life to face a crisis like this. I've retired, starting to take things easy, and now I have to put everything on the line with the odds of a successful outcome remote, to say the very least. Strangely, I'm not worried about myself; it's my family who concern me most because, once again, they will have to pay the price and that's what sickens me.

I paused when I reached the top of the hill and gazed out over the beautiful countryside below me, bathed in full moonlight. This is what my retirement is supposed to be about, having the time to enjoy the natural beauty that surrounds me, not fighting some criminal organisation intent on overthrowing international governments. Anyway, while I'm here I'm going to enjoy as much of the scenery as I can, as who knows what the future holds?

While I trudged on, my mind kept wandering back to some of the terminology used by Dr. John during our meeting; at the time, it struck me as being exaggerated. He said that we are involved in a war, but is that true? The rules have changed so much I'm not certain if it is. However, on reflection I suppose it is a war because, if somebody wishes to change governments without majority consent, using coercion and deception, it would definitely result in a war. If anybody, or a group of people, or even a government attempted to change the ruling government without majority consent using traditional methods, such as through the barrel of a gun, it would definitely result in war. This is the central premise to creating a war. The fact that somebody has ingeniously changed the rules as to how they take over the government, to the extent that we don't even know we are under threat and consequently, don't know who our real enemy is, doesn't change the central premise of what creates a war. Furthermore, this conflict could involve all the free democracies around the world as they are all under threat. Therefore, by definition, I suppose this is actually a World War. By so radically changing the rules, Alvarez has created 'a silent war', as nobody knows we are fighting it and even worse, nobody has identified him as the enemy. Also, no shots, or very few, will be fired in our overthrow; so Dr. John's description of a silent war appears to be most apt.

It's strange when you think about it; during the First World War, hundreds of millions lost their lives. In the Second World War, tens of millions lost their lives. In subsequent wars, thankfully, there have been far fewer fatalities. And now in this, the Third World War, there may be fewer than a few hundred fatalities. Not that this is particularly reassuring when I consider that Dr. John and I are two distinct possibilities among those fatalities.

I followed the same route home as I had taken to get to Rosewood Cottage. It was a relief when I finally reached the outbuildings. Fiona would be worrying where I was as I hadn't told her I was going out this afternoon. I hurried on up to the house. As I approached it, I noticed the outside lights weren't on again. I quickened my pace as I know how much she hated being in the house on her own, particularly in the dark. On entering the house I made straight for our bedroom, calling her name as I ran so as not to alarm her wondering who may be in the house. She was sat huddled on the bed, with her knees tucked under her chin.

"Where have you been, James?" she enquired in a quivering voice. "I have been worried sick about you."

I sat on the bed and put my arms around her.

"I'm so sorry, my darling, I didn't wish to alarm you," I said.

A tear rolled down her face.

"I have been so worried and scared," she said.

"What happened to the electricity?" I asked.

"I don't know," she replied. "It's the same as last night; it went off as soon as it became dark."

"Are you alright?" she enquired.

"Yes, I'm fine, thank you – nothing wrong with me," I said.

"Well, where on earth have you been?" she said as her confidence returned.

"I will explain everything to you tomorrow," I said, "because unfortunately the walls have ears."

"Stop talking in riddles," she said.

"Can we please leave it for now; I will explain everything to you tomorrow. Right now, I need to make you a nice, strong cup of hot tea," I say changing the subject. Now is not the right time to tell her and if the house is bugged, I can't do it inside anyway.

"Thank goodness for our gas cooker," she said. "At least we can have a cup of tea and a hot meal. I have tried calling some local electricians to come and sort out the problem, but have been given just about every excuse under the sun why they can't make it until late next week, at the earliest."

"Don't worry," I said, "I will get an electrician all the way from Edinburgh if needs be, but the electricity will be sorted out by tomorrow, come what may."

The next morning the electricity was working again. Despite this, I decided to get an electrician to come in and sort out our intermittent supply problem once and for all. After phoning a few businesses unsuccessfully, I was able to locate one from Taunton who was quite prepared and willing to charge me an extortionist price. As he so eloquently put it, 'I ain't workin' on a Saturday, mate, unless you're gonna pay me double time for a minimum of five hours, plus travelling time and travel expenses at one pound twenty per mile. You know what I mean, mate?'

Any price to sort out our electrical problems, is cheap at the price; although I hate been ripped off by anybody.

I now needed to book my flight to Istanbul, but before that, I face the difficult task of telling Fiona what is happening. Assuming that the house is bugged, and I have no reason to doubt this, I would have to explain everything to her in the garden. After breakfast, I suggested that she and I take a stroll through the garden.

It was another pleasant day and we strolled through the garden arm-in-arm. She excitedly pointed out plants and shrubs she had planted earlier, and how she was looking forward to seeing them blossom this summer. I felt terrible when I thought this might not happen. She, almost single-handed, had restored the house and gardens to their former glory, and to think this could all be taken from her as a result of me confronting a ruthless criminal. She is such a good person, always caring and

150

concerned for others; it just isn't fair! However, if I bailed out now and events unfold as described by Dr. John, I could not live with myself knowing that when I was called upon, I was not man enough for the task, putting my own interests before those of my fellow beings. Hopefully, she will see this in the same light. I will definitely be reprimanded for having become involved in the first place when she explicitly asked me not to. Telling her this story is more stressful than when I first proposed to her all those years ago; I don't know what I would have done if she'd rejected me then, and now it's even worse. I took her in my arms, gave her a big hug, kissed her on her forehead and told her I loved her more than anything else in the world. With my heart in my mouth, I began telling her the full story. When I was finished, I walked her to a bench under a large oak tree in the garden and sat her down. She just stared ahead with a vacant look on her face.

"I'm sorry," I said, "truly sorry!"

She sat quietly for a few moments, probably gathering her thoughts.

"No, James," she said, "you were just in the wrong place at the wrong time. You have been caught up in circumstances beyond your control, and I understand that you have little choice but to follow them through whatever the consequences. Whatever happens, please promise me one thing – that you will take great care of yourself. You are the most precious gift that I have and if that's all I'm left with, I will still be happy and content."

I'm blessed to have been given a soul-mate in life. Although we have the trappings of a wealthy family today, we've had a hard life, working hard everyday, foregoing many essentials throughout our life, yet despite all this, we have grown closer together everyday. Hopefully, this strong bond will see us through further hardship.

Quite suddenly, she slapped both her hands on her knees and stood up. "Right," she said, "you had better get on with it.

You've got the world to save, and I've a few household chores to complete."

Relieved that she has taken it all so well and given me her blessing, despite knowing that in her heart, she, like I, wished we had never become embroiled in this matter. I suggested that she makes arrangements with her friend Dorothy, who lives in the village, to stay with her while I'm away.

"That's exactly what I intend doing," she said.

"When do you intend leaving?" she enquired further.

"As soon as I can get a booking," I said.

"Surely not before Monday?" she queried.

"No, from Monday onwards," I replied.

"Fine – that gives me time to make arrangements".

"You are taking this all very well," I remarked.

"There is no point crying over spilt milk," she said, "and as much as I wished you had not become involved, you are, and now, as a consequence, you bear great responsibility. You won't deliver against this responsibility unless you have a supportive family standing by you. I will support you in whatever you do as I know what you have done you have done for good reason. Had I stood in your shoes and had your courage, I would have done no differently."

Around mid-morning the electrician arrived and started busying himself. Meanwhile, I went onto the Internet to make my bookings for Istanbul. I had assumed it would be a relatively simple task, but it proved to be anything but. Difficulties arose around timings. After a fairly lengthy process, I managed to make a booking from Bristol to Hamburg and then from there to Istanbul, arriving late on Monday afternoon. I also made a hotel reservation at one of the Istanbul airport hotels for that evening. I had decided that I would drive to the airport and leave my car in the long-stay parking as my return date, at this stage, is uncertain.

I looked at my watch. The electrician has been with us for nearly two hours. I wondered what progress he had made and decided to find him and get a progress report. After looking for him in the house, I eventually found him sitting in his van in the driveway.

"Found the problem?" I asked.

"No, mate, there ain't noffing wrong with your electricity supply," he said.

"I would beg to differ," I said, "there is definitely something wrong with it."

"Well, mate, I checked it at the supply point and at the distribution board and there is power at both points."

"Have you checked between these two points?" I asked.

"No need, mate. If you've got power at one end and power at the other end, there ain't noffing wrong."

"I'm no electrician, but logic tells me the problem must lie between these two points, so I would suggest that you check this out."

"That will be like a very big job, mate," he said.

"That shouldn't concern you," I said, "after all, you are earning double time."

"Yeah – okay, I'll have a look," he said rather begrudgingly.

I get the distinct feeling I haven't employed the services of a workaholic.

I returned to my study to prepare myself for Tuesday's meeting with Gonan. Under these circumstances, it wouldn't be advisable for me to carry any written notes, in case they fell into the wrong hands. It's always more difficult to prepare yourself for a meeting when you can only rely on mental notes. Things are so easily forgotten, or the order in which you present them can change and this can often change the nature of the message itself. I just needed to memorise a logical framework for the meeting to ensure I get the full story across as succinctly as possible. Once I have this framework, I can easily embellish upon it as I go along. While scribbling some notes, I heard the electrician calling me from the foyer.

"Hello... hello, Your Lordship? Hello... hello, yahoo?"

I got up and called out, "I'm coming."

The man was standing in the foyer with a big smile on his face.

"What is it?" I said.

"I've found sommit very interesting," he said.

"Well, what is it?"

"I don't rightly know," he said, "I ain't seen noffing like it in me life before. It looks like a remotely-controlled switch or a fancy timing gadget. What da you put sommit like this in your house for?"

"I didn't have it put in, and I certainly didn't know of its existence either," I said.

"It looks like its been put in recent like," he said. "Somebody wants to mess with your electricity supply. What da you want me to do about it? "he asked.

"Can you remove it?" I enquired.

"Sure can, but you'll be without electricity for a while," he replied.

"That's no problem, we've become accustomed to living without it over the past few days," I replied.

"Why are people trying to mess with you, gov? Are you some sort of spy or sommit?" he enquires.

"No, far from it," I said," I'm just a retried solicitor."

"Well, whatever," he said, "somebody is trying to mess with you."

'Intimidate' was a better word, I thought. How effective low key intimidation can be. You have no idea how unsettling it is to have your electricity switched off every night. You feel helpless and vulnerable. Two nights of it were enough for me. I can just imagine what would happen if it was off for weeks. The message they have been trying to send me has been received loud and clear. Perhaps now is the time for me to use their bugs against them, by spreading disinformation through Fiona and I openly discussing how we no longer intend pursuing this matter and that it's out of our hands. Give them the message they want to hear.

This is the first tangible evidence I have had which backs up Dr. John's story. He said that they would bug the house, and that they would try to intimidate me. Even though it is low key intimidation, it is highly effective. It isn't so much the loss of electricity, but the fact that somebody is 'trying to mess with me', as the electrician so eloquently put it, that is unsettling.

The weekend passed uneventfully. It was a great relief to have the electricity working; I could enjoy my History channel on TV once again. Fiona made her regular weekend calls to the family, including Felicity, to whom she would speak for hours. I also received an unexpected call from Richard. Normally, I would phone him to keep me up-to-date with events in the City, so it was most pleasant to hear from him for a change. While talking to him, I had a strong urge to tell him about current events. It is so difficult to bottle up such things; you need to tell somebody, particularly a confidant, to get their opinion and views. It's therapeutic and stress relieving to hear the opinions of others whom you respect. So strong was the urge that I started explaining events to him, before commonsense prevailed and I bit my tongue. I had no right to involve a young person like this and place him at unnecessary risk. Perhaps the time will come when I need to call on his assistance, but not right now. Fortunately, I told him very little, except that I had met somebody who had shed a completely different light on the

Marketing legal debacle unfolding internationally. As soon as I returned to my senses, I told him the story I had heard carried little credence and was probably not plausible, so I would not waste his time explaining it any further. He didn't push me on the matter, rather suggesting I leave such affairs well alone and enjoy a well-earned retirement. I wish that I had the wisdom of his youth.

I'm certainly not cut out for any undercover work. I felt conspicuous and paranoid when in the Bristol Airport, believing I was being watched, particularly by the police, of whom there appeared to be a particularly large presence. The flight to Hamburg, and from there to Istanbul, passed uneventfully, so much so that when we touched down at Istanbul's Atatürk International Airport, I was feeling completely relaxed and looking forward to my meeting with Gonan.

On entering the terminus, I headed for the 'Hand Luggage Only' queue, which is normally short and clears quickly. To my dismay, I found a long queue which was moving extremely slowly. The two officials on duty seemed to be checking everything rather thoroughly, oblivious to the huge bottleneck they had caused. Eventually, after nearly half an hour, my turn arrived. One of the officials snatched my passport from me without a word, glanced at my photo and handed it over to his colleague. His colleague glanced at the photo, got up from his desk and came over to me. He grabbed me firmly by the upper arm and said, "Please come."

It all happened so quickly I didn't have time to be frightened. In fact, as I was frog-marched away, I felt angry and annoyed. "What are you doing? You have no right to do this to me," I declared.

"Our Captain wants to speak to you," he said in broken English.

"What about?" I demanded, "I haven't broken any laws."

"I don't know, you speak to him," he said, marching me down a long corridor with doors along one side of it. Near the end of the corridor, he opened a door with some writing on it. I

156

only glanced at it, but somewhere on the list I'm sure I saw the words 'Interview Room'. He pushed me into the room.

"Wait here," he said, turning on his heels and slamming the door closed.

It was a small room with a desk in the middle. Two chairs on the one side and one on the other. The furniture was simple and cheap; just what you would expect in a government department office. There was one small window high up; more like a vent than a window. There was one large, neon light in the middle of the ceiling. On the wall behind the single chair was a large clock that ticked rather loudly. Maybe I had read the words on the door incorrectly, perhaps it said 'Interrogation Room'; it certainly looked like one.

Having little other option than to sit and wait, I sat down and waited... and waited... and waited. Under these circumstances, your thoughts go through a distinct sequence of events. Initially, you are angry and annoyed, then your thoughts change to frustration and doubt, before moving on to insecurity and fear. It doesn't take long before your thoughts reach the fear level; thereafter, the fear starts feeding itself. I'm no expert in this matter, but I estimate that it takes about an hour and a half before you become fearful. If you have reasons to be fearful in the first instance, reaching the fear threshold is a lot quicker and the fear intensified. I had on numerous occasions tried the door despite having learnt on the first occasion that it was locked.

I have been a prisoner in this horrible little room for almost three hours now, believing quite firmly that I had fallen foul of Alvarez's cohorts. What would happen to me now – would I just disappear, as Dr. John had suggested earlier? The loud ticking of the clock was driving me crazy. Suddenly, the door burst open and in walked an urbane, middle-aged gentleman dressed in an expensive suit. He had a broad smile on his face and extended his hand in greeting.

"Mr. Barton-Marshall, I do apologise," he said. "My name is Abad Saatci, I am responsible for airport security and immigration control. There has been an unfortunate case of mistaken identity. One of my over-zealous officers mistakenly identified you as a wanted criminal, whose arrival in Istanbul we had anticipated. Passport names are meaningless, it is facial features they go on and the similarity between you and the wanted criminal are quite remarkable. It was this that led to the confusion. It has taken me all this time to verify who you are, through our Scotland Yard contacts. Once again, I apologise for the delay and inconvenience this has caused you."

From a state of fear to euphoria; his words sounded like pure honey to me. "No... no, that's alright," I said, "as long as the matter has now been cleared up."

"I think it has," he said sitting down at the table and producing my passport from his pocket. He started flipping through it. "What are you in Istanbul for?" he asked.

"I'm here on business," I replied.

"Aren't you a retired lawyer?" he enquired.

"That's correct."

"If you have retired, what business matters would that be?" he enquired further.

"Personal business," I replied.

"Ah... you have a mistress in the city," he said with a laugh.

"No, nothing like that, I'm a happily married man."

"What then is your business here?" he said in a brusque manner.

"I'm here to interview somebody who may be able to help me with some research I'm doing into a book my wife is considering writing."

"I understand," he said staring at me closely for sometime. I get the feeling this isn't somebody you cross without considerable trouble.

After staring at me for what seemed an age he said, "I hope the book has a happy ending?"

This comment almost sounded like a warning.

After flipping through my passport repeatedly, as if hoping to reveal something he had not already picked up, he suddenly stopped and said, "Right, I have kept you long enough, time for you to be on your way. Can I perhaps give you a lift to your hotel?"

"That would be most kind of you," I said.

"Where are you staying – at the Hilton?" he enquired.

"No, I'm staying at the Holiday Inn near the airport," I replied.

"Oh, that's only a few minutes away," he said. "Do you have any luggage you need collecting?"

"No, I only have this hand luggage."

"Good, then let us be on our way," he said.

Our drive to the hotel took only a few minutes. He pulled up outside and walked in with me.

"Are you being picked up tomorrow?" he asked.

"No, I will need to hire a taxi."

"I will make arrangements with the receptionist to ensure they get you a reliable driver that can speak English well," he said.

"Thank you, that would be most helpful," I said.

I started booking in while he chatted away to one of the receptionists. When he had finished, he came over to me with his hand outstretched in greeting. "I hope your research doesn't lead you astray, Mr. Barton-Marshall," he said. He shook my hand, turned around and walked out. I was pleased to see the back of him, even though he had been fairly pleasant, he was the source of my anxiety over the past few hours.

I was so relieved to get into my bedroom; I was totally exhausted. The travelling together with the anxiety of the past few hours had taken their toll. I will phone Fiona to let her know that I'm alright, although I won't tell her of my ordeal as this would upset her unnecessarily. I will take a shower and then pop down and have dinner in one of the restaurants in the foyer.

While taking my shower, I kept thinking of today's events. I didn't believe for one moment that I was held because of a mistaken identity. They were looking for me, and they wanted to frighten me. The interesting thing is, how did they know I was coming? The whole episode shows the extent of Alvarez's influence; he can pluck anybody from a queue in an international airport, anywhere in the world, and do whatever he wants with them. That is positively scary! I know I was only subjected to low key intimidation, but, nonetheless, it is very effective. Mr. Saatci's reference to the book I'm supposed to be researching having a happy ending, was, in my opinion, a direct warning – 'Don't meddle and your life will have a happy ending'. Also, his comment when we parted that he hopes my research doesn't lead me astray, is another reference to stop meddling. The message is loud and clear – back off and leave things be. I understand that I'm pushing my luck by pursuing this matter further. Soon they will drop their intimidation tactics and resort to overt violence. Although this afternoon's ordeal was unpleasant, I actually feel more determined to put an end to Alvarez's activities, but I remain fearful for my family, who may have to pay for the consequences of my actions.

After I had my shower, I lay on the bed for a few minutes as it was too early to go down for dinner. I woke with a sudden start; realising immediately that I must have fallen into a deep sleep. I glanced at the bedside clock. It was half past two in the morning. I pulled the bedcovers over me and promptly went back to sleep.

Next morning, after having booked out, a young female receptionist approached me. "Good morning, Sir," she said in impeccable English. "I have arranged a taxi for you. He is waiting outside for you right now."

"Thank you, that is most kind of you," I said.

She smiled and returned to her duties behind the desk.

Outside, propped up against a tired, dilapidated, looking, old car was my taxi driver.

"Good morning, I'm your taxi driver," I was heralded.

How he had identified me as his client from among all the people leaving the hotel, I'm not quite sure. He opened the back door and I climbed in.

"Where you going?" he asked in a rather heavy accent.

I gave him a slip of paper upon which I had printed Gonan's address.

"Okay – no problem," he said and with that, sped off in what can only be described as a terrifying journey. If there are any traffic rules, nobody seems to be aware of them or concerned about obeying them. It was absolute bedlam; people hooting and gesticulating and driving anywhere there was an opening. For the sake of sanity, I thought it best to close my eyes.

Istanbul is a very large city, so I had anticipated a fairly lengthy journey to my destination; not that I know Istanbul at all, or where I was going relative to the airport. It was just a simple assumption that the journey may be lengthy based on the size of the city alone. However, this journey seemed to be taking an unreasonable length of time. The airport is located in the west and I think we had now crossed the Bosphorus and were in the eastern part of the city. We were travelling a lot slower than before, but the hooting and gesticulation continued. We entered an old and rather run-down suburb of the city, with very narrow roads and old buildings on both sides. After driving for about ten minutes through this dilapidated neighbourhood, we came to a stop. The driver announced, "We here now," pointing to a door on the opposite side of the road.

My first impression was that it doesn't pay to work for the CIA or Mossad, having to live in this rather seedy neighbourhood.

"Me wait," announced the driver as I got out and headed for the door.

I knocked on it a few times before it was opened by an old, scruffily-dressed woman, who had a rather quizzical look on her face on seeing me.

"Hello," I said speaking very slowly and pronouncing my words correctly. "I am looking for Gonan Mehad?"

"No, no, no," she said shaking her head and gesticulating with her hands.

"Has he moved away?" I enquired further.

"No, no, no," she said, continuing to babble on. She then turned and started shouting into the bowels of the building; I assumed she was calling somebody. True enough, within a few minutes an old man appeared. He was fat, unshaven with a huge paunch. He was filthy, wearing an old, sleeveless vest, shorts and sandals. She carried on talking to him. He pushed past her and came and stood a few inches in front of me, adopting a rather threatening manner. I step back slightly.

"Good morning, I am looking for Gonan Mehad," I said placing the emphasis on Gonan's name.

He made some loud exclamation sounds as he threw his hands up in the air and started babbling on at me in a annoyed manner. Whatever I have said or done has certainly upset this duo. The old man and woman continued their cacophony of complaint at the top of their voices.

I stepped back and glanced at the driver. "Please help me, I don't know what these people are saying."

He got out the car, cigarette dangling from the side of his mouth; sauntered over to the old couple as if there was no tomorrow, propped himself up against the doorpost and started talking to the old man. After chatting to him for a few minutes, he stood up and came over to me.

"The person you are looking for doesn't live there anymore. He has left with their young daughter and owes them a lot of money. They do not know where he has gone," he said.

My heart sunk. What now? How am I ever going to find this man in a huge metropolis where I cannot speak or read the language? I would certainly prefer trying to find a needle in a haystack. What's more, Gonan doesn't sound like a particularly pleasant character, or even a likely CIA researcher that could add any value to our cause, but what do I know of these things and the world of secret services?

"What do you want to do now?" asks the driver.

I walked back to the car and got in. I need a place where I can sit quietly and think through my options. The driver got into the car.

"Take me to a hotel," I instructed him.

As we drove off, the old couple remained in the doorway gesticulating and babbling away at the top of their voices. What a particularly unpleasant encounter.

We hadn't gone far before we came to a screeching halt with the driver announcing, "Hotel."

You could have fooled me. It looked as sleazy and dilapidated as the house we had just come from. I wouldn't stay in this place for any reason. However, I wanted to get rid of the driver, as I didn't like or trust him, and I needed a quiet spot where I could sit for a few moments to gather my thoughts and plan a course of action; this hotel would serve that purpose for now.

"Please give me the paper I gave you." I asked the driver.

"What paper?" he said.

"The address I gave you, can I please have it back?" I asked.

"Oh, this," he said, producing a crumpled piece of paper.

"Yes, that," I said, taking it from him and ironing it on my leg.

I got out of the car.

"You want me to wait?" he asked.

"No, thank you, I have finished with your services," I said, paying him his fare.

I pushed the hotel door open and entered the building. There appeared to be a reception desk on the left hand side of this dimly-lit room. It had a pungent tobacco smell. To the right, there were a few chairs placed against the walls, like a waiting room. I assumed this was their reception area. There was nobody at reception, although they had a small brass bell on the counter which I presumed was for the purpose of summoning assistance. All I wanted was a place to sit and think for a few minutes. Although this place is as sleazy as it gets, it will serve my purpose for now. I went and sat down on one of their rather hard and uncomfortable chairs at the farthest end of the room.

I felt absolutely dejected. How could I possibly find this man in this huge city? I placed my elbows on my knees, lent forward and placed my head in my hands. I sat like this for some time with random thoughts rushing through my head. I wasn't focusing on anything; my thoughts were just running wild. Then suddenly the penny dropped. How stupid have I been? I have allowed one of Alvarez's henchmen to organise me a taxi which promptly took me on a wild goose chase to the wrong address. Then they stage a charade with the old couple to make me think they know him, and that he has run off and is impossible to find. They also stage this event in a sleazy part of town to make me doubt Gonan's credentials and concoct a story that he has run off with a younger woman owing money, just to make sure my doubts about Gonan are heightened. This all makes sense now; it also gives me hope. All I need do now is find another taxi driver and put the theory to the test. I must admit, although their plan was simple, it could easily have worked.

I picked up my luggage and headed for the front door. Outside, parked where he had left me was my taxi driver. Why is he still here, surely he has other fares to collect? Obviously, he has been paid to keep an eye on me. I quickly stepped back into the building so he didn't see me. I would have to leave through the back and take a side alley to avoid him. Inside, immediately opposite the front door, was a door which led onto the reception area. I headed for it. It led onto a corridor which ran parallel to the road. I turned left and walked down the passage. I don't like walking around other people's property uninvited and unannounced; it makes me feel uneasy. At the end of the passage, on the right-hand side, was a door. I knocked on it gently and tried turning the door knob, but it was locked. I started making my way back down the passage, trying each door as I went. After my third attempt, a door opened; this door led onto another passage which ran the full length of the building. There was a door at the end of the passage which was slightly ajar as I could see the sunlight pouring in around its frame. What relief, I could escape this building without coming across anybody. I pushed the door open. It led into a courtyard used for refuse collection and guessing by the smell, it hadn't been collected for a few weeks. There was another building in front of me and on the left was a high wall, but on the right there was a wooden gate six or seven feet high. Unfortunately, it was locked. I'm not agile or fit, but had no hesitation in deciding that I needed to climb it. This wasn't going to be easy carrying my luggage, but at least it was an old gate with ample opportunities to find a foothold. I started scrambling the gate. When I reached the top, I looked up and down the alleyway onto which it led. All seemed quiet so I hoisted my luggage over the top and let it drop onto the street below. I then hoisted myself over the gate and slid down its front. Once back on terra firma, I picked up my luggage and headed up the alleyway, away from where the taxi was parked. Unsurprisingly, I discovered my shirt and jacket had been covered in some oily substance during my descent of the gate, which upon rubbing, worsened its appearance. I decided to leave it as it was for the time being.

The alleyway was not that long. It led onto a road similar to the one where the taxi was parked. I turned left, attempting to put as much distance between me and the taxi as possible. As long as I remain in a fairly built-up, residential area, I should come across another taxi fairly soon. If I could find a shopping centre or some point where the community gathers, this should increase the opportunity of finding one. Having no clue as to where I am, or where I am going, such thoughts are academic. I just kept on walking. I asked a few people I met in the street for a taxi but just received blank stares in response. After over an hour, I started to become quite desperate. I thought it would be a simple task, but now have visions of wandering the streets of Istanbul late at night trying to find a taxi or hotel. As built up and as populated as it is, the place reminds me of a complicated maze where I cannot ask for, or expect, any assistance in finding my way out. Half an hour later, I seriously doubted the wisdom of my choice. Perhaps if I could find a police station? Then, as if by chance, I spotted a board which appeared to be advertising the services of a taxi company. I went over and stood in front of it to find a telephone number. What would be the point, if I could find a number and get through to it they probably won't understand any English, and I don't know where I am to give them instructions to pick me up. I was now quite despondent. I leant against the wall to take a short break. I looked down the street and amazingly enough I saw a taxi coming towards me. I stepped into the road and waved my hands frantically. The vehicle slowed down and came to a stop, much to my relief. The back door opened and I got in. The driver started speaking to me in Turkish. I put my hand into my jacket pocket and produced the slip of paper with Gonan's address on it. I gave it to him. He read it and started speaking in Turkish again.

"I'm sorry, I don't understand," I said.

"Oh, you are English, I should have spotted that earlier," he said speaking perfect English, although with a strong accent. "You Pommies stick out like sore thumbs. I worked in London for four years, so I know you Pommies well. This address you have given me is on the other side of the city, is that where you want to go? "

166

You have no idea what a relief it was to get into this taxi, hear a friendly voice and have my theory confirmed that I was led on a wild goose chase. Suddenly, I felt refreshed and alive again. As we sped off back through the city, I was regaled with the driver's experiences as a London cabby. He was a friendly and totally likable character, who, by the end of our journey, had me quite homesick for London.

Chapter Eight

We had been travelling for sometime before we entered a modern, upmarket suburb of the city. The houses are large and attractive and surrounded by parks and tree-lined avenues. We stopped outside one of these houses, which looked particularly large and impressive.

"This is it, Gov," said the driver.

"Thank you. Do you mind waiting for me until I'm inside?" I asked.

"No problem, but don't you think you should change your jacket before going in? This is a posh suburb, and they won't let anybody in looking like you," he said in a jovial manner.

"Good idea," I said opening my case to retrieve my spare jacket. As I opened it there was a strong smell of aftershave. To my dismay, I discovered that when I dropped my case over the gate, I had either broken the bottle of aftershave or its lid had been dislodged and its contents leaked into my case. Whatever had happened my spare clothes were equally un-wearable. I felt disappointed, as I believe it's important to create a positive first impression, and how you dress plays an important part. I took a folder from my briefcase; I would hold this strategically across my chest partially to hide the stain.

I crossed the road and pressed the large, brass doorbell. I could hear the bell chiming inside. After a few minutes, I pressed it again; this time much longer. Not soon after, I could hear a bolt being undone on the door. It opened and there stood an old, thin man in a black suit and tie. My first impression was that he was the butler. He stared at me, up-and-down, for what seemed to be an age.

"Good morning," I said pronouncing my words slowly. "May I please speak to Mr. Gonan Mehad?"

"Who is calling, and what is the nature of your business?" he said with a slight American accent.

"My name is James Barton-Marshall, I'm from the United Kingdom, and I have some rather important information that I need to give Mr. Mehad," I said.

"Phone his office and make an appointment. He is extremely busy and does not see people from the street," he said turning to go.

"Wait a moment, please," I pleaded. "I have travelled far with extremely important information that I know Mr. Mehad will find invaluable. I appreciate that he is busy and I don't have an appointment, but circumstances have prevented me from following procedures, as Mr. Mehad will appreciate. Can you please let him know I'm here so he can decide what to do?"

"I doubt he will see you as his diary is booked at least three weeks ahead," he said walking back inside.

"Please, this is a matter of national and international security and you must let him know I'm here, otherwise, you personally will have to bear the consequences of any delays caused by me not seeing him today," I said.

"Wait here," he said closing the door behind him.

I could hear him bolting the door behind him. At least I had located Gonan and there is a possibility I will see him today.

I walked back to the taxi and paid him. I asked that he wait until I had gone inside. I also took his mobile number to contact him should I require his services further. I returned to Gonan's house and waited. A quarter of an hour later I heard the door being unbolted again. The old man peered from behind it.

"Come in," he said.

I turned and waved to the taxi driver as I entered the house. The front door led onto a foyer with a closed door in front of it.

The old man was standing in the foyer with a portable metal detector in his hand.

"I will have to scan you for weapons before you enter the house," he said.

"Is that necessary?" I asked.

"This is the property of the United States Of America, who are under threat of attack from radical elements at anytime. We cannot allow strangers onto our property without conducting a security search-and-check first," he said. "If you do not wish to subject yourself to this search-and-check, then you may leave now."

"No, everything is in order," I said. "I was not aware that this is a diplomatic residence."

He paid no attention to me and started scanning me up-and-down. He then asked to look inside my luggage. I apologised for the state of my luggage and my own appearance, but he seemed totally disinterested.

He took a card from inside his jacket and passed it through a reader on the side of the foyer door. The door opened and he walked through, beckoning that I should follow. He then led me into a reception room near the foyer. It was a large room with a boardroom table in the middle; it was beautifully appointed, with original paintings of Istanbul appearing along its walls. He produced a piece of paper and asked me to fill in my name and address and to give him my passport, which I duly did. He then left me in the room on my own.

A short time later he returned and handed my passport back to me. He sat down at the table opposite me.

"Mr. Mehad is too busy to see you but has instructed that I hear what you have to say," he said.

"I'm sorry, but the information I have for Mr. Mehad is too sensitive and can only be given to him personally," I responded.

He pushed his chair back and got up.

"I'm a Personal Assistant of Mr. Mehad who trusts me implicitly and instructs me what to do. If this is unacceptable to you, you may leave now," he said.

"I'm sorry, I did not mean to offend you," I said.

"I have taken no offence," he said, "but this is how Mr. Mehad wishes events to be conducted. He cannot be here personally right now, so has asked me to deputise for him."

"Right, I understand and apologise for appearing rude," I said.

I suppose I have no option but to tell this man my story?

He made no comment or gesture; he just stared at me as if to say, "get on with it".

I gave him the full presentation, as if I was speaking to Gonan directly. He just sat there and listened, making no comments or asking any questions. It was like giving a presentation to a robot. He showed no reaction or emotion whatsoever; it was quite remarkable and unsettling.

"Have you finished?" he enquired in a matter-of-fact voice.

"Yes, I have," I said, a little irritated at his attitude, as if what I had to say meant nothing and that I was wasting his time.

"I will relay your story to Mr. Mehad when he finishes his current meeting, which should be in about twenty minutes time," he said looking at his watch. "Please remain here until I return."

He got up and left the room.

He isn't a particularly gracious host, I thought. I hadn't had anything to drink for hours and was feeling parched, yet had received no offer of refreshment from this unpleasant, old man.

The waiting continued for hours and I was becoming desperately thirsty. I placed my head on the table and closed my eyes for a few minutes. I don't know how long I had been like this before I heard somebody clearing their throat to rouse me. I looked up and in front of me stood a very large, middle-aged man with a dark complexion, full, black beard and broad smile, with flashing white teeth.

"James, it's a pleasure to meet you, my name is Gonan Mehad," he said.

What a relief, finally I get to meet Gonan. I stood up and extended my hand. He took it in a firm grasp and shook it warmly.

"I'm very pleased to meet you finally. I've been through a few unpleasant scrapes to be here," I said.

"David has told me your story and I need to speak to you. However, I still have a few meetings to get through this afternoon, so what I would like to suggest is that you make use of our guest suite to freshen up, and I can meet you for dinner this evening where we can discuss your rather disturbing story further; if that is acceptable to you?"

"That would be ideal," I said.

"If you have no hotel reservations, you are more than welcome to use our guest suite tonight," he said.

"That is most kind of you as I have made no reservations," I said.

"Good," he said, "I look forward to our meeting this evening. Meanwhile, I will leave you in the capable hands of David who will show you around. Oh, and by the way, if you need any laundry being done, just ask David to sort it out for you," he said with a broad smile while rubbing the front of his jacket.

As he left, David, the old man, entered the room.

"Please follow me to the guest suite," he said, picking up my luggage.

I followed him as we walked through the house. I don't know what Gonan's position is, but this house is palatial in size and furnishings. The guest suite is suitable for the President. I have never had the privilege of living in such luxury. We have a very comfortable house by most standards, but this dwarfs everything I've ever known.

On depositing my luggage in the room, David enquired, "Do you have any laundry requirements?"

"Yes, I do, but first, I'm absolutely parched. Do you have any bottled water?" I enquired.

"There is a fully stocked bar over there," he said pointing towards it. "I will ask the maid to collect your laundry shortly. I will call back at seven this evening to direct you to the dining room."

What a day it has been. From my nondescript Holiday Inn's room, to the sleaziest hotel in the city, and now to this palatial luxury, all in one day, with a few scrapes and bumps along the way. It's been exhausting, so I will take a bath and try to get a few hours sleep before dinner and my meeting with Gonan.

That evening, at precisely seven o'clock, David escorted me down to a bar adjoining the dining room. Sitting at the bar on his own was Gonan. He got up when I entered the room.

"Good to see you again, James," he said. "Can I offer you something to drink?"

"Scotch, ice and water, thank you," I replied.

He went behind the bar and poured my drink. He then produced a menu and suggested I make my choice as he likes to let his staff go off as early as possible. Having made my choice, he lifted a telephone receiver at the bar and ordered our dinner from the kitchen. He then came and sat down at the bar next to me.

"I am meeting you in an unofficial capacity – as a friend," he said. "Whatever is discussed here tonight is off the record. It is a conversation between two friends trying to help one another."

"I understand fully," I said. "May I enquire as to what your job function is?"

"Yes, certainly, I am the USA Trade & Industries attaché in Turkey," he said.

Sensing that I may ask why a trade attaché should be afforded such luxurious living quarters, he hastened to explain.

"This used to be our ambassadorial house in Turkey before the government moved to Ankara. It's still used for certain state events and so it was decided to retain it. I'm not complaining; I get to live in this beautiful place which is way above my station in life," he said laughing aloud.

"I'm sorry to have to do this to you, but I would like to hear your story again, but this time from the horse's mouth, so to speak," he said.

"No problem at all. I know a lot can be lost in the telling," I replied.

Just before I had finished my story, a young lady interrupted us, announcing that dinner was ready. We went through to the dining room where over a most delightful meal, I finished my story. Gonan paid very close attention to what I was saying; interrupting me occasionally to get clarity on an issue or to ask a question.

After dinner, we returned to the bar where Gonan poured us both a large port.

"A fascinating hypothesis and one which provides a crucial piece to this complicated jigsaw puzzle. Critical to the cause of defeating Alvarez will be the availability of documented evidence, which you have intimated you have. However, I must say that it is highly irregular for any researcher in the employ of a secret service to make and keep duplicate copies of their research. It goes against every tenant of conduct in the service. Having said that, I appreciate the unique situation that he found himself in, and acknowledge his irregular and unethical behaviour may be our saving grace.

"Let me tell you my part of the story.

"Many years ago I worked for the CIA as a researcher, investigating the funding and involvement in radical Islamic groups by organised crime syndicates. More specifically, I was involved in researching Alvarez and his Al-Qaeda connection. My colleagues were involved in researching other radical groups which Alvarez and his syndicates were involved with. While I am no longer directly involved in these projects, I have remained on a Review Board directly responsible for reviewing, vetting and providing research direction.

"One of the most fundamental questions that has concerned and perplexed researchers over the years has been the motive behind the crime syndicates involvement with radical groups. If ever an odd marriage – this is it. Many theories have been propounded, but none has withstood rigorous analysis. This hypothesis, on the other hand, makes good sense, where Alvarez uses these radical groups to strike in unison at the time when he has our financial markets in free fall. The effects of this will be devastating, and then to sustain these attacks thereafter, backed up by civil unrest, will bring governments to their knees. His control of the networks then renders governments ineffective and useless. This provides the ideal situation for him to install illegitimate puppet governments who are miraculously able to return things to normality very quickly and in the process deliver up the terrorist groups, who the masses think are responsible for these catastrophes. These two acts alone will legitimise these governments in the eyes of the masses. It's a very clever plan that has caught us completely offguard. You referred to this as a silent war; I don't think you could have given it a more apt name. Furthermore, your conclusion that we are involved in an international war is one I concur with completely.

The nub of the matter is that we have totally underestimated Alvarez. We all tend to think within the box, and yet we are dealing with an individual that takes the box, turns it upside down, sits on top of it while he thinks of a more appropriate plan that in no way conforms to previous thinking. We are ten steps behind this man. He's thinking of ways to catch us out, and we are sitting on our fat backsides doing nothing about serious and known problems. If you think about it, our stock markets, and therefore our economies, are highly exposed to a malicious attack like this. Our economy is our heart – attack our economy in this way, and you have us on our knees as if you'd launched a thousand A-Bombs. Have we been so stupid as to think this impossible? Alvarez has used known weaknesses within business to catch us unaware. So what the heck – we know the Accounting Model doesn't work, but it won't harm anybody, and anyway, vested interest in keeping it remains high, so let sleeping dogs lie. The same applies to the shortcomings in our stock market trading procedures. We knew there were problems, but for the same reasons, we did nothing. Wrong answer – wrong attitude! I'm a Trade & Industry attaché, so I know what I'm talking about, when I say our Accounting Model is entirely inappropriate as a universal business measurement standard. I should have been more vocal about the problem and supported the free thinkers who promoted the concepts of modern value management; I now wish I had, as I'm sure many of my colleagues around the world would have done. The same applies to the stock market – we should have made the changes when we could.

"If only business, with all its resources, and knowing it had a problem had not carried on like sheep; it's truly shameful! Granted, they may not have foreseen how their indolence could cause the demise of the free world. If business had only taken a leaf out of Alvarez's book and thought about the problem completely differently and come up with a truly innovative solution, you, and I would not be meeting under such dire circumstances. However, I suppose there's no point moaning about what we should have done."

He paused for a while as he sipped his drink. He was very pensive as he reflected on what might have been. We sat quietly for some time before he continued.

"Let me tell you what I know about Alvarez's organisation, and its involvement in radical religious groups, before we discuss a possible course of action. However, it may be advisable that I tell you a little about myself as my critics may claim that my past experience clouds my judgment. I don't think it does, but as we will be working closely together, you may as well hear it from me rather than from my critics so that you may draw your own conclusions.

As a young man working in Tel Aviv, I lost my entire family in one of the first suicide bombings in a public place. My wife and young son, together with my mother and I, were enjoying some refreshments in a café, in a section of the city frequented by tourists, when a suicide bomber blew himself up right next to my family. I escaped as minutes before I had gone to the toilet. As I was leaving the toilet, there was a terrific explosion which threw me back inside the toilet and rendered me unconscious. I only suffered minor injuries, but my family, who were nearest to the bomber, never survived. There is no doubt that this event has affected me. To have those you love most dearly killed in this horrific manner, right in front of your own eyes, has left me bitter and determined to do whatever I can to fight terrorist organisations to my dying day. I have not been able to reconcile myself with their deaths, no matter how hard I have tried. I had hoped that advancing age would heal my hatred but, unfortunately, it has not. Despite these feelings, I try at all times to keep my feet firmly on the ground and to make fair and informed decisions. I believe if I don't do this and allow emotion and hatred to take hold, I will make the wrong decisions and thereby minimise my effectiveness. In fact, I could become totally counterproductive if I allowed these emotions to take hold, and my life's work dedicated to stopping indiscriminate terrorist attacks wasted. I want to do everything I can to ensure others don't have to go through what I had to."

"I'm very sorry to hear of this horrendous attack on your family," I said.

"It wasn't an attack on my family as much as an attack on society," he said biting his lip and fighting back a flood of emotion. It was sad to see a man who had clearly not got over the trauma of these events.

"Normally, I don't talk of these things," he said, "as they upset me unnecessarily, but I felt it important you understand my past so that if you think I'm leaving the straight and narrow, allowing emotion to take hold, you tap me on the shoulder for a reality check."

"I understand," I said.

"Returning to Alvarez and his involvement with Al-Qaeda," he said.

"Sorry to interrupt you, Gonan, but can you tell me a little more about Alvarez?"

"I don't think I have much more to tell you about him personally, because soon after taking control of his organisation in 1989, he became increasingly reclusive, to the extent that over the past five years or more, he has never left his island fortress. We do, however, see Alvarez figuratively all around the world, virtually on a daily basis, through the workings of his vast empire, yet he has never been seen. The only other bit of personal information I know about him is that in the early 80s he was shot in the face in a bungled police raid. The bullet evidently shattered his lower jaw and left him badly scarred. He went through considerable reconstructive surgery, but the scar was still visible on his last sighting. Since then, he may have had further surgery; nobody really knows."

"Thank you," I said.

"Getting back to Alvarez and his involvement with Al-Qaeda," he said, "Al-Qaeda was formed in 1988, approximately one year before Alvarez took control of the World's largest crime syndicate. By the early 1990s, we noticed significant funds being poured into Al-Qaeda. They were using them to launder vast amounts of money, using non-traditional laundering methods. The 'dirty' money appeared to come in with little or nothing going out. By the mid-nineties, Alvarez's involvement included technological and armaments support. He was equipping them with the latest and most sophisticated communications equipment, and access to the latest and most expensive armaments.

"You must realise that terrorist organisations take on frightening proportions when they have the support of local communities, but this isn't as frightening as when fanatical groups are paired with organised crime syndicates. It is a lethal concoction of frightening proportions. Local communities can provide cover and local knowledge to terrorist groups and their activities, but organised crime syndicates not only provide this, but also access to sophisticated technologies, weaponry, vast amounts of money and an underworld network of ruthless thugs to do their bidding. Its potency over local community involvement can hardly be measured.

"We saw this for the first time in the 2001 7/11 attack. We have irrefutable evidence that Alvarez was involved in this attack. His organisation provided some of the logistical support to enable the attack to take place, but his greatest involvement was in booby-trapping the Twin Towers. It was their technology and know-how that brought the Twin Towers down, through a series of controlled demolitions. I know the conspiracy theories about this have been debunked, but the facts are, it did happen, and it was Alvarez's involvement and their technical expertise which ensured the buildings collapsed. The American government has enough evidence to prove this, but clearly they didn't want to alarm the public that Al-Qaeda has the backing of organised crime. You can imagine the panic this would cause, for reasons elaborated on earlier. It would also have complicated George Bush's 'War on Terror', so they put a lid on it. One thing that amazed me was how they managed to rig these buildings without being detected, as it was a big job. I had always put it down to the mobs influence, which I'm sure played a big part, but now I can see how the influence of the networks guaranteed its secrecy, and maintains it today.

"Alvarez used this attack as a trial run for several reasons. Firstly, to lift the profile of Al-Qaeda, as they are to play a key role in his unfolding plot, but unbeknown to them, they will become his 'fall guys', or sacrificial lambs, as you put it. Secondly, to test the two organisations ability to cooperate on a large scale. Thirdly, to entrench his control within Al-Qaeda. In his opinion, these are small men thinking on a small scale. The more control he has over them, the more effective and dramatic the results he can produce. He had to prove to their leadership that he has the capacity to produce better results than them, and that he truly shares their desire for the destruction of Western capitalism.

"He came up trumps in all his objectives, but the most important objective of all was for him to play a more leading and dominant role in their planning. The reason for this being, he wishes to use Al-Qaeda as his storm troopers; for them to lead the initial attacks across a broad front, on a scale never before seen.

"Since 2002, we have seen how Alvarez has started to influence their strategies. Their plans have become more ambitious and sophisticated and if carried out, would result in optimum panic and terror. His strategy appears to be directed at all forms of transportation. In light of what you have told me, all the pieces of the puzzle start falling into place. Why they had exclusively targeted transportation was unclear to us. Now in the light of your revelation, explaining how they will attack stock markets first, setting off a run on shares, followed by an attack on most forms of commercial transport makes perfect sense. He attacks commercial transportation to immobilise business, driving financial markets down further and faster. His strategy requires the terrorist attack to coincide with his attack on the stock markets, but he cleverly targets these so called 'terrorist attacks' to cripple business; a clever dual purpose to his plan.

"Many elements of the puzzle were missing until now, leaving us wondering what he was up to. We know that he has put into motion a number of his plans, but as yet, has not executed them. It now makes sense; he is waiting for one massive, coordinated attack. He has allowed a few minor attacks to take place in the interim to ensure Al-Qaeda maintains a high profile, but the serious firepower has been held back in the wings. He has been marshalling and positioning his troops for one big coordinated attack. Each of the numerous plots we are aware of are potentially much more devastating than the Twin Tower attack. In that attack, he used technology to optimum effect. Remember, we are dealing with a forward-thinking man who embraces every facet of evolving technology to further his aims. He has vast amounts of money to spend on developing and, or purchasing solutions to aid his plans. I am aware of one such plot where he intends using drone airplanes, utilising technology far more advanced than even the US military has in operation right now. It's now all so clear to me why he invested so heavily in creating these sophisticated and devastating plots; they represent a key component in his destabilisation strategy."

He pauses for a few seconds, probably reflecting on what he has just said, before continuing.

"Using Al-Qaeda and other terrorist groups to play a crucial part in his strategy, unbeknown to them, is clever and devious, but his control over social and business networks is a stroke of absolute genius, and it this which will prove to be our nemesis. It is something you cannot prove exists, and you may not even be aware of until you bump your head against it, like you have done with MI6. I will face the same problem as you in taking this matter forward; who will I be able to trust and who will try to stop me? His control over the networks will turn previously highly effective organisations, such as the CIA and MI6, into introspective, indecisive and bungling organisations, fed half truths and lies by individuals continuously watching their backs and untrusting of their colleagues. For these reasons, we need as much documented evidence as we can lay our hands on as in all likelihood, we may have to bypass normal communication protocols and go straight to the top. If this is how events pan out, and I suspect they will, we will only be given one shot at talking to the top man, so we had better have our facts and figures correct."

He paused again, sipping his drink, "I just can't get over the brilliance of Alvarez's strategy in dominating every facet of society. I'm aware of the conspiracy theories regarding World domination, often called the New World Order. It is claimed that a small group of international elite control and manipulate governments, industry and media organisations worldwide and are said to have funded, and in some cases caused, most of the major wars over the past two hundred years. I'm sure many of these events may have involved a conspiracy, but I remain of the opinion that they did not emanate from the same source. If such groups like the Bilderberg Group, the Illuminati or the Bohemian Grove, to name only a few, are behind such conspiracies, the rug has been firmly pulled from under their feet. Alvarez's approach of dominating every facet of society, including its knowledge, is absolutely brilliant. These other secret societies may have attempted to manipulate events through control of financial markets, yet Alvarez realised that was insufficient and took his influence and control to a new level, which most of us find difficult to even conceive. You have to hand it to the man – he's brilliant and far-sighted.

"Returning to the present, I'm going to call a meeting of as many people as I think I can trust to convene here on Wednesday evening to form a task group to tackle the problem. I would appreciate it if you could do the introductory presentation highlighting the dangers we face, and incorporating what I have told you tonight. You are more than welcome to stay here over this period; in fact, I think it would be advisable."

"Thank you, I will gladly do the presentation if you think it will help," I said.

Assuming our meeting was drawing to a close, I told him of my experience the day before at the airport and my taxi ride in the morning.

"Welcome to Istanbul," he said with a broad smile. He seemed to be amused about my experiences, but soon returned to the seriousness of the situation.

"I'm pleased you gave them the slip. They will, however, be watching this place so it's probably best you don't go out over the next few days. I'll have you flown home after the meeting well under the Alvarez radar. Next thing they'll know is that you will be back home, having been off their radar for a few days.

"We have an extensive library and a beautiful garden to keep you amused during your stay. However, I would respectfully ask that you use your time, and that keen mind of yours, to consider a practical course of action to rid us of this curse. Clearly, a strike at the serpents head will be totally inadequate.

"I have a long day ahead of me tomorrow, not least of all organising people from around the World to attend our meeting at short notice. So, if you don't mind, I would like to be excused?

"No, that's fine," I said.

"Do you know your way back to your room?" he enquired.

"I think I do, thank you."

"Up the stairs to the first floor and it's the second door on the right," he said. "If you need any help, just lift the receiver in the bedroom and David will help you. Goodnight."

This is not the way I thought things would pan out. I had imagined that all I had to do was get our message over to the experts at the CIA, and they would know exactly what to do. Now, to be asked to consider and propose possible solutions to a group of experts appears to be well beyond my realm. I have no experience or knowledge in this field, but then I suppose neither do they; this is a totally new threat conducted according to a new set of rules.

Believing that finding solutions to this problem was not my responsibility, I have paid scant regard to it. My first naïve thought was to think that a strike at the 'serpents head', as he put it, would solve our problem, yet the astute wisdom of Gonan has quickly put paid to that idea.

Dr. John had always referred to Alvarez's control of the networks as a parasitic invasion, and I tend to support his analogy. This isn't like fighting a snake or dragon where, if you sever its head, the body dies. Parasitic entities are completely different. One of the problems of killing a parasite at an advanced stage of development is that you risk killing the host as well. Let us assume we can kill Alvarez and destroy his computer systems in one fell swoop; that removes his threat and central control of the networks, but the networks remain. They remain under the control of undesirable elements. These controllers could form coalitions with other controllers, or people higher up the Alvarez hierarchy could take control of multiple networks, making them powerful people. Whatever happens, we will end up with many self-serving agendas that will pull us in all directions, debilitating government and making them ineffective. Over a period of time, this could lead to the government's demise and result in their replacement by a form of dictatorship, as the public will soon become fed up with bungling and indecisive governments, favouring instead strong, centralised leadership that can purge us of the cause – the networks. The irony is that our ultimate savour may be what Alvarez wishes to establish; a totalitarian state.

When you think of it, we have been at war for almost two decades and over that period we have suffered many casualties on a daily basis. By now, our 'casualties' account for millions of people who have fallen under the influence of Alvarez's network; many of which are rich, powerful and influential. These are not casualties of war as you would expect from a conventional war, but, nonetheless, they are casualties. In fact, the casualties we suffer are substantially more costly to us because when we suffer a casualty through the network taking over control of an individual's soul, our loss is their direct gain. This individual now dances to their tune and no longer exercises freedom of choice. The millions we have lost, unbeknown to them, now work against us. We have been losing little battles every day over the past two decades. Such huge losses are not overturned through winning one big battle, namely removing Alvarez. We have been taking body blows all this time without being aware of it, and will soon pay the price.

On that rather sobering note, I thought it advisable to get to bed. Perhaps a good night's rest would reinvigorate tired brain cells, allowing me to offer some insightful advice at our meeting on Wednesday.

Over the next two days, I spent most of my time in their large, beautifully appointed and well stocked library; with the occasional sojourn into the garden to enjoy the sunlight and fresh air. I took all my meals alone in the library as Gonan was tied up in meetings and dinner parties. David has been most helpful and attentive over the past few days. He's not the sombre, miserable, old gent I took him to be. He is, in fact, very friendly and has a sharp, but rather dry sense of humour. He was kind enough to pop in and chat to me occasionally. I don't know if this was of his own volition or whether Gonan had asked him to pay me regular visits on his behalf. It transpires that he is a well-educated man, with a Masters degree in Religious History, who has worked as one of Gonan's personal assistants for many years.

One thing that has struck me over the past couple of days is the size of the Trade & Industry department operating out of this building. It appears to be very large, although that's just a guess on my part as much of the house is off limits to me; requiring a security card to enter. David was rather reticent on answering any questions regarding the department and their activities. Things just don't seem to stack up for me. I know people make big career changes, but a person who is emotionally driven to bring terrorists to justice doesn't give up careers in Mossad and the CIA, working directly to achieve that aim, to become trade attachés – it doesn't jell with me. Gonan also told me he now plays a role in determining strategic direction for a department he supposedly doesn't work for. It makes even less sense now. Why does the Trade & Industries department require such a big staff, with Gonan requiring more than one personal assistant, one of which appears more qualified in religious matters than trade and financial affairs? Add to the melting pot Gonan calling a meeting which will consider a course of action against Alvarez; this shows somebody acting well beyond their remit, unless of course this is a CIA front and possibly a counter-terrorist department placed here on the cusp of east and west for strategic reasons. Furthermore, why would Dr. John pin his hopes on a Trade & Industries attaché? Perhaps because Dr. John didn't know that many people, but then he did look on the computer and would have known he was no longer a CIA employee, unless it showed up differently. Dr. John did indicate Gonan was our doorway into the CIA, unless he was just hoping, Gonan would have some old leads he could call on. I really don't know what to make of it. It would be reassuring to know I had entered the heart of the CIA and wasn't playing around on the fringes. Perhaps I'm just imagining things, hoping our position is a lot stronger than just having found the sympathetic ear of a Trade & Industry attaché who has some old contacts that may or may not be of any use.

I have had no flash of brilliance or any illuminating moments when considering a course of action against the threat of the networks. I have, however, had time to reflect on the enormity of the problem. Each network works as an independent cell. Each network may or may not know of the existence of another. In all likelihood, they don't know of each other's existence. Members of a network may know some, but not necessarily all members of the same network. This is not a fraternity brought together through commonality of interest or objectives, but rather through their own avarice. Hence, the networks are isolated and highly secretive. Loyalty, or should I rather say compliance with network requests or orders, are enforced through fear in numerous forms. Consequently, the problem we face is huge because we don't know how many networks there are or who directly controls each network, and, or what organisational infrastructure, if any, controls the networks. Therefore, we need to capture his computer systems intact to be successful, but that objective appears remote. I'm no military man, but an attack on a stronghold to capture a computer system, or its information, intact would seem to be highly improbable. The authorities best bet would be to launch some form of cyber attack where our computers could infiltrate theirs and communicate their data back to us. Dr. John did, however, tell me that Alvarez was technologically very savvy, investing more than large international banks into his systems, so I should imagine such an attack will be difficult, if not impossible. One thing I have learnt so far in dealing with Alvarez; don't look for the answer in the obvious and known places. His attacks and counter-attacks will border on the unexpected and brilliant. This is what sets the greatest military or businessmen apart – doing the unexpected brilliantly.

What a different war we face today. It is a war over the control of information, with our best option being for one computer to attack another. The problem with this is that the information we wish to control resides in the ether. It is very difficult for us to pin it down, read or destroy it, if the owner knows it's under attack. Alvarez and his cadres can transfer information from one computer to another, on the other side of the world, in nanoseconds, and leave no trace.

I think in formulating strategies to attack Alvarez, it is critical to understand the top echelons of his organisation and his relationships with these people, because power and control over the networks could be transferred to one of them and the threat will remain; perhaps even worse, because at least Alvarez is a known adversary, even though brilliantly unpredictable.

So as I see it, Plan A is to destroy Alvarez and capture his network information intact. Such an outcome appears remote to say the very least. An attack on his stronghold may result in his death, but I would imagine the organisation will continue as before under new, possibly less capable, but equally determined leadership. Plan B might be to attempt to negotiate with the new leadership, if we can identify them, because clearly we cannot obliterate its command as we don't know who, or where they are, and we cannot gain control over their information, so in essence, we have lost the war. If an attack on his stronghold kills Alvarez and destroys the 'collective' information about the networks, we still face the threat of the networks that could debilitate and bring down governments over a prolonged period, as 'fragmented' network knowledge will still be known by each network controller. Plan C would involve dealing with this scenario; the control of the networks by many undesirable and unscrupulous individuals. I don't know how to handle this problem, except perhaps to go public and tell people the nature of the threat we face, and get people within the networks to rebel. I'm probably a little naïve in believing such an approach will work as the 'glue' of the networks, namely fear, will still remain and people may not think their 'arrangement' has anything to do with this massive international network plot.

When I came to Istanbul, I thought it would be straightforward – I would tell Gonan the problem, and he would get experts with all the answers, backed up by the might of the CIA, to slew the beast. What a reality check I have faced; there are no experts and the problem has been allowed to grow unchecked for so long, that it now appears insoluble. The only possible scenario I foresee is a slide backwards into a totalitarian state.

On the Wednesday evening, I took dinner alone in the library as Gonan was attending another dinner party. David popped in and informed me that Gonan would see me at nine and take me to the presentation room. At precisely ten to nine, Gonan made his appearance.

"I must apologise for having left you to your own devices over the past couple of days," he said.

"It has given me the opportunity to review the situation," I replied.

"Good," he said "and what is your prognosis?"

"Whatever way I look at it the outcome is bleak, unless you have some technical wizardry up your sleeve that can capture Alvarez's computers," I replied.

"My colleagues and I anxiously await your presentation and evaluation."

"I don't think I can add to this debate as I don't have any idea of how much knowledge you already have on the subject. Furthermore, I don't have adequate understanding of how you work or what resources are available to you as the CIA. I definitely believe you know more than what you have told me."

"It would appear that you have spent your time fruitfully. Yes, we do know a little more than what I have told you, but you have some very important information I would like you to tell my colleagues directly. Secondly, your prognosis is important to us because it represents an outsider's or lay interpretation of the situation, because, as you correctly pointed out, you don't know how we work or what resources we have. Your view may represent the view our enemies have of us, so it's important for us to get that perspective. The more in the dark our enemy is of our capabilities and the more hopeless they think our situation, the more prone they are to making mistakes.

"This brings me onto the procedures for this evening. I will take you to our presentation theatre where you will be introduced as Mr. A. You will do your presentation and give your considered opinion on how we are to handle this threat. Afterwards, you may be asked a few questions which you may answer freely. This will complete your presentation and David will escort you from the room. Please understand that we request you leave to protect you and the interests of the State. This is no insult to you. Your efforts are acknowledged and appreciated.

"I will meet you tomorrow morning to explain the arrangements I have made to return you home, and any further instructions or requests we may have of you. Is that quite clear to you?"

"Quite clear," I responded in a matter-of-fact way.

"Let me make it very clear to you – we are grateful to you, but from here on in your involvement should be minimal, if at all."

"That is what I had hoped to hear all along. I'm just an old retired lawyer, I don't want to become embroiled in matters where I could become a liability," I responded.

"Good, then let's get going," he said.

We walked down the passage, went through two security doors then turned right into another passage. At the end of this passage, we entered a lift which took us to the basement. In front of us was a short passage with two large double doors at the end, which led us into the theatre.

Gonan pushed the doors open and strode up to the lectern, which was on our left. It is a large theatre. The lights are dimmed over the audience and only the stage is lit, so you can't see who's in the audience. I followed Gonan. From the wings, David emerged and handed both Gonan and myself a set of earpieces with integrated microphones. We placed these on our heads and Gonan started addressing the audience.

"Thank you all for making the effort to attend this emergency meeting. As I have explained to you all, although very briefly, Mr. A, my friend here, approached me a few days ago, Tuesday to be precise, with a very interesting scenario. I have asked him to re-tell this scenario, in person, to you tonight. Although my friend is an intelligent and learned man, he has no experience beyond his profession as a lawyer: nevertheless, I have asked for his opinion on how he would see us tackling the threat, which he will explain in his presentation. Once he has finished his presentation and given his prognosis of the situation, you may ask him questions. Please refrain from making suggestions as Mr. A will leave us after his presentation, at which stage we will open the debate. Thank you."

Gonan gestured for me to step forward. I peered into the audience; all I could make out is what appeared to be a sea of heads. I estimate there must be between thirty to forty people. I felt encouraged by seeing so many. I had thought there may be a few people; not more than ten at the most, so this is most pleasing.

On completing my presentation and prognosis, I thanked the audience for their time. After what seemed to be an age, my earpiece crackled into life.

"This question is directed at the Chairman and Mr. A. Do we have documented proof of these events, as I would see this as being a critical part of our future plans?"

"Mr. A should be in possession of documented proof of the Alvarez organisation's involvement in underwriting business and learning institutions, all, or most of which, are involved in the first phase of his strategy, namely, the destabilisation of the international economy. Alvarez's involvement in funding and guiding Al-Qaeda is widely known in the upper echelons of most major powers, although I have seen to it over the past few hours that this evidence has been secured by us, independent of any government agency, as we do not want a repeat of the MI6 experience where documented proof is destroyed. With regard to documented proof on Alvarez's control over the networks, this is difficult to prove. Often 'dirty money' is used so there is no or little trail as to who has received what. We have to rely on hearsay and anecdotal stories. No – this is not ideal, but then this is the brilliance of the strategy," replied Gonan.

"If there are no more questions for Mr. A, I would like to thank him for his time and express our gratitude to him," said Gonan.

With that, David reappeared from the wings and led me off the stage. We walked back to my room in silence.

Early next morning, Gonan was knocking on my door.

"Good morning, James, I hope you slept well? I have arranged a flight back to Bristol for you this morning on a friend's private jet. You will slip back into Britain undetected by Alvarez. I'm also going to give you a special mobile phone that you can use to contact me at anytime. This phone cannot be tracked or calls monitored. It's a safe and secure method for contacting me, or for me to contact you. Don't use any other method. As soon as you are in possession of the documents, let me know so that I may arrange for their safe collection and keeping. I don't have to remind you, these documents will play a critical role in our strategy; without them, we may be hamstrung. We are convinced that somebody from the Alvarez organisation will attempt to contact you within the week. They will do this to find out what we know, but more importantly, they may be on the trail of the documents as well. Believe me, they will not hesitate to kill to secure such information. Once you know of their whereabouts, you must let us know immediately and we will secure them rapidly, no matter where they are in the UK. Don't try and store them, or delay contacting me, as you will be sitting on a time bomb.

"On a more positive note, I can let you know that my colleagues do not share your bleak prognosis. We do have a few tricks up our sleeves which will even the odds substantially. I

would like you to leave here feeling optimistic about the future –
we are certainly not beaten, I can assure you of that."

Gonan got up and shook my hand.

"Thank you, James. Good luck and I will hear from you
shortly. David will be here shortly, and he will take you to the
airport. Goodbye."

Chapter Nine

My flight back to Bristol was most pleasant. I had a ten-seater executive jet all to myself. What a contrast to my outward bound flight in a cramped budget airline.

The flight landed just after two in the afternoon. It will be dark in about three hour's time, and I need to be home well before that for a possible rendezvous with Dr. John. We had agreed that we would meet any day from Wednesday onwards. The sooner we can meet and the documents handed over to Gonan the better. I still have to collect the car from the long-stay parking area, and then drive all the way to Dorothy's cottage to collect Fiona. I had phoned her earlier to let her know of my ETA so she can be ready, but I still need to spend some time at Dorothy's to show my gratitude for having taken Fiona in over the past few days. All this will take at least two hours without any unforeseen delays, so I will need to hurry.

I'm sure Dr. John will be pleased with the outcome of my meeting with Gonan. I suppose the meeting went well enough in the sense that I got our message through to the CIA, but it has left me with a sense of despondency. I remain of the opinion that the prognosis is bleak, despite Gonan's reassurances. The reality is we are playing catch-up and time is not on our side. We have been fighting and losing a war for the past two decades; under these circumstances, you don't reverse your fortunes in one or two easy moves. I look forward to hearing Dr. John's opinion on the matter. I didn't ask Gonan for the information he holds on Alvarez as, in my opinion, we have nobody to give it to and by us sitting on such information, it endangers us unnecessarily and could compromise our efforts if it falls into Alvarez's hands.

When I think about my meeting with Gonan, I am sure he asked for my prognosis to get me to think the problem through logically, as a means of subtly letting me know we've been caught offside and not to expect a favourable outcome. Then, in retrospect, he has thought it a bad idea to leave me with a pessimistic opinion, particularly as I still have a role to play in securing the documents for him. He therefore attempted to reassure me before I left. I'm convinced our only salvation lies in a technology solution; perhaps they have one and our cause is not lost. I can only hope this is the case and must act as if we are fighting this war on a level playing field, but my gut tells me differently.

Fiona and I arrived home at around ten past four. I headed straight for my study and waited anxiously for a signal from Dr. John. By half past six, it had been dark for well over an hour and I hadn't seen any signal. I was disappointed and fearful at the same time. I hope nothing has happened to Dr. John. Gonan's warning that they would have no compunction in killing to secure this information rang in my ears. I just wanted the documents handed over as quickly as possible.

Friday came and went with no contact with Dr. John. On Saturday morning, I decided to give Gonan a call to let him know I had not yet seen Dr. John, as I was sure he would be anxious for an update. After the third attempt at getting through, and receiving the message 'No Connection Available', I managed to speak to him. The line was as clear as a bell, which vindicated the connection problems and my doubts about the technology.

Gonan didn't appear to be at all surprised or concerned about the non-appearance of Dr. John. Perhaps it was just a façade to help calm me down. I am anxious about this matter. I believe that every second we waste our enemy consolidates, or even strengthens their position. I don't believe we can afford to sit on our hands waiting for events to unfold. Maybe Gonan isn't sitting around waiting, but I am and it is extremely frustrating. I know it's not doing me any good fretting about the situation, so I may as well take a leaf out of Gonan's book and let events unfold in a calm and collected manner. It's going to be difficult as my mind is preoccupied with these events, and I've never been one for sitting around. I'm going to go and help Fiona in the garden, which should clear my mind and prove to be therapeutic.

The weekend came and went with no contact with Dr. John. Monday came and went with no contact either. By Tuesday morning I was feeling quite ill with anxiety, not only for the well-being of Dr. John, but more importantly, knowing that without the documents our cause is lost. Horrible, apocalyptic images of the future engulf me. I see Adolph Hitler-type dictators implementing ethnic cleansing on a scale which makes the horrors of the Holocaust pale in insignificance. I see totalitarian states more brutal and ineffective than Russian Communism. I can't stay in the house, and I can't go to my study, because there my thoughts will revolve around nothing other than this matter; so I head for the garden and another day of digging flower beds to help numb my mind.

At around mid-morning, while sitting on the front lawn nursing blisters on both hands, I received a surprise call from Sir Andrew Sweetman. He informed me that there had been some interesting developments on the case and that MI6 had reopened it. He asked if he could meet me to discuss a few issues regarding it. He would be at his Gloucestershire estate over the next few days and suggested we meet there. As it is less than three hours from here, and a lot more convenient than going all the way to his London office, I agreed to meet him there. Anything I could do to move this matter forward was welcome news to me, so I set the meeting up for tomorrow morning just after ten. This should give me sufficient time to hold the meeting with him and get back before dark to see Dr. John, if I don't see him tonight. I was elated with this news. My meeting with Gonan has borne some early fruit; progress has been made, no matter how small it may be, at least something positive was happening at last. I'll probably hear from MI6 shortly, as technically I'm not supposed to discuss this matter with anybody. Perhaps I will meet them at Sir Andrew's?

That evening, again no contact was made with Dr. John. Tomorrow it will be one week since we were scheduled to meet. I find it difficult to believe that he would have been delayed for this length of time. He knew where he was going and how long it should take him. There is definitely something wrong, and I fear the worst.

I left early on Wednesday morning for Sir Andrew's country estate, which is near Stow-on-the-Wold in Gloucestershire. Thank goodness for the modern wonders of satellite navigation whose services proved invaluable in finding Sir Andrew's estate.

Sir Andrew has made a lot of money during his life and if first appearances of his country estate are anything to go by, then he has been equally successful in spending it. You enter the estate through a huge stone archway and impressive gatehouse. He has sophisticated electronic surveillance at the gate where you have to announce yourself before being let in.

There is a long driveway leading up to a beautiful Georgian mansion. The house alone must be worth every penny of twelve million pounds.

I parked in front of the house and started climbing the stairs to the front entrance. Before I reached the top, I met Sir Andrew who had come out to meet me.

"Hello, James, good to see you again. Hope you found the place with no difficulties?" he enquired.

"Hello, Sir Andrew, it's good to see you as well. Unfortunately, I cannot claim any of the credit for finding my way here, that's all thanks to my ingenious little satellite navigation unit."

"Isn't technology amazing; I absolutely love it," he said.

"Come on in. Come on in," he said, gesturing towards the entrance hall.

"You have an absolutely beautiful place here, Sir Andrew."

"James – how many times must I ask you to please call me Andy, as do all my friends?"

He then turned and admired his property. "Yes, this is a beautiful place, and I try to spend as much time as I can here or down in Poole, where I have another lovely house and where my pride and joy, a ninety-foot motor launch, is moored. Do you do any boating, James?"

"No, I'm no seafarer," I said

"That doesn't matter at all," he said, "this boat is designed to pamper you as you rock up and down on a few gentle waves. If it gets rough, we just go back into the harbour. I believe it's designed to handle rough seas, but I'm certainly not going to put it to the test. You and the wife must come down one weekend, preferably in the summer."

"I may take you up on that offer," I said.

"Good," he said, "come inside."

He led me through a huge entrance hall, paved in marble with beautiful staircases on both sides. It looks truly magnificent. The sheer grandeur of the place takes your breath away.

On entering the hall we immediately turned left and went down a passage in front of the house. At the end of this passage was Sir Andrew's office. The office looked out over the front gardens with a beautiful view of the estate, which seemed to stretch for miles. The office itself was beautifully appointed; what you would expect of a multi-million pound mansion.

"Wow – this is beautiful," I said, "I'm most impressed with your house and estate, Andy."

"It's cost me a fortune, but it's worth every penny," he said.

"Sit down, James. Can I get you something to drink?" he enquired.

"A cup of tea would be appreciated – thank you."

He went behind his desk and pressed an intercom button on his telephone. He stood there with his finger on the button for well over a minute, before he got any response.

"Hello, Nelly, can you please organise a cup of tea for my guest, Mr. Barton-Marshall. We are in my office, thank you."

It struck me as being a little odd the way he announced who I was to his kitchen staff. Surely 'one cup of tea' would have sufficed. Anyway – no big deal.

"Thanks for making the effort to come and see me, it is much appreciated," said Sir Andrew. "There is somebody here that would like to meet you and discuss developments with you privately. Let me go and call him right now," he said standing up and leaving the room.

I was quite intrigued. Who could he possibly be referring to? The only likely candidate that came to mind was perhaps a senior MI6 official.

A few minutes later the door burst open and in walked a fairly dark skinned, debonair, middle-aged gentleman with a broad smile and gleaming white teeth. He strode straight up to me with his hand outstretched in greeting.

"Hello, James, what a pleasure it is finally to meet you."

I stood up and extended my hand. He grasped it firmly and shook my hand so vigorously that I thought he would dislocate my shoulder.

"My name is Manuel Alvarez," he said.

You could have bowled me over with a feather, and it must have shown on my face.

"You are surprised to meet me?" asked Alvarez.

I just nodded my head.

"Sit down," he said, "I can understand why. My enemies make me out to be some kind of monster, but I can assure you I am not the person they claim me to be."

I sat down and he came and sat in the chair next to me, still with a broad smile on his face.

"I asked my good friend, Andy, to set up this meeting as I need to ask for your help."

This is like one shock after another. Firstly, the most powerful man in the world deems it necessary to speak to me; for what purpose I have no idea. Then, he asks for my help; how extraordinary.

"Let me explain," he said. "You have been used as a pawn by my enemies, in a game of high stakes, to set off a sequence of events which may have dire consequences for the entire world. I know this request might sound strange coming from somebody who you, no doubt, don't have a particularly favourable opinion of, but then that is because you have been fed lies and half truths about me. I am not the man or the person you think I am. I'm not 'Snow White' and I'm no angel, but equally, I am not some megalomaniac hell bent on dominating the world, as my enemies portray me to be. As I have said, you have been fed part truth and part lies. It is always difficult under these circumstances to differentiate between the two, so let me speak plainly to you about the problem so you can make your own informed decision.

You know some of the story but not all of it. I'm therefore going to start right at the beginning, when over twenty years ago, I noticed major shortcomings in our financial accounting procedures, recognising that it is entirely inappropriate for the task of recording or reporting business value. I also recognised the weaknesses in our share trading practices; these markets are driven mainly by fear or avarice, not by logical evaluation, and if logical analysis drove them, the only tool they have for the purpose, the Accounting Model, is entirely inappropriate for the job. Consequently, these major shortcomings in our financial systems offered an ideal opportunity for an entrepreneurially-minded individual like myself to make immense wealth quite easily. Knowing the business world and how staid they are in their thinking, and their lassitude in addressing what is clearly a flawed system, the problem would worsen over years and the opportunity for me would improve, until the time came for me to implement my plan.

"I realised that if I could create, big enough fear across a wide cross-section of financial markets, I could drive markets down substantially, and then step in and buy the shares at bargain basement prices. This is what is happening on our stock exchanges on a daily basis, but only on a much smaller scale. Stockbrokers are continually looking for opportunities to buy low and sell high, and they use the principles of fear and greed to achieve this.

The Stock Exchange is nothing more than a commodity market. It's lost its core value as a sensible investment mechanism to nurture and protect the principles of wise, long-term investment. Instead, it fosters a punter mentality, where people are more interested in buying and selling shares regularly just to make a fraction of a percentage on the deal. It shouldn't be about trading, but about investing. There needs to be a return to the fundamentals, with a complete overhaul of the Stock Exchange. The Stock Exchange should be a vehicle to help people invest and to nurture an investment culture, not foster a short-term trading culture. We've lost our way. In the recent past we have seen many otherwise sound businesses lose huge value overnight, not because there was anything wrong with these businesses, but because traders received unfounded, adverse information about them, which made them panic. This is absurd and does little good for the wider economy. What else can you expect if the principles of trading rather than investing exist?

"Think about this; during the 2008/09 Credit Crunch, some of the major banks started returning exceptionally high profits from early 2009 onwards. These profits weren't generated from their retail, business or mortgage divisions. In fact, these divisions remained unprofitable for many years to come due to the international recession caused by the Credit Crunch. These huge profits were generated from their investment divisions. Yet, how could this be possible when the underlying markets had stagnated or declined around the world? Clearly, they knew how to work the system; a system designed to benefit an elite few at the expense of the masses. By clever or more often devious trading practices, which I have mentioned earlier, they can earn massive profits when the underlying fundamentals of our economy are weak. Tell me these people are not our modern day highwaymen, because they are not creating wealth through their trading activities; they are simply taking money off somebody else to make themselves rich. Their gain is somebody else's loss. In fact, some of the big losers in this episode were the pension funds. It is people like this who ensure our current stock market trading systems and procedures remain in force, unchanged, because they are the people who benefit from and control the system. I will now play them at their own game and crush them in the process, while doing a service for the man in the street. If my efforts can get the system to work as a proper investment mechanism, serving the interests of all, then am I really that bad in doing what I am? Sure, I'm not a philanthropic person. I'm not doing this for others; I'm doing it for the challenge and the huge financial rewards it offers. The irony is that it will ultimately benefit all. I'm the vital catalyst that will bring about a complete revamp of the system. I'm doing the economies of the free world a service by shaking them to the very core, making them realise that the current inefficiencies of the stock markets cannot continue. It is unfortunate that they let things slide for decades, knowing the system is flawed, but then they thought nobody within their exclusive 'club' would want to rock the boat. It wouldn't make any sense for anybody capable of joining this elite club to topple a system designed to serve their needs. This ineffective, one-sided system is perpetuated to serve the greed of this very exclusive club. Unfortunately for them, I will play them at their own game, but on a much larger scale than they could ever imagine. I will bring these 'fat cats' tumbling down. To do this I need to affect a wide cross-section of businesses, across international markets, not just in New York or London. Furthermore, I realised that if I created civil unease at the same time I created financial crisis, through say an Al-Qaeda attack, the impact on financial markets would increase exponentially and I could buy up shares at even better prices. This much of the story I gather you already understand, but beyond this you have been fed lies. You have been told that I work alone, and that I control this entire operation and that I am using these events as part of a wider strategy to ultimately take over the governments of the free democracies of the world. This is absolute nonsense and just what my enemies want you to think."

There was a knock on the door. Alvarez stopped speaking and bid the person enter. Into the room came a middle-aged woman dressed in a business suit carrying a tray of tea.

"Oh, hello, Nelly," said Alvarez in a very friendly manner. "You have brought Mr. Barton-Marshall something to drink have you?"

"Yes, Mr. Alvarez," she replied. "Could I perhaps get you something to drink?" she enquired of him.

"Yes, Nelly, a cup of strong black coffee, please."

She put my tray down and enquired if she should pour it, which I gratefully accepted.

Who are his enemies and why involve me; I'm nobody of any influence or consequence?

As soon as Nelly left the room I put these questions to him.

"As you are aware I run a fairly large, international business organisation, but in the broader picture, it is relatively small. I control no more than twenty percent of the market at the most. So, to increase my international coverage for this programme, I enlisted the support of other similar organisations around the world. Part of my plans, as I have already explained, involved the cooperation and support of militant groups around the world to help stir up social unease through so called 'terrorist attacks'. However, it would now appear that rather than controlling and using these militant groups as part of the strategy, in some areas they have, over the years, usurped control over this aspect of the strategy. It would appear that they are no longer intent on achieving our financial objective, they want to carry this through to its full conclusion, which is the destruction of the free economies of the world. They see the free economies of the West, and our apparent love of money, as the source of

Western decadence and wish to destroy it. I, on the other hand, wish to capitalise on the weaknesses within the system. I do not wish to destroy it! It makes little sense in destroying what ultimately sustains me. These people now wish to take me out of the equation as I will not support their objectives under any circumstances, and will fight tooth and nail to stop them. It is these enemies that have used you to set me up."

"How have I set you up?" I asked, perplexed as to how I had achieved this.

"You were approached by a certain Dr. John Abromovitz, who claimed to have worked for MI6 his entire life, and yet MI6 has never heard of him. He then feeds you a story which you fall for hook, line and sinker about how I am intent on ruling the world, etcetera. He then directs you to the one person, Gonan Mehad, who will blindly believe any Al-Qaeda/Alvarez conspiracy theory he is fed, due to his unstable background and hatred towards Al-Qaeda and other terrorist groups, and towards me because of my involvement with them. He, in turn, starts putting into motion plans that could see my demise."

He pauses, sensing my shock and dismay on learning that Dr. John does not exist, and that he is a complete fabrication; cleverly used to point the finger in the wrong direction. How could I have been so gullible?

"I saw his MI6 identification," I protested.

"James, I carry more authentic international passports than you can care to name, yet only one is genuine. Identification cards, no matter how authentic they look, mean absolutely nothing."

"What about his website?" I asked.

"What about it?" he enquired. "I'm no computer expert, but I know anybody can set up a web page within minutes and publish whatever they like on it. I had one of my computer experts have a look at his website, and he told me it had been constructed within the last six to eight weeks; how convenient. And what does the website tell us – a pack of lies."

We were interrupted again by Nelly bringing in Alvarez's coffee.

He is a very gracious man; he stood up and thanked her for the coffee. He has a very friendly disposition, with a permanent smile on his face. He certainly doesn't fit my archetype, syndicate-boss profile. I couldn't imagine him ordering or being involved in the death of anybody.

"When you met Gonan Mehad in Istanbul, did he ever indicate he knew or worked with this impostor Dr. John Abromovitz?" Alvarez asked.

"I can't remember," I replied.

"Think about it for a few minutes," he said.

I can't recall him referring to, or ever mentioning Dr. John's name, but then neither was it appropriate that he did. Gonan didn't question the source of my information, so I assumed he was satisfied with it. At the time, it all seemed above board, but now, when I think about, it is strange that he never made any reference to Dr. John.

"No – no reference was made to Dr. John," I replied.

"Exactly!" he said. "When you were first told the story by Dr. John Abromovitz, or whoever he is, what struck you as the most implausible part of his story?"

I don't know if I want to tell him; I just don't know who to trust.

"Come on, James, we are being open and frank with one another here," he said.

"Okay, it was the scale of the operation," I said.

"Precisely," he replied. "It is totally inconceivable that an individual can mount an operation on the scale I have been accused of, that is why I told you earlier that I had enlisted the support of similar organisations worldwide. It is now these organisations that are attempting to achieve what they accuse me of. I also believe that the impostor, Dr. Abromovitz, is supposed to be in possession of incriminating evidence that places me at the centre of all these events. If this is correct, I ask you, where are these documents – do you have them? Of course not, because they don't exist. You see, James, they are trying to make me the fall guy. If governments react to this bullshit, excuse my French, given to them by you, and they eliminated me from the equation, they would be fools to believe the problem has gone away. In fact, they now face a worse enemy and have made a fatal error by eliminating the one person best qualified to help them.

"Because you have been fed such bullshit about me, I understand you hold a prejudiced view about me, but that's exactly what they want. They have probably told you I am a recluse who never leaves my island, and yet you know that to be a blatant lie. What other lies have they told you to discredit me? Quite frankly, it suits me to let people think I am a recluse as it allows me to travel the world freely, in total anonymity, using any one of many different aliases. The poor fools think I have a disfigured face."

I sat in my chair dumbfounded. I have been caught off guard – totally unprepared and unsuspecting of what I have heard here today. What I had believed to be true and correct until now, has been attacked and all but shredded by some rather convincing and plausible arguments.

I'm not the quickest thinker in the world, but I do think through all options very carefully and make what I believe are well informed decisions. Right now, too many thoughts and ideas are swirling around my head for me to make any sense of them, apart from the obvious one – what does he want from me? So I put the question to him.

"You can help me in one of two ways. Firstly, don't attempt to make any further contact with Mehad in Istanbul. Secondly, if you do contact him, then you need to feed him as much disinformation as possible. He has set in motion a number of actions which I now need to counteract. This will not involve you. All I ask is that you do one of these two things, and if through some miraculous event you come by some documentation purporting to come from, or belong to Dr.

Abromovitz, you not give it to them, because then you will have, in a single-handed way, betrayed the free world. I'm convinced my enemies will attempt to produce fake documentation which they will try to palm off as originals and authentic. Some of it may be true, but the vast bulk will not be."

"They don't have to fool me," I said, "they have to fool the experts."

"That's the point I have been trying to make; it doesn't matter if any documents are false or authentic, if they land in the hands of Mehad, he will use it against me, irrespective, because he has an axe to grind," he said.

"Surely he would put truth and the well-being of the free world ahead of personal vendettas?" I asked.

"People say I'm 'messed up' because of a difficult adolescence. Perhaps they are correct, but what of Mehad who had his family blown up in front of him? Now there is one screwed-up guy fighting his own holy war."

"I don't know who, or what to believe anymore. Why should I support anything you do as you are planning to enrich yourself at the misery and death of others, when you have no need for money or power?" I said.

"You are not entirely correct," he replied. "Now that there has been a falling out among thieves, as you would put it, I am secretly working with an American government agency to deliver my enemies on a plate to them. My enemies are more vulnerable than I, but they are too stupid to realise that. I know their organisations inside out. That is why the government is prepared to allow bygones be bygones and to work closely with me in wrapping up their 'War on Terror'. However, this association is highly secretive and known only by a few. You can therefore imagine that anything Mehad does in conducting his own holy war jeopardises the success of this liaison, and complicates the work of those I am working with in the government. In fact, it was one of these officials that suggested I have this chat with you, which I thought was a goods idea.

"As this is a frank and open meeting, I can let you know that there have been some concessions on both sides in my dealings with the government. I have spent billions over the past two decades on setting up and managing this scheme to manipulate international stock markets, to the point where it has reached critical mass, and can unfold with or without me. Without me, it will run an unmanaged course with dire consequences for the free economies of the world. Consequently, it has been agreed that I may create a few waves on the stock market to recoup my investment. I think this is a small price to pay. The Phoenix which will rise from these ashes will be a new business measurement and evaluation standard, and a totally revamped investment system nurturing the principles of sound investment; placing investment at the heart of our financial markets and not trading. Only a major crisis is going to jolt the business world out of the rut they are in. I'm doing the world a service, and I'm sure history will come to view this event as a catharsis for the business world; a rebirth almost."

Alvarez makes a compelling and plausible argument. No doubt his government contacts have their eyes on the vast wealth his scheme could make for them, and consequently, are prepared to go along with it.

"So, as you can see, I'm going to cost the rich a few dollars, but I'm not pursuing the route of civil unrest to propel the markets to their knees as my enemies, or ex-colleagues wish to do. My proposal holds benefits for the free world, and immense wealth for a few privileged individuals, like you, James."

"I have enough money to keep me comfortably well-off for the rest of my life and leave a little for my children, thank you. I cannot understand why a person like you, with immense wealth, continues to try and amass even more. What compelled you to devise and implement these plans all those years ago when you didn't need the money? Is there any truth in the claim that you are attempting to protect mankind from his own follies?" I asked.

"I'm driven by the need to make money – plain and simple," he replied. "Why this is the case, I have no idea; it is a question I have asked myself many times. By anybody's standards I am a wealthy man, and yet I have an insatiable desire for more wealth. It's like a disease similar to alcoholism, where you just want more and more and yet the path it leads you on is almost certainly self-destructive, but you cannot stop. The consequences of this endeavour could destroy me and my family, and yet I pursue it with a passion. Many times have I wished to have an attitude similar to yours, where I would be content with an income sufficient to allow me to enjoy life and not be obsessed with making money. Life changes radically when you can have anything money can buy; your value standards change to such a degree, where everything loses its value for you. When you have to struggle and save to buy something, you cherish it, but when you can buy anything without thinking twice, you don't cherish it or savour the moment you bought it; it has no meaning or value for you. Amassing money rather than spending it is more important to me; that is a sad situation, as after all, money should only be a means to an end not an end, in itself. You could say I have the Midas touch, but I suffer for it because it's all about making money and not about enjoying life. I get up everyday to make more money, not to enjoy life, and that is a sad state of affairs."

I suppose when you think about it, people living on the extremes of life; the super rich like Alvarez and the alcoholic in the gutter, all have misshapen values which drive them towards a destiny where they miss out on the joys of life. I suppose it's all about harmony and balance. I'm certainly not one to preach on the subject; I didn't get the work and family balance right and as a consequence, I missed out on some of the joys of life. Despite his immense wealth and power, Alvarez is a miserable and unfulfilled individual. Metaphorically, he is in the gutter of life together with the alcoholics and drug abusers he helped create.

"Well, James, can I count on receiving your support?" he enquired.

"You said that this meeting is a frank and open one, so I put it to you, I cannot consider working with you while you continue to bug my house," I replied.

"What, James – bug your house? I have never bugged your house."

"Well then, how would you explain the timing device placed on my electricity supply to cut off supply as soon as it got dark?" I asked.

"Who told you your house was bugged?"

"Dr. John," I replied.

"Precisely, and when you found a bug or a device to tamper with your electricity supply, you immediately assume it is me – correct?"

"Yes," I said.

"Again, that is exactly what they want you to think; it adds credibility to their story. That device was placed in your house by Dr. John and, or his accomplices."

Now that I come to think about it, Dr. John did have an intimate knowledge of my house which I had assumed he had acquired from MI6, which he said had me under surveillance.

"I can tell you I place little reliance on bugs and other listening devices," he said. "As far as I am concerned, they provide little insight into the individual being observed and are what I call 'reactionary devices'. I prefer to have insiders who get to know the person I am monitoring intimately; I then know, or have a very good idea, how they will react in a given situation. I call this 'pre-emptive monitoring'."

"That is most interesting, and it leads me onto the obvious question – do you know me intimately and do you know or believe you know, how I would react under certain circumstances?" I enquired.

"I do indeed, James," he replied, "that is why I had no need to bug your home or put you under any surveillance."

"I would have preferred you bugged my house," I replied. "May I enquire as to who your 'insider' is, as such a disclosure would indicate your goodwill, particularly as you wish to work with me, and in your own words, this is an open and frank meeting?"

He sat silent in his chair for a while looking at me intently. He then got up and walked around the desk.

"James, this maybe something you do not want to hear. If I give you the assurance that I shall no longer use them, you will be none the wiser and will not be hurt either."

"Mr. Alvarez, with due respect, you know that's no option."

My mind was racing who could this be? Matt Todd's name kept coming up.

"That's fine," he said, "it's your choice and in the spirit of working together I will disclose who they are, although this may hurt you."

I accept that," I said, "but would rather know."

He walked back to his chair and sat down.

"Richard Petrada and Felicity Marchant," he said.

I repeated his words in total disbelief.

"That is correct," he replied, "and I warned you it would hurt."

That is an under-statement, I am absolutely distraught.

These two people are practically family. What a betrayal! It feels like somebody has taken a plug out of my body and let the life drain out. Betrayal is one thing, but when it is committed by those for whom you have great affection and trust, it's a lot more than betrayal. It feels like everything precious in life, the values and standards you hold dear, are worthless. This is hard for me, but I hate to think what affect it will have on Fiona, she thinks of Felicity as her daughter; meantime, it has all been a charade to watch over and monitor me.

"I know you fairly intimately," says Alvarez, "women in private discuss the most amazing things. I feel I know you inside out. You are a good and honourable man, and I know you will do what's right for the wider good of mankind, which is why I knew I could approach you with confidence to help us; you know the good of the free World is best served through me and my colleagues in the American government."

"May I enquire, when I decided to go to Istanbul to meet Gonan Mehad, were you fed all this information through either of these two insiders?" I asked.

"That's correct, James. That's why I don't need listening devices."

"And who specifically gave you this information?" I enquired further.

"I'm not sure as I don't deal with them directly, but I think most of our information came via Felicity. Women like to chat, James – that's a fact."

I slumped back into my chair disappointed and disillusioned.

"What of Matt Todd?" I enquired. "Is he one of your insiders as well?"

"No, Matt Todd holds no appeal for me or my objectives. I tend to recruit more visionary and capable individuals, such as you, James."

What a relief to hear that Matt is not embroiled in this odious affair.

"Well, James, are you onboard?"

I hesitated. "I don't know, there are so many things to think about," I said.

"The choices aren't that complicated, James."

"No, the choices may not be that complicated, but I have to sift through a lot of contradictory information which I have been fed over the past few weeks and determine what represents the truth. I need a bit of time to consider and reflect on everything I have been told."

"But, James, what I have told you is the truth, so there is no need to reflect or consider."

"I hear what you say, but it is in my nature to reflect on things in some detail and only to accept them when there are no, or very few doubts. You should know this of me as your insiders should already have told you this is how I work."

"Indeed they have, James, and I will not push you for an answer today, but I do urge you to act with some haste or at least stall any actions you had anticipated, until you have arrived at your thoughtful consideration."

"Thank you," I said.

"I know you are not a great holiday taker, James, but when all this is behind us, I am inviting you and your good wife Fiona to come and spend a nice, long holiday with me and my family on our beautiful island in the Pacific; there we will show you what it is like to have a truly fantastic holiday."

I thanked him, despite knowing Fiona would never accept his offer as he is the reason for tainting Felicity, and she would never condone living off ill-gotten money, particularly drugs and blood money.

"Remember, James, if you ever need any help or support, no matter what, I am always there to support my friends. Loyalty is important to me, and I feel I can rely on you, James."

Then without further ado he stood up, "Good, then that concludes our business. It has been a pleasure meeting you and I look forward to seeing you again, perhaps under more convivial circumstances, standing on an island paradise," he said with a broad smile on his face.

I put my hand out to shake his. He came forward and wrapped both his arms around me and gave me a huge bear-hug; something I am unaccustomed to. After receiving my bone-crushing bear-hug, we walked back through the house to the spectacular entrance hall. There he turned to me and said, "Wealth like this and considerably more are all within your grasp. Work with me and you and your family will be fabulously wealthy – that I can promise you."

Just then, as if on cue, Sir Andrew and another gentleman, clad in a black suit, appeared from a room in the corridor running right of the entrance hall.

"You gentlemen finished already?" he bellowed across the entrance hall as he walked towards us.

"Manuel, this is Ian McKinnon, one of my operations managers. Neil, this is Mr. Manuel Alvarez and a friend and colleague of mine, Mr. James Barton-Marshall, who has been holding what I hope have been fruitful discussions," said Sir Andrew.

We shook one another's hands.

"It's almost lunchtime, James," said Sir Andrew, "can I interest you in some lunch?"

"Thank you for the kind offer, but I shall decline as I would like to get home early and consider today's meeting while everything remains fresh in my mind," I said.

"Always the lawyer, James – off to consider your verdict rather than enjoy a pleasant lunch among friends," laughs Sir Andrew.

"The leopard doesn't change its spots, Andy," I remarked.

"No, it definitely doesn't," he replied.

I felt my comments regarding the leopard rather appropriate for Sir Andrew, considering who his bedfellow is. His business profile accurately fits one of Dr. John's money laundering scenarios, where he described how a business on the brink of collapse makes a remarkable and inexplicable recovery, and goes on to grow into an enormous entity because of almost unlimited cash resources pumped into it by Alvarez's money laundering activities. So now I know it wasn't Sir Andrew's brilliance as a businessman that earned him a knighthood and immense wealth, but rather his dirty dealings. These are not my friends and never will be, despite the great show and claims of friendship they lavish upon me. All this is just a show, attempting to win me over to their cause. They are shallow people, and I have nothing in common with them.

On bidding my host farewell, I had a strong urge to run down the stairs, jump in my car, slam the doors and lock them. I just needed to get away from these people and be in my own quiet, secluded place where I could sift through what I have been told. As a lawyer, an important part of your job is to sift the chaff from the wheat. The only practical way of doing that is to sit your client down and get them to understand the importance of being totally honest with you and to give you the facts, and drop the liars. If this relationship does not exist, you will ultimately fail your client, and they, themselves. Nothing worse can happen in a case than you open up a can of worms because you weren't told the truth, or only part of it. I always asked my clients 'to let me know what lies beneath', then in court or in arbitration, I'm never caught off-guard, and it's so much easier to hear when the other party is lying. Right now, I have two parties claiming that they are telling me the truth yet their stories are conflicting; so I have no anchor as to what is possibly the truth. The only way I can do this is to go through the information I have been given, one at a time, and using a process of elimination, eventually arrive at what I think represents the truth. Most of it hinges on the existence and reliability of Dr. John; is he genuine or not? In many respects, I feel like a naïve, little schoolboy because, when somebody appears on the scene and tells me a story, I fall for it. As Alvarez said, I swallowed Dr. John's story hook, line and sinker. Perhaps it was the almost theatrical circumstances under which we met that added credence to his story; who knows? Alvarez claims he has never worked for MI6, and Gonan, as far as I can recall, never referred to him directly. Thirdly, he has not reappeared on the scene as arranged. The odds certainly don't favour his existence. However, there is one aspect that points to his possible existence and that concerns his illusive documents. Both Alvarez and Mehad indicated the possibility of their existence, yet if the man who is purported to have compiled and stored these documents does not exist, then surely the documents themselves don't exist? Alvarez did warn me that they may produce fake documentation. I would find it strange if Gonan would accept fake documentation, despite the holy war he is evidently fighting, as this would definitely harm his cause. I will need to get verification from Gonan that Dr. John exists. However, Alvarez has explicitly asked me not to make any further contact with Gonan.

What about the credibility of Gonan? Alvarez says this is a man blinded by personal rage, conducting a holy war against him and terrorist organisations; a person who will use anything, including fake documents, to frame them. I am aware of Gonan's past, but he claims that while you cannot eradicate your past you equally cannot allow it to blur your future. Alvarez attempts to paint an entirely different picture of the man, so who to believe? In some respects, it's more difficult to believe Gonan as he lives in a cloak-and-dagger world – a trade attaché who is possibly a CIA boss, who calls secretive meetings and applies a mushroom culture to those he is supposed to be working with. At least Alvarez appeared to be open and frank. He even gave up 'insiders' when, in reality, he had no need to go that far. I cannot like or approve of the man, but I am trying to determine right and wrong here.

What of Alvarez himself? He certainly wasn't the person I had imagined. He is charming and friendly. As much as I tried to see the ruthless gangster and megalomaniac beneath the surface, I simply could not. They have him down as a recluse, who Dr. John and Gonan have indicated could possibly be taken out in a single strike. Clearly, such a strategy is flawed. Their belief that he is a recluse enables him to travel freely as nobody is looking for him. Therefore, all things considered, and on balance of the evidence, I would have to support the Alvarez camp.

I am not looking forward to breaking the news about Felicity and Richard to Fiona. This isn't something you get over, like the flu. It's something that leaves you scared for life. Only time can partially heal the wounds.

My journey home seemed extremely short, no doubt because I was preoccupied with thoughts regarding my meeting with Alvarez.

Fiona was working in the garden, so I took the opportunity to break the news to her outside. I would prefer to do it away from the house because it may still be bugged, perhaps not by Alvarez, but by others. As soon as I told her about Felicity and Richard, she stopped me saying, "He lies... he lies. How can you trust this despicable man, a known drugs trafficker and murderer?"

"I don't know who to believe or trust," I said. "I simply have to take it on the balance of the evidence presented to me, which appears to favour him presently."

Tears welled in her eyes. She turned away and walked off to a rose garden she had been tendering. I thought it best to leave her for a few minutes with her own thoughts. This is worse than having to tell somebody that they have lost somebody dear to them, because then at least they still have cherished memories to cling to. Under these circumstances, you have lost the person and the memories are hurtful because you know the person was not genuine, you were just used. Your feelings and emotions meant nothing to the abuser.

I walked up to her and put my arms around her and for the first time ever, I got a sense of her fragility. She was sobbing quietly.

"Oh, James, how can people do this to one another?" she asked.

I just held her tight. I know no words could comfort her at this time.

"The human race has lost its way somewhere along its evolutionary path, James; we put wealth and affluence at the centre of our lives, and yet it will never bring us true happiness. I would gladly forsake the fancy house, cars and other trappings for loving family and friends. People don't appreciate how wealthy they are when they have such relationships and their good health.

These two things together will lead to happiness, and yet money can never buy them."

I could not respond as I was too choked up.

"Our predecessor of a few thousand years ago lived the idyllic life; they probably had very strong family and community relationships as their well-being depended upon it, and they would have been a lot healthier than us as they ate natural, unprocessed food, and lived in close harmony with nature. Unless man can return to these basics, he will self-destruct."

She is babbling a little, which is understandable as she tries to make sense of these events, while also taking her mind off Felicity. She is right when she points towards our financial greed and its consequential negative impact on the environment as being man's potential undoing.

"Let's go inside, my dear, and I will make you a nice, hot cup of tea," I said leading her towards the kitchen. I put my arm around her as we walked. Her head was bowed and her shoulders hunched. For the first time ever, I have seen her as an old person. She has always been so sprightly and full of the joys of spring; now she almost shuffled along, the wind taken from her sail.

Chapter Ten

The following day, around about mid-morning, I received a phone call from my bank manager in Exeter.

"Good morning, Sir," he said, "I have been asked to let you know that the sum of three million pounds Sterling has been transferred into your account this morning from the Alvarez Family Trust."

"No," I said, "there must be some error, I am not expecting any funds from anybody."

"There is definitely no error, Sir. I was left with explicit instructions to let you know personally when the funds were transferred, and to read a short note attached to the transfer, which says, 'Thank you for services rendered – Manuel'."

"Well, I don't want to accept it," I said.

"There is nothing we can do except credit your account according to instructions given. Should you wish to return the funds, then you have to initiate a new transaction reversing it."

"Well then, go ahead and reverse it," I said. "I'm not accepting this man's money under any circumstances."

"I cannot take instructions like this over the phone, Sir. You will need to initiate the transaction through the proper channels."

"Very good then, and thank you for letting me know," I said putting the receiver down.

What a cheek! This man thinks that he can buy any and everything. I wouldn't accept a penny from this man, even if I were destitute, not least of all because it's dirty, tainted money.

I picked up the receiver and phoned my accountants in London, who handle all my financial affairs, and instructed them to have the transaction reversed.

I won't let Fiona know of this little affair as it would absolutely infuriate her; trying to buy my support for a few pounds. Surely his 'insiders' would have told him I would never accept a bribe like this, and that the money would be returned promptly? Clearly, he doesn't listen.

It's been a week now since I met Alvarez.

During this time Gonan has made a few attempts to contact me, but I have not returned his calls.

I did however contact Matt Todd as I wanted to get an update on the legal front and had a strong urge to discuss this matter with somebody I could trust.

According to Matt, several rulings had been handed down internationally, all of a similar nature to ours. Other rulings were expected shortly; none of which were expected to buck the norm. This means the third phase of the Alvarez plot could be launched imminently, namely where they take out class actions against major corporations around the world, claiming multiple million pound damages for misappropriating company resources. Their argument will be based on the rulings currently being handed down, which have found that Marketing, as a discipline, were aware of the possibilities of misappropriating funds, yet did nothing to attempt to rectify the problem. The legal argument which would be used is that the corporations were aware of, or should have been aware of the problems through their membership of the Marketing Institute or Association, who has received the court ruling, and that therefore, individually, they are as guilty as their Association and potentially squanderers of shareholder capital. They don't even have to prove this. Simply by bringing these actions against all the major corporations around the world, they will start panic selling on the international stock markets which could possibly shed trillions of pounds in a matter of hours, all to Alvarez and his associates benefit. All Alvarez needs now is to wait for rulings to be handed down against Marketing Institutes from all the major economies, as then he could implicate virtually every major corporation in the world, as each major corporation will no doubt be members of their local Marketing Institute or association. Matt estimates that all the important rulings could be handed down within a couple of weeks.

I told Matt the full story of my meetings with Dr. John, Gonan and recently Alvarez. In typical Matt fashion, he wanted to rush out and tell the world. I explained the die had already been cast and that there was little we could do to stop the inevitable collapse of the stock markets. I explained that it was possibly a good thing as this would be the catalyst for changing our business management, recording and stock trading practices forever. It's a pity we have to face disaster of this scale to rectify known problems, but once again, this is an indication of man's hubris and greed which dictates his stupidity. Matt disagreed and felt we needed to launch a massive PR programme that would highlight the problem and stop it in its tracks. After an intensive argument lasting well over an hour, I got him to see my point of view, which was that mass media around the free world are owned and controlled by huge corporations, and that these corporations are more than likely controlled by Alvarez's networks, either directly or indirectly, and that we could never hope to get our message out into the market. They would more than likely turn against us and discredit us, thereby reducing our chances of making any difference remote. He suggested that we look towards the Internet as a possible medium for spreading our message, as it is an independent resource. I agreed with him that this maybe an avenue we need to investigate, but that he was only to consider the possibilities and do nothing without my consent, as potentially he may play into Alvarez's enemies hands with the result that we not only have a collapse of the stock markets, but also of the free governments of the world.

Fiona has slowly been getting over the shock of Felicity, although she has been deeply hurt by the whole affair. To try to help her put Felicity and this unpleasant affair behind her, we have been taking regular outings, finding new pubs and restaurants where we can enjoy the local cuisine and scenery.

We try to get out as much as we can and today is Thursday; our regular shopping visit to the village. This week the Woman's Institute is putting on a fête to help raise funds for African AID Orphans, which Fiona has been deeply involved in. She has already touched me for a significant, anonymous donation.

After our visit to the library and coffee shop, we headed off to the village hall, where the fête was being held. I find these events extremely boring, but there is normally a consolation in it for me; the local women appear to be excellent cooks, and I'm allowed to buy one or two of my favourite savoury tarts or custard slices. Normally, I'm on a strict diet of tasteless, boring food I refer to as 'recycled cardboard', imposed by Fiona under strict instructions from my doctor. I'm like an excited, little boy who has been given a penny by his Mom and told he can go and buy a sweet from the local shop.

I certainly haven't been let down by the local ladies. I have had some good fun acquiring two rather tasty looking bacon and egg quiches, which I can't wait to get stuck into.

While browsing around some stalls, I bumped into Mrs. Morgan, the owner of Rosewood Cottage, who was very busy looking through some knitwear on a table.

"Oh – Mr. Barton-Marshall, how nice it is to see you again," she said.

I returned the compliment.

"My deep condolences on the loss of your friend," she said.

I must have looked quite puzzled, so she quickly explained.

"Oh – the tragic accident your friend Mr. Edwards had a few weeks ago," she said.

"What are you talking about, Mrs. Morgan?" I enquired.

"Oh – don't you know?" she said.

"Know what, Mrs. Morgan?"

"Mr. Edwards was knocked off his bicycle one evening about two weeks ago, not far from your house, and died instantly at the scene. It was most tragic," she said.

"How did you find out about this, Mrs. Morgan?" I asked.

"He was staying with Shirley Williams at The Meadows. I had recommended Shirley to Mr. Edwards when he left me as he said he could not stay in one place twice and wanted a B&B fairly close to your house," she said.

"Did you see the accident?" I asked.

"Oh, yes," she said, "the accident took place close to Shirley's house. She heard a terrific bang and went out to have a look. It was dusk and visibility was not that good. Two youngsters driving a small, blue car had collided with Mr. Edwards, sending him flying over the wall into the paddock next to Shirley's house. He stood no chance. I think the youngsters were speeding as Mr. Edwards was lying in a peculiar position, as if all his bones had been broken. It was quite terrible. Shirley is still shaken by the whole incident."

"Why has there been nothing about this in the local papers?" I asked.

"I don't know; it is rather peculiar that they haven't reported on it. We don't get fatal accidents around here, so it should have been big news. Mind you, the policeman did say there was some confusion as to Mr. Edwards's identity. He had registered at Shirley's as Mr. Phillips, but I assured the policeman his name was definitely Mr. Edwards, and that they should call you to verify this."

"They certainly didn't call on me to clear up the matter," I said.

"That's strange, as the policeman said he would go and see you straight away," she said.

"How did you hear of the accident as Rosewood Cottage is some way away?" I asked.

"Shirley phoned me straight after phoning the police, and I cycled down immediately. I got there a few minutes before the police," she said.

"What of the youngsters?" I asked.

"The policemen took them away in their car. They were not local lads. I think one had a Londoner's accent."

"Thanks for the information, Mrs. Morgan. I can tell you I did not know Mr. Edwards that well; in fact, I had only met him on three occasions, one of which was at your house. I believe he was a brave man who died putting the interests of others above his own. I think we all owe him a debt of gratitude."

"Have you any idea where he was going to or coming from at the time of his accident?" I asked.

"The policeman asked Shirley the same question," she said. "Shirley told them she thought he had gone to your house, but was not sure about this at all."

"Do you know if he had any large trunks or suitcases with him?" I asked.

"Oh – I don't know that Mr. Barton-Marshall, but Shirley might be able to help you. I think she is around here somewhere. Let me try to find her for you."

"Thank you, that would be most kind of you, Mrs. Morgan. I will wait around the entrance for you."

About ten minutes later, Mrs. Morgan appeared dragging a rather reluctant, elderly lady behind her.

"Mr. Barton-Marshall, this is Mrs. Shirley Williams," she announced.

"How do you do, madam? It is a pleasure to meet you," I said.

She smiled faintly but appeared very nervous.

"Mr. Barton-Marshall just wants to ask you a few questions about his friend, Mr. Edwards, Shirley," said Mrs. Morgan.

"When Mr. Edwards, or Mr. Phillips as you knew him, booked in, was he carrying a number of large suitcases or trunks with him?" I enquired.

"Not that I can recall," she said.

"And when you and the police came to clear out his room, did you come across any suitcases or trunks containing documentation."

"No, there was only one small suitcase containing a few clothes, nothing else. The police took the case," she said.

"Were you with the police when they inspected his room?" I asked.

"Yes, I was," she said.

"So, as far as you are concerned, you didn't see any suitcases or metal trunks containing documentation?" I asked.

"No, there was nothing like that," she said.

"And when did the accident happen precisely?" I asked.

"It happened on the previous Wednesday at around half past five," she said.

"Was he returning or leaving the house?" I enquired further.

"He was returning, as he had left the house at around about three o'clock."

"When did he book in?" I asked.

"The previous day, in the afternoon."

"How did he get here, did a taxi drop him off?" I asked.

"I did not see, but I know he was dropped off by somebody as I could hear doors slamming."

"Thank you, ladies, you have been most helpful," I said.

I went back into the hall and found Fiona chatting to some of her friends. I called her aside and told her I needed to go to the police station as it appears that Dr. John had been killed, and I needed to get some clarity on a few issues from them. I would meet her back in the hall as soon as I had been able to clear up the matter.

At the police station, I met a rather officious constable who refused to divulge any information pertaining to the accident.

"I'm not allowed to divulge any information regarding this accident as it is no longer a police matter and is being handled by Security Services."

"And what department would that be?" I asked.

"I am not at liberty to disclose that, Sir."

"Could you at least confirm the date and time of the accident?" I asked.

"We have been given strict instructions not to discuss this matter in any way, with anybody," he said.

"As a citizen, I am entitled to have a look at your Incident Book," I said.

"The Incident Book is a police document and as this is not a police matter, it has not been recorded. You are welcome to look at the book, but there are no entries regarding this alleged incident," he said.

"The police were at the scene, they interviewed people, removed evidence and evidently arrested two youths in connection with the accident, and you have no record of this?"

"We are only one of many organs of the State. If a department with greater authority assumes responsibility for an incident because there are wider issues affecting the case, which do not involve the local police, then we are duty bound to serve the wider good of the government and its people, and relinquishing control of the case. We are equally duty bound to adhere to all requests made by the new investigating authority, which may involve not discussing the matter with anybody," he said.

"The greatest authority in the land is the individual and when we try to conceal the truth from them by claiming to serve the wider interest of the state, we are on a slippery slope towards a police state and loss of liberties," I said rather angrily.

"That is your opinion, Sir, to which you are entitled."

"At the rate we are going, I soon won't be entitled to any freedom of speech or thought in our new police state, where decisions are made for us and we are told what's best for us," I said.

Clearly, this line of investigation was leading nowhere, so I turned on my heels and returned to the village hall to pick up Fiona.

This changes everything. It brings into doubt what Alvarez has told me. As a matter of urgency, I have to verify the existence of Dr. John and the only way I can do that is to speak to Gonan.

As soon as I got home, I tried to get hold of him. An hour later and after my fourth attempt, I managed to get through.

"James – I have been trying to get through to you – what's happened?"

"I will explain shortly," I said, "but first of all, I need a few straight answers from you."

"Sounds like Alvarez has got to you, James?"

"Perhaps," I said, "I just need a few straight answers to clear up some issues."

"I would be happy to oblige, James. What are your concerns?"

"Have you worked with Dr. John Abromovitz in the past?"

"Yes," he said.

"So you can vouch that the man exists. Can you also vouch for the fact that he worked for MI6, and more specifically that he was in their employ until recently?" I asked.

"Dr. John Abromovitz has worked for MI6 his entire working life. I dealt with him many years ago where he provided us a lot of support and guidance on how Alvarez was laundering money through terrorist groups. Over the past few years, I have had little or no dealings with him. However, when you appeared at my door and told David your story, we had both of you checked through our system and our international contacts to verify your credentials. Had you not been truthful, you wouldn't have got any further," said Gonan.

"Why then, throughout our discussions, did you never acknowledge or make any reference to Dr. John?" I asked.

"I'm not sure," he said, "perhaps it is because old habits die hard. I have worked in the Secret Service for most of my life and one of the principles you adopt early on is not to refer to, or make reference to, an individual unless it is entirely necessary. If I had concerns about Dr, John, I would have raised them with you at the time. Why all these questions about Dr. John? When we met you were quite happy with his credentials. Has one of Alvarez's henchmen been in contact with you and attempted to bring Dr. John's credibility into question?"

"One final question," I said, "do you work for the CIA?"

"I do, James. I head a division responsible for researching terrorist group activities."

"Why then didn't you tell me this when we met?" I asked.

"It didn't seem relevant at the time, and such information is only divulged on a need to know basis," he said.

"One further thing," I said, "can you describe what Dr. John looks like?"

"I only met him once many years ago, James, but having looked through his file recently, I don't think he has changed much over the years. Perhaps he has aged a little but still easily identified as Dr. John. He is of average height, slender build, narrow, drawn face with thick, bushy eyebrows, a mop of black hair and thick rimmed glasses. Does that description suffice?" he said.

Dr. John's existence, and his possible murder, brings everything Alvarez said into doubt. I have no choice; I must tell Gonan the full story of my meeting with Alvarez, which I promptly did, sparing no details.

When I had finished, Gonan said, "You didn't meet Alvarez."

"What do you mean?" I said rather indignantly.

"When we met recently and you asked me if there was any other information I could tell you about Alvarez, I told you I didn't. That was an oversight on my part. We have known for sometime that Alvarez uses actors to impersonate him, but only on very important occasions, and I had no reason to believe they would use this on you."

"Why not?" I asked.

"Because I didn't think you were a big enough fish, but clearly I was wrong. That means the documentation Dr. John has are potentially more damming than I had originally estimated."

"If you are right, then why go through this elaborate charade with me?" I asked.

"The most important reason I would surmise is to find out whether or not you have the documents in your possession, and secondly, to buy themselves more time, which right now is a critical component of their strategy. Let me tell you categorically, Alvarez is in total control of this operation; there are definitely no rebellious factions. He is pulling all the strings, nobody else, and he is driving this towards his goal of worldwide domination, nothing less.

"Let me ask you, this character you met, who said he was Alvarez, what was your gut feeling about him?" he asked.

"I don't know, he seemed a very pleasant, well-mannered person," I said.

"Essential ingredients to win you over," interrupted Gonan. "If I was to ask you to rate him as a gentleman or as a ruthless megalomaniac, which option would you choose?" asked Gonan.

"He certainly didn't strike me as a ruthless person at all, or even a hard-nosed businessman," I said.

"Precisely, because he is neither of those, just an accomplished actor," said Gonan.

I then told Gonan about Dr. John's accident and how I suspected it was possibly murder, as it appears the two youngsters who almost ran me over were the two involved in his death.

"That's proof enough; all the proof you need to show Alvarez is implicated. Who benefits through Dr. John's death – Alvarez, nobody else. Tell me, were you given, or were you able to recover, any of his documents?" he asked.

"No," I said.

"That's unfortunate as they are critical to our cause. That's definitely the reason Alvarez was fishing with you, to see if you had them. Without this documentation things are complicated. We need documented proof to strengthen our hand," said Gonan.

"It appears that Dr. John had booked into his B&B the day before, and was returning from my place at the time of the accident. To me, this shows that he had successfully retrieved the documentation and was ready to hand them over to me. I base this assumption on the fact that he set the appointment time, which must have been based on him knowing he could complete his tasks within the allotted time. As he had fully adhered to his own timing, I can only assume he was successful," I said.

"But you said there were no documents," said Gonan.

"Nobody saw any documentation. That does not mean there are no documents," I said.

"That's all a little academic for me," said Gonan, "because everything is time critical. Find the documents in six months time and they will be worthless. Have you any idea where he may have stashed them?"

"No, I'm afraid I don't," I said.

"Are you aware that Alvarez will be ready to launch the third phase of his campaign, namely bringing law suits against all the major corporations around the world for misappropriating shareholder funds, and that this will be the trigger for terrorist strikes?" I said.

"I am too acutely aware of these circumstances," said Gonan, "over the last few weeks we have noticed heightened activity among terrorist groups. Numerous plots and participants have been identified, but we are aware of many others for which we only have scant information, and yet we believe them to be a serious threat."

"Can't you take action without the documentation?" I asked.

"You and I know the extent of Alvarez's influence through his networks and, unless I can present an extremely strong and plausible case backed up by as much documented evidence as possible, our plan could easily be derailed," said Gonan.

"Well, if you don't have the documents then you don't have much other choice than to act now," I remarked.

"We still have a little time, and I would prefer to wait and see if these documents appear, if not, then you are right, we have to proceed without them. You must remember, James, that we are not without our own spies and insiders as well, so if Alvarez does come by these documents, there is a strong possibility that we may learn of this," he said.

"That's hardly reassuring," I said, "if he's got the documents, we have lost."

"We then know we have to strike straight away, don't we, James?"

"I suppose so, but it's hard to sit around waiting for the unlikely event of the documents turning up when time is so critical. Consequently, Matt Todd and I, or more correctly Matt on his own, is working on a campaign to inform the general public of this threat using the Internet as the communications medium. Why don't we go ahead and launch this campaign as soon as possible, as it may help our cause and bring the worms out the woodwork?" I said.

"No – definitely not at this stage, you may upset a lot of the groundwork that I and my team have put in place. It may have undesirable affects, particularly for you and Matt, as they will deal with you quickly and ruthlessly. You will be trampled and trashed by the media and even possibly killed, just as they dispatched Dr. John, and our efforts laid to waste. Follow my advice and give it a little more time," said Gonan.

"That's the ingredient we don't have a lot of," I said.

"No, we don't have a lot of it so what we do have, we have to use wisely," he said.

"James, I have to go now, but please keep in regular contact and don't allow Matt, who is known to be a hothead, to talk you into doing anything rash," and with that he put the phone down.

I sat quietly for a few moments gathering my thoughts.

Dr. John was killed the day before I returned home. The police may have come to my house when I wasn't in and subsequently, when the case was taken out of their hands, no further contact was made with me and the whole affair hushed. If it had not been for the fortuitous meeting with Mrs. Morgan, weeks or even months may have passed without me even being aware of the incident, by which time it would all be too late. By keeping his death quiet, Alvarez was able to get me to question Dr. John's existence, thereby getting me to support him and effectively neutralising me.

Why did they wait until Dr. John's return until they killed him, as they could have done that at anytime? They must have been waiting to take the documents off him on his return; but how would they have known he had gone to collect his documents and return with them when only the two of us knew of this plan. Alvarez knew of the possibility of such documents, but not necessarily that this meeting was for the express purpose of handing them over to me, so when his agents saw Dr. John with no documents, they must have decided to silence him and let him take his secrets to the grave. They knew if they acted immediately, and in my absence, they could cover it up before my return and then a few days later stage the charade at Sir Andrew's house to see if their plan had worked, and in the process neutralise me for long enough not to be a fly in the ointment; very clever.

I'm, however, convinced that Dr. John did return with the documents, but he's a shrewd old fox and wouldn't make a public display of the fact. The documents must be here somewhere, but the question is where? He didn't know the area well enough, so how could he confidently hide such important documentation without them being discovered by unwanted individuals?

Gonan has said that we must wait and see if the documents turn up, but they won't because Alvarez doesn't have them, and I'm convinced they are securely stored in the vicinity, but I have no clue as to where they may be. It would prove a futile exercise for me to even attempt to look, so I think we should take action right now while we have time.

I immediately phoned Matt and filled him in on the latest developments. He agreed with me that we need to take action. I, however, suggested we give Gonan one week's grace before we take matters into our own hands, to which he agreed. This would give Matt additional time to prepare the campaign.

As a lawyer, I believe in following the right channels and not taking matters into my own hands, but when the local police and MI6, together with the CIA, are dancing Alvarez's tune or have been rendered impotent through his networks, one is left with no choice. To do nothing is not an option. I suggested to Matt that we meet at our earliest opportunity to discuss the format and content of the campaign, to which he agreed. Rather than him fly to my house and draw attention to our meeting, I suggested we meet at Exeter Airport where we could hold our meeting at one of the nearby hotels. Matt suggested we meet the following morning at nine o'clock, to which I agreed.

Next morning, as arranged, I met Matt and two of his colleagues at the airport. We then proceeded to a local hotel where we had booked one of their conference rooms for the day.

Before the meeting started, I pulled Matt aside.

"Matt, do your two colleagues have an understanding of the nature of the campaign we are about to embark upon and if so, are they equally aware of the potential dangers they may face in helping us?" I asked.

"The guys do have a good idea of what it's all about, but I think it would be useful if you gave them a more detailed account of the situation and explained the potential dangers to them," he said.

"Good," I said, "I don't want anybody going into this not being fully aware of what we are trying to achieve and the dangers it imposes. They have to do this of their own volition and conviction, and not through coercion and money."

"I agree fully," said Matt walking back to join the others.

"Let's start the meeting guys. James is going to start with an overview of the situation and explain the potential dangers you face by becoming involved. Having heard his introduction, if either of you do not wish to proceed, I and James fully understand and will not pressure you into continuing, although we would appreciate your help," said Matt.

"I'm going to spend quite a bit of time explaining the threat we face," I said standing up. "The reason for this is to leave you under no illusion as to the potential danger you face, and if you wish to proceed, it will give you valuable insight into the problem and how we need to address it."

After I had finished explaining the full situation, I said, "Basically we are going up against the most powerful crime syndicate ever known, which wields enormous power and influence throughout the world. We will be seen as a threat; somebody intent on thwarting their plans. Therefore, they won't stop at anything to silence us; of this I am convinced. Personally, I believe it is incumbent upon me to stop these people.

Strangely, I am not fearful for myself, but I do fear for my family, and also the effects on my family should I perish. Consequently, I take this decision with a heavy heart, but one I know my family will support, and one I need to make on behalf of my fellow citizens. We are asking you today to make one of the hardest decisions you are ever likely to face. As a result, I am going to call for a tea break to allow you time to reflect on your decision. If after this you are still undecided, I would recommend that you declare yourself out."

The younger of the two men immediately responded, "The decision is easy for me, I have no family apart from elderly parents who live in New Zealand, and like you, James, I feel duty bound to serve my fellow citizens in their hour of need. In fact, I feel honoured and proud to be able to play a part in bringing a heinous criminal like Alvarez to justice. Matt's offered me a pretty good financial deal to work on this campaign, but let me tell you I won't accept a penny; it's the least I can do."

"Thank you," I said, "such fire and passion is a welcome ingredient."

This young man's declaration had clearly put his colleague under a lot of pressure. I could see him squirming in his seat. He cleared his throat a few times before beginning to speak.

"I have a very young family of two children. My family is entirely dependant upon me as my wife doesn't work; so the decision is considerably more difficult for me from both the perspective of my family's well-being, and financially. I am not a man of means and cannot afford to donate my time, no matter how worthy the cause."

"I understand your situation completely, so please don't feel pressurised into making a decision you will regret. Everybody's circumstances are different and your decisions have to be based on your own unique circumstances. Take a break and consider your options carefully; don't rush it and if you wish to decline, we will understand," I said.

After tea, when we reconvened, the young man declared his intentions.

"This has not been an easy decision," he said, "but I believe it is the correct one. Young men with families have been called upon, time in memorial, to defend their country from external threats. Most were given little or no choice in the matter. I am, at least, fortunate in that I have been given a choice. As much as I love my family, I can't turn my back on my fellow citizens when so little stands between us slipping back into the Dark Ages. I wish there were others we could call upon, but the reality is there aren't, and time is running out. So I, like James, commit myself with a heavy heart. However, now that I have committed myself, you can expect one hundred and one percent commitment from me, as I am not going to let our enemy get the better of us and destroy me and my family."

"You two young men restore my faith in humanity, which Alvarez and the like have destroyed. I am so pleased to see people display such fundamental good, where they put the collective interests of their fellow beings above their own. In the recent past, I have come across so much greed and self-interest that I had begun to lose faith in humanity, believing this was all people cared about. Such a path leads us to destruction. We are a social animal dependent upon one another to survive; as soon as we lose this sense of society and only consider ourselves, and not the well-being of others as well, we are doomed. You have shown me that I should not lose faith, and that I should put more trust in the fundamental good within most people. It gives me a lot more hope for this campaign. If we can get our message out to enough people, maybe we will have a much better chance to succeed than I had ever hoped for. Gentlemen, thank you once again for your unselfish and brave support."

"Thanks, guys," said Matt, "I didn't choose you just because you are the best in your profession, but also because I knew you would come through and make the right choice, as you two are made of stern stuff. Now, let's get down to some hard work, guys."

"If I could start the meeting," I suggested, "by describing our so called 'target audience' and the message I believe we should attempt to get to them. There are four major target audiences who can influence the outcome of events. The first group is the general public. If they are made fully aware of the threat and how it is likely to unfold, they can hold governments more accountable. The masses have to be able to say 'that's the way those people predicted it' and be mobilised to stop it in its tracks. For this to happen, we have to give them easily identifiable milestones in our enemy's strategy and suggest what they should do when they are reached.

"The second target audience are those people involved in Alvarez's networks. Many people are involved in Alvarez's networks, yet the vast bulk will be totally oblivious to this fact. If they are in some dubious network, and they are instructed, or asked to do some counter-intuitive task, they are to ignore these instructions as they are more than likely coming from the Alvarez organisation. For example, a Police Chief who may in the past have received cash or favours from a network of 'friends', is given instructions by this network for him to drag his heels and not mobilise all his forces when faced with a major terrorist threat. The Police Chief will find such a request counter-intuitive and should ignore it, even although he may face unpleasant repercussions. These people must be left in no doubt that they are receiving their instructions from Alvarez, the enemy, and the network to which they belong has more sinister roots. The power of the networks can only be broken if people make a stand against them and realise that with the demise of the Alvarez organisation, its power and influence will rapidly dissipate.

"The third target audience, that of investors, must be convinced not to react negatively when these law suits are brought against the major corporations around the world, because it will be their negative reactions which will drive us over the brink.

"Finally, the fourth group, namely participating terrorist groups, must be convinced that they will be offered up like sacrificial lambs as soon as Alvarez gains power. This is a crucial element of Alvarez's strategy. It adds credibility to his puppet governments, and helps bring about rapid stability in a tumultuous situation. While these terrorist groups may enjoy some short-term successes, they will certainly be snuffed out. Alvarez's new regime will more than likely show less religious and ethnic tolerance than the free world shows now. Alvarez will definitely embark on an 'ethnic cleansing' programme on an unimaginable scale, and the terrorist groups ethnic backgrounds are probably at highest risk. Their support of Alvarez will be their ultimate demise and that of their ethnic group.

"I understand that being able to achieve all this is a tall order; almost mission impossible, but I leave it in your creative and capable hands to achieve the impossible.

"I'm no Marketing man and I'm not suggesting how you should design and conduct this campaign, but I believe we must be totally honest and brutally frank as this will probably pack the greatest punch," I said.

"Thanks for that," said Matt.

"My idea is to make a professional, highly polished video presentation where we can set out all the facts and address all four target audiences at once. We would then launch this through all the video websites such as You Tube, backed up by an extensive email marketing campaign targeted at many millions. That should get the ball rolling, but the video message must be used to get everybody to spread the word urgently. We have to use viral marketing to its fullest. I also intend setting up a website where we will post statistics on the number of people who have viewed our video across all the video websites, plus give them the opportunity to blog on the subject," said Matt.

His two colleagues nodded in agreement.

"Right then, let's get down to composing this video production," said Matt continuing.

Early that evening, Matt called a halt to our work. I was very pleased with the progress made and thought the draft for the video presentation exceptionally good and convincing. Matt made arrangements to fly back to London that evening with his two colleagues. They felt confident that within the next couple of days they will have finished production and fully edited the video, ready for launch. The compilation of the email database and emails would also be ready by then.

Matt wanted me to stay for dinner, but as I faced an hour's drive home, and as it was getting late, I declined his offer. I didn't want to leave Fiona in the house alone as she appears to have become very jittery over the last few days.

Chapter Eleven

The last few days have been rather unnerving for me. I had been hoping to hear from Gonan with a message that he has everything under control, and that we need do nothing but sit back and wait for a successful outcome; reality tells me differently. It is unnerving, knowing that I am going to have to take matters into my own hands; fully aware of the consequences such action could bring.

Three days after my meeting with Matt and his team, I gave Gonan a call and told him that we had gone ahead and prepared a video presentation and email campaign, which was ready to be launched almost immediately. He implored me not to proceed as yet.

"Gonan, unless you can tell me specifically what you are doing about this threat, apart from waiting for the documents to turn up, which I think is highly unlikely, I feel compelled to take what I and others deem effective action," I said.

"James, do you honestly think we are sitting on our hands doing nothing? I'm also not obliged to tell you what we are doing, except to say that you stand a good chance of disrupting a lot of good work my team and I have done. Therefore, I would appeal to you not to take any action right now."

"You said if the documents did not surface, you would have little other choice than to take action without them. Let's face it, these documents, in my opinion, are in the vicinity, yet we have no idea where they are. Therefore, it is highly unlikely that they will surface within the foreseeable future, so there is no point delaying the inevitable; we must take action now," I said.

"Perhaps you are right," said Gonan, "but the action we take is not what you are proposing. If you implement your plans now, it could potentially result in undesirable effects for us and complicate our efforts."

"How?" I asked.

"Can you confidently predict the outcome of your campaign?" he asked.

"No, I can't," I replied.

"Exactly," said Gonan, "you are adopting a cavalier approach where the outcome is difficult to predict. Perhaps it may favour us, but then perhaps it may not. I'm not prepared to take a chance on such a risky strategy."

"I disagree with you. I think all parties involved in this plot, most of whom are ignorant of it and their role in it, have a right to know about it so that they can play a part in stopping it. Keeping people in the dark, which you are so good at, Gonan, means we cannot call upon the collective goodwill and ability of millions to stop this threat in its tracks. You don't even want me involved; encouraging me to sit on the side and wait, doing nothing. What if we could mobilise millions like me, who are not content in allowing Alvarez to achieve his objectives, and are prepared to put everything on the line to fight it? Believe me, I think when our story is known we will have more than a few million clambering to fight our cause. They will immediately demand explanations from their governments as to how we have allowed an enemy to sneak up on us undetected until the eleventh hour. Such a situation should strengthen your hand considerably," I said.

I then went onto explain the message we intended sending each target audience.

When I had finished, he said, "It sounds all very good, James, but I still have my doubts. I would appreciate it if Matt could forward me a copy of the video and email campaign. Once I have had sight of these, give me a couple more days and I won't stand in your way. You do, of course, realise that by launching this campaign you are on your own. You are putting reputations and lives on the line, and I cannot help or protect you. Be assured, Alvarez will come after you with the ferocity and might of a trapped and wounded tiger. I doubt either of you will survive; think carefully before you proceed."

"Both Matt and I understand the risk, but somebody somewhere has to stick their necks out to stop this megalomaniac. I'm pleased for at least one small mercy and that is, you have come around to our way of thinking. I would hate to have to launch this campaign without your prior knowledge and consent. If we are to pay the ultimate price, then at least we know it has not been in vain because our efforts may help you, even in a small way, to strengthen your efforts. After all, it will be your actions, not ours, that will deliver Alvarez's fatal blow. All we can hope to be is the catalyst, which may strengthen your efforts; a substitute if you will for Dr. John's missing documents. Perhaps that's not correct; what we are doing is more than a document substitution. I believe in the benefits of informing the populace and getting them to protect their own interests, rather than keeping them in the dark, making decisions on their behalf regarding critical matters we haven't even told them about. The populace will make the right decisions and act appropriately on their own to swing the balance of power in our favour. Isn't this what democracies are all about? Isn't this what we are fighting to retain?

"I realise the future is going to be messy, no matter the outcome of our efforts. As long as it helps us fight and win this war, we will have been successful."

"I admire your courage, James, and only wish I could do more to help. Good luck! I will speak to you in a couple of days time."

I immediately contacted Matt and asked him to forward a copy of the video and email campaign to Gonan at a London address he had provided. Matt also agreed to courier me a copy, which meant it would be with me early tomorrow.

I felt pleased that it was likely that Gonan would consent to us launching this campaign, yet his warning to both Matt and I rang loud in my ears. We are only a few days away from our D-Day. I know this war is totally different to a conventional war, and that therefore we cannot draw any parallels, yet, in some respects, there are some similarities with what we are about to do and that of the D-Day landings. Both are pivotal events where enormous power was unleashed on the enemy. Matt and I intend unleashing the enormous power of the populace and the inherent good within man, to battle with a person who has built his strength on the inherent weaknesses of man; I feel confident that our cause will prevail, just as Allied Forces prevailed against evil in the 1940s.

Next morning, early, I received a copy of the video which I played to Fiona to gauge her reaction; as a possible barometer of public reaction.

"It's very well presented and the message is clear and powerful," said Fiona. "It should succeed in getting the message across and stir people into action. However, my concern is a personal one; you and Matt will be marked men and will pay the price. A price I can't even contemplate, but one which I know will be too high. I ask the question 'why us'? Couldn't it have been somebody else?" she said.

"I don't know, perhaps it's destiny. I can assure you I didn't want to be in this position. I would much prefer to be living in ignorant bliss right now, but I would hate to learn that somebody could have done something about it but did nothing. I have no choice, I have to do this," I said.

Fiona nodded with a forlorn look on her face. She got up and left the room. She knew as well as I that I had no choice.

Two days later I heard from Gonan.

"James, my colleagues and I have reviewed the material Matt sent us. On reflection, we believe this campaign has a lot of merit and think we can help by providing the email addresses of an extensive database, comprising highly influential individuals whose email addresses are generally not in the public domain.

This database will almost guarantee that you reach all the influential shakers and movers within the political and big business arena around the World. I'm convinced this will put the cat among the pigeons in our favour. Many of the people on our database will appreciate that when the public knows of this threat, they will be held accountable for taking action, which I believe will strengthen my position.

"Please let Matt know the database will be delivered to his office later today.

"It goes without saying, you don't know where this data came from; it was delivered to your office by an anonymous source.

"And finally, James, I am morally bound to warn you again that by launching and running this campaign, both your's and Matt's lives are in danger. I can't help by providing you any protection; in fact, I have very limited resources to offer, so if you wish to continue you are on your own against the considerable might of Alvarez. He will come after you with all guns blazing," said Gonan.

"I know that and am as scared as Hell. I wish there was an alternative," I said.

"You are both brave men stepping into the lion's den. I just hope that when this is all over, the world acknowledges, with gratitude, the brave and courageous stand you both took."

"Thanks, Gonan, but I would prefer to have retired peacefully in the countryside with my lovely wife."

"That was never to happen; destiny has already plotted your course, James.

"Before I leave you, it is important that we coordinate the launch of your campaign. It would be preferable if it is launched this coming Monday at twelve hundred hours, New York time. Can you please relay this request to Matt and his team?

"I probably won't talk to you until after the launch, so let me wish you all the best. May God be with you and protect you."

After I had relayed the message to Matt, I sat in my study and contemplated what we were about to do. Single-handed, Matt and I are about to take on the most powerful man in the World, whose tentacles of power and influence extend everywhere. It's like two men with one musket and one lead shot between them, up against a squadron of Apache Attack helicopters. My nerves are all a-jingle and butterflies dance wildly in my stomach. I don't know how I am going to remain sane until D-Day. I had thought about going away for the weekend, as that may take my mind off things, but I don't think so. No matter where I am, these events will remain foremost in my mind. Sitting doing nothing, just counting down the time, is probably one of the most stressful things you can do, as I am learning.

As thoughts of past events keep tumbling through my mind, I keep returning to Richard and Felicity. Alvarez lied about Dr. John. He also lied about the device used to tamper with my electricity supply. So why then should he have not lied about Richard and Felicity? When I consider how easily he gave them up; it just doesn't make any sense. Perhaps he thought I posed no more threat and that there was no need to monitor me any further, and that by giving them up improved his credentials with me and bought my silence. Naturally, I am assuming the person impersonating Alvarez was acting with his full consent. Perhaps it's all a lie and they never worked for Alvarez? Perhaps he just spun this elaborate story to help improve his credentials? Who knows, but one thing is for certain, I am not prepared to risk communicating with either of them until the dust has settled on this matter.

D-Day had finally arrived and Matt and his team were ready to 'unleash hell' on our enemy. I think these were the words used in one of the opening scenes from the film 'The Gladiator', where the Roman Legions were about to attack a barbarian horde. It just makes me feel good to think in these terms.

I logged onto the website, keen to monitor the progress of the campaign. The statistical counters started whirring almost immediately. People had started blogging fast and furiously. I started reading some of these blogs and was ecstatic about the comments made. Unanimous outrage, indignation and determination to stop the threat was the underlying theme of every blog I read.

Late that evening, Matt posted a message on the website declaring that the video had smashed all previous viewing records hours after being released. It is the most-watched video of all time and becoming more popular, every hour.

As it was getting fairly late, I decided to call it a night. I'm very pleased with the results and can't wait to see the statistics tomorrow morning.

In bed, I couldn't get to sleep, tossing and turning, thinking about the results and hoping for bigger and better things, like the little boy who can't get to sleep on Christmas Eve thinking about all those presents waiting for him under the tree in the morning.

The next morning, early, straight after breakfast, I checked the website for the latest statistics and was absolutely amazed. I thought I had better give Matt a call to get him to verify the figures, and confirm that he hadn't massaged them in an imaginative way.

"Hello, James, aren't our results amazing – the power of the Internet. It just shows you, if you have a good story it will spread like wildfire."

"Are all your stats accurate, Matt?" I asked.

"No," he said, "most of the stats on the website are a few hours behind, so in reality we are understating our success. I would have adjusted for this had our figures not been so strong, but there's no need for that."

"I agree. The figures are quite astonishing," I said. "While going through the blogs, I note that many are in a foreign language. Do you think there is any merit in recording the video in one or more of the more popular languages? "

"While you are sleeping, James, some of us are working. We have already launched a Spanish, French and German video with by-lines. We are working on a full Spanish version right now, which should be ready shortly. We will follow this up with a French version."

"Some of us need to get as much sleep as we can to preserve our good looks, which others who do not sleep that much have lost," I said jokingly.

"I prefer to be ugly but productive," said Matt, responding with his usual sharp wit.

"Do you have people monitoring the blogs?" I asked.

"I have about ten people monitoring them around-the-clock."

"Are they all positive?" I asked.

"Absolutely," he said. "I get the team to highlight and extract the more interesting ones, which are then forwarded to me. I will forward them onto you so that you can post an erudite response."

"I'm not so sure about the erudite response, but I would like to read them and respond if I am able," I said.

"We are estimating that within the first twenty-four hours of launch, we would have had over seven million video hits. Many of the video websites have been unable to cope with the volumes, and viewers have switched to less popular websites to view and download it. The demand is increasing exponentially as more and more people are becoming aware of its existence and spreading the word. At this rate, we could have over seventy million hits. I know it's too early to call, but I think we have a resounding success on our hands," said Matt.

"We will definitely have to wait and see," I said. "People may have responded positively through their comments on the blog, but at the end of the day, our success is not measured in these terms but rather through their actions in stopping Alvarez dead in his tracks, ensuring his plans do not unfold as he had hoped.

"How have the financial markets reacted to the news so far?" I asked Matt.

"It's probably a little too early to gauge, but as discussed with you at our meeting, we did anticipate some initial panic selling, but no stampede. To what extent it affected yesterday's drop in the Dow Jones is hard to estimate. As long as we can contain it at these levels, we are okay," he said.

"I will be watching the markets carefully over the next few days as this will be a critical period," I said

"I won't keep phoning you, Matt, as I know you have a lot on your plate. I'll keep in contact via the website and probably give you a call at the end of the week."

The figures just kept rising and rising. The number of video hits and blogs has reached staggering proportions over the past couple of days.

Normally, when there is a phenomenon like this, news of it spreads quickly into mainstream communication channels and is broadcasted across national TV, and in the daily press. Coverage of our campaign is conspicuous through its absence. Not the slightest comment appeared anywhere. We didn't expect good international coverage, but a total lack of it is alarming. Alvarez's control over the media is a lot more effective than I had ever imagined. A critical and obvious component of his strategy is to control the media. It is not the fact that he has done this so well, but how well he has concealed his control over them. This is quite remarkable. He doesn't appear to have any direct financial control over the media, yet through convoluted investment bodies and his networks, he has total and effective control over virtually all traditional media channels. We thought we may get a little coverage from some of the smaller, independent groups who, on seeing that the big players are not running news on the event, would try to cash in. It is frightening when you think how far his tentacles stretch. A few months ago, I didn't know the man existed; today, I realise just how powerful he is. His total control over conventional media is going to make things a lot more difficult for us. While the Internet is an effective tool, it's no match for national TV and press coverage.

After having returned home from our weekly Thursday shopping trip in the village, I decided to take a rest as I had been spending many late hours reading and responding to some of the more interesting blogs forwarded to me by Matt. I must have read and replied to well over fifty blogs since Tuesday; all of which required some thought and individualisation. I think this, plus the anxiety I have been feeling over the past few days, has finally caught up with me. I was feeling quite exhausted and drained and thought it best to take a short nap, as I intended spending the evening replying to the ever-increasing pile of interesting blogs.

Fiona has been trying to put a brave face on things, not mentioning matters much; trying to carry on with life as normal. I know current events have taken a big toll on her; she seems to be so much older. Perhaps she thinks the same of me. I seldom take a nap in the afternoon, so I'm showing my age by doing so.

No sooner had my head touched the pillow than I drifted off into a deep sleep. It felt as if I had only been asleep a few minutes when I heard Fiona shouting for me from our TV lounge. It was dark, so I must have been asleep for some hours.

"James, come quickly… hurry, hurry, or you will miss it," she said.

I staggered to my feet and rushed down to the lounge as fast as I could go. The seven o'clock news was on.

"Matt has committed suicide," stammered Fiona.

"Rubbish – not Matt," I responded.

"That's what they are saying on the news – watch," she said. "The full story should be viewed shortly."

248

I sat down in my chair feeling quite dazed and nauseous. This can't be true! Anybody else but Matt. This is Alvarez and his doing.

"It's coming on now," said Fiona, turning up the volume.

"A prominent businessman, Mr. Matt Todd, of the Global Marketing Association, committed suicide early this evening by jumping from his central London office block, according to the latest police report. It is believed that he left a suicide note apologising for his involvement in a recent Internet scam. Mr. Todd and his accomplice hatched a scheme which claimed that there was a plot to overthrow the free governments around the World. Their idea was to cause stock markets to panic, thereby driving down price so that they could buy shares well below market value, making themselves multiple billions overnight. He sincerely regretted becoming involved with his accomplice, the prominent ex-lawyer, Mr. James Barton-Marshall, but was forced into the matter through his long-standing relationship with Mr. Barton-Marshall. He regrets his actions and the harm and anxiety it must have caused many, and felt the only way to redeem himself was to make a full and honest disclosure of events before taking his own life," said the newsreader.

"God – they have killed poor, old Matt. He was a good man, quite prepared to put his life on the line to protect the interests of others and these lying criminals go and kill him, and trash his good name in the process," I said angrily.

"Gonan warned you that they would come after both of you, fast and furiously. Did you think he was joking? You are next, James," said Fiona.

I sat jellified in my seat. You know what it's like after you've had a huge fright, where your body is pumped full of adrenalin; after the threat has gone you feel like a bag of jelly and ache all over. I sat like that for a few minutes. The TV continued playing, but I have no idea what they were saying.

While sitting in this quiescent state, I felt Fiona's hand touch my shoulder. She had brought me a cup of hot, sweet tea. I sipped the tea slowly and felt myself returning to normality with every sip.

"I think we are at risk staying here," I said to Fiona.

"Phone Mrs. Morgan or one of the other B&B owners hereabouts and see if they can put us up for a couple of nights. It may be best if you go and stay with Dorothy, and I stay at one of these local B&Bs."

"No, James, I am not leaving you," she said.

"It may be riskier for you," I said.

"I don't care," she said, "I am not leaving you."

"Alright then – can you please find us a local B&B?" I said.

"That won't be necessary. Dorothy will put us up for a couple of nights. She has the room and would be pleased to help," said Fiona.

"Good," I said. "Pack a few things and let her know we are coming straight away. We'll take your car and leave a few lights on, to create the impression we are in. We'll come back tomorrow and pack for a lengthy stay."

Next morning, early, I attempted to get onto our website using my laptop, but it kept returning an error message that the site couldn't be found. Alvarez had clearly closed down our website. Other websites have set up blogs on the subject but the whole credibility of our campaign has been brought into doubt through the murder of Matt and its international coverage. Unless we can keep communicating with our audience, defending our position, this whole thing could backfire on us. Our lines of communication have effectively been closed down and theirs have been opened on a scale we could only have dreamt of. Our campaign is being trashed every minute of the day; our credibility is dwindling rapidly under this blizzard. So, called experts are being put on TV to discredit everything we said on our video and website.

I also checked a couple of the more popular websites to see if our video was still listed. Unsurprisingly, they have been removed from every website.

I am sure what we have done has caused Alvarez some damage. His whole strategy is based on silence. Until now, nobody knew him or knew what he was getting up to. Our little campaign has upset the apple cart by making public his plans at the eleventh hour. While he may have gained the upper hand right now by silencing us, it's not in his interest to keep this matter in the public eye for longer than necessary. He will want to hush things up very quickly so the public will forget about it. He will have to shelve his plans for at least eighteen months to two years, by which time this will all be a distant memory in the public's mind and he could proceed once again. He may have a lot of convincing to do when it comes to his relationship with the terrorist groups, but then he is an imaginative, resourceful and determined person who will overcome these small problems. Having said that, I don't think Alvarez's strategy will ever be as effective had he been able to launch it undetected. Now that he and his intentions have been fully identified, his ambitions will become considerably more difficult to achieve. This does not mean we can write him off; far from it. He will learn from this experience and come at us with renewed vigour and even more ingenious threats: in short, he remains as dangerous as ever.

Later that morning, as I was preparing to return home to pack our cases and collect some personal belongings, Dorothy came up to our bedroom carrying the telephone.

"James, I have a Sir Andrew Sweetman on the line for you," she said.

So Alvarez knows exactly where I am. What's the point of running and hiding? I took the telephone from Dorothy.

"What do you want?" I said in curt and rude manner.

"James, I have been asked to have a chat with you," he said.

"You're just a message boy," I said, "which probably reflects your true station in life."

"I can understand you are a little angry and upset right now," said Sir Andrew, "but what I have to tell you is very important for you."

"Alvarez doesn't do anything important for others, only for himself; so what is it that your Master wants me to do now?" I asked.

"James, you and Matt have seriously disrupted Alvarez's plans and have cost him many billions. As a result, he is seriously pissed off. Despite this, he is prepared to spare your life and that of your family if you are prepared to recant fully all the statements and claims you have made in your video presentation."

"Never," I said, "he can go and rot in hell as far as I am concerned!"

"Think very carefully about your reply," said Sir Andrew, "as it is not just your life that is at risk. Are you prepared to sacrifice your family's life for a lost cause?"

"It may be an easy enough call for you to make as you have no moral fibre and only think of you and your own family's interests. You are a person who has bullshitted and pulled the wool over the British public's eyes for too long. You accepted their honours and accolades when you knew you were not worthy of them. So don't tell me what I should or shouldn't do," I said.

"I take that as a no then," he said.

"You are damn right," I said.

"Just remember you are fighting a lost cause. Alvarez may have taken a flesh wound through your actions, but give him a little time to recuperate and learn from this experience, and he will be back stronger than ever, while you will be pushing up daisies. What's the point, man? You can't win and are a fool for believing you could in the first instance. You have no idea how powerful this man is. Look how quickly he closed your puny little act down, discrediting both you and Matt, and dealing with Matt in the rough justice that has made him so powerful. You have had your moment of madness – for God's sake, don't perpetuate it. Give it up, man!"

"I would rather have fought him and failed than have done nothing at all. If I perish, that is a risk I knowingly accepted," I said.

"Did you take this risk on behalf of your family as well?" asked Sir Andrew.

"Yes, and we are not backing down," I said slamming the telephone down.

I called Fiona and told her what had happened. She looked quite ashen and clearly disturbed.

I put my hand on her shoulder to reassure her.

"Tell the boys to bring their leave forward immediately and to disappear for a couple of weeks. They must not let anybody know where they are going, and I mean nobody!" I said.

"They may not have any money to do that, James," said Fiona.

"That's no problem," I said, "I will transfer funds into their account today. Please get onto them immediately, and if they ask too many questions, tell them I will phone them later and explain everything, but please get them to leave work and home immediately. It's a matter of life and death.

"I'm going to Taunton right now to transfer funds. I can't do it online as I'm using a special savings account which isn't linked to my other accounts.

"I shouldn't be long. When I get back, we will go home and pack some clothes, and then head for London. It's probably easier to hide in a big city."

When I got to the bank, I requested to see the Bank Manager or his assistant so that I could get the transaction processed quickly.

Within a few minutes, I was ushered into the Manager's office, where I explained that I wanted to transfer twenty thousand pounds into both my sons' current accounts. He produced a form which I duly completed and handed back to him. He then scurried off to process the transaction.

He returned a few minutes later with a rather baffled look on his face.

"I don't know what has happened, Mr. Barton-Marshall, but all your accounts have been frozen," he said.

"What do you mean, frozen?" I asked.

"No transactions can be processed against them," he said.

"Why? Under whose authority has this been done?" I demanded.

"I have no idea. I checked all your accounts just to see if this was an error on this specific account, but found that all your accounts have been put on hold," he said.

"It's my money and you have frozen every single penny of it, effectively making me penniless. It's absolutely iniquitous and I demand an immediate explanation."

"I have already phoned Head Office requesting an explanation," he said.

"I can't wait around for an explanation; I have other urgent matters to attend to. As soon you have cleared up this mess, can you transfer the funds as requested," I said leaving his office.

This clearly smacks of Alvarez's doing, but by what authority has he been able to do this? I hope it is nothing too serious and that my accounts will be freed shortly, but I must admit, I don't hold much chance of that happening. This effectively leaves my family penniless. My two boys hold down regular jobs, so they won't have any spare money to run and hide. I will have to try and borrow money from friends to facilitate our escape. I haven't been in this impecunious situation since my early university days; at least then I had my father to fall back on. It's a horrible feeling, knowing you are penniless and dependent on the benevolence of others.

When I got back to Dorothy's house, I told Fiona what had happened and asked her whether she would explain our situation to Dorothy, and ask if she could extend us a small loan?

"That's not necessary," said Fiona, "I have been putting a little money aside for the past couple of years, as a nest egg for a rainy day; to be used on a special occasion like our African holiday. The account is in my maiden name and with another bank, so hopefully it should be safe and accessible."

"Oh, you clever girl," I said. "How much money do you have in this account?"

"I'm not sure of the exact amount, but I think it's between twelve and fifteen thousand pounds."

"That's fantastic news," I said. "Tomorrow we can transfer three thousand pounds each into the boys' accounts. Have you spoken to them and sorted things out?"

"Yes, I have. Everything's fine with Michael, but Anthony said taking leave right now would strain his already fragile relationship with his employer," said Fiona.

"I hope you got the message across that such concerns are of no consequence right now," I said.

"I did, but he is leaving under some protest."

"That's understandable, we are all leaving under protest," I said.

"Let's pack up and head for home around dusk; hopefully missing any prying eyes."

After we had packed our bags, I went and sat in the lounge to watch television to catch up on any events that may have unfolded over the past few hours. Dorothy had satellite television and access to all the major news channels around the world. All, without exception, were running lead stories on Matt's supposed suicide and trashing our story with their one-sided and totally bias reporting. Whatever support base we may have had was retreating like snow on the Equator.

Just before six o'clock, as I was about to switch off the TV and leave for home, they announced they had an important newsflash about the story. I waited keenly to hear this news, as they ploughed through one mindless ad after another.

Finally, they returned to the news with the newsreader announcing, "It has emerged today that Matt Todd's co-conspirator in the plot to swindle international stock markets of billions of pounds was definitely the ringleader and instigator of this serious crime. Several prominent business people have today confirmed that they were approached by Mr. James Barton-Marshall to invest multiple millions into a scheme, where he was guaranteeing returns in excess of two hundred percent within six months. The details of the scheme were not made known to the investors, apart from Mr. Barton-Marshall explaining that he was capitalising on inherent weaknesses within the stock markets to be able to generate such substantial returns. As a result of these allegations, the Serious Fraud Division has started investigations into the affairs of Mr. Barton-Marshall and in the process, frozen all his assets. According to a senior officer within the Serious Fraud Division, they have documentary proof of one transaction where he elicited funds from an investor for his scheme. Mr. Manuel Alvarez, an international businessman, transferred three million pounds into Mr. Barton-Marshall's account. Mr. Alvarez subsequently wished to withdraw from the scheme as he did not wish to become involved in any underhand or illegal activities, but Mr. Barton-Marshall refused to refund his money and subsequently accused Mr. Alvarez as being the instigator of the plot in an elaborate hoax, which Mr. Barton-Marshall posted on the Internet. Mr. Alvarez has been deeply hurt and upset through this incident where, he, as an innocent party, has been dragged into this sordid affair. Sir Andrew Sweetman, another prominent businessman, has also confirmed that he was approached by Mr. Barton-Marshall with an identical proposal, but because Mr. Barton-Marshall could not be specific on how the scheme worked, Sir Andrew declined to become involved. All these allegations appear to confirm what Mr. Matt Todd said in his suicide note.

"The Serious Fraud Division has appealed to Mr. Barton-Marshall to hand himself over for questioning."

My God, things are going from bad to worse! This story, which is no doubt being aired around the world right now, will be the final nail in our coffin. Nobody will believe our story now; many will feel angry towards us, believing we have deliberately misled them for our own personal gain. The Alvarez communication machine has made short work of us. How stupid I have been to think we ever stood a chance. I have now had a glimpse of how effectively Alvarez controls the media, and how he would use this control to mould events and opinions in his favour once he launched his plot. Media control is a critical and powerful tool, over which he exercises total mastery. In this silent war, Alvarez has a phenomenal arsenal. Nonetheless, I know Matt and I have put a big spoke in his wheel. Maybe it's not a David and Goliath clash, as Goliath succumbed; I will console myself with the fact that at least we made Goliath stumble.

I got up to leave the room and noticed Fiona and Dorothy standing in the doorway. They had obviously been listening to the same news broadcast. Dorothy had her arms around Fiona comforting her as tears rolled uncontrollably down Fiona's face. I went up to her and patted her shoulder gently.

"We still have one another, if nothing else," I said smiling at her.

"Thank you for being such a good friend," I said, turning towards Dorothy. "Unfortunately, I embarked upon a cause which I thought would do some good, but it would now appear to have done little, yet it may cost my family dearly. Fiona and I need to leave now; we don't want to endanger you as I fear my enemies are ruthless and will stop at nothing in dispensing their rough justice. This could include people who aid-and-abet us."

The two ladies embraced one another and started sobbing uncontrollably.

I left them like that and went to the car.

We made the journey home in total silence, broken only by an occasional sob from Fiona. She is a strong person and has been able to bring her emotions under control quickly, particularly when you consider her whole life has come tumbling down about her ears.

As I drove into our driveway, I was sure I saw a light flickering in one of the upstairs bedrooms.

"Did you see that light flickering in the Rose bedroom?" I asked.

"No, I didn't see anything," she said.

"I can't risk driving up to the house. What I will do is park in the farm lane below the woods," I said.

"That's a long way from the house," she said.

"I know that, but it means I can approach the house undercover through the woods, past the outbuildings and into the house undetected. If it's all clear, I will come back and we can drive up to the house."

She nodded her head in approval.

I turned the car around, and headed for the farm lane. I drove the car as far down the lane as possible, making sure it was not visible from the main road.

I told Fiona not to remain in the car, but to hide at the edge of the woods, in case somebody saw the car in the lane.

I then started making my way through the woods, up towards the house.

It's quite a long way from the car to the top of the woods. It was almost dark and the incline fairly steep. Consequently, I fell a few times and found the going hard.

After twenty minutes, I reached the spot where I had previously met Dr. John, and decided to catch my breath and survey the house, as you get a good view of the house from this vantage point.

I could definitely see somebody was in the house. There could be more than one person as I could see a light flickering in different rooms simultaneously. People appear to be moving around the house using a torch.

I crept closer to the edge of the woods to get a better view.

Suddenly, a huge ball of fire erupted in my study.

I gasped and pushed myself back from the edge of the woods.

Immediately thereafter, similar eruptions occurred in the dining room and one of the lounges. The ferocity of the fire had to be seen to be believed. Within minutes the window in my study had burst, sending a shroud of glass flying over the lawn. The whole study was engulfed in flames. At this rate, the house would be reduced to rubble and ash within the hour. Clearly, the arsonists had doused the house in a flammable liquid before igniting the fire. I must have witnessed them moving about the house doing just that.

I moved back into the woods, watching in horror as this beautiful old manor house and all our possessions are engulfed in flames.

I should have run but was fixated by the blaze. I kept moving back slowly. The flames from the house illuminated the entire sky. As I moved back, I noticed a small cairn of stones which hadn't been there before. My mind raced – could this be a marker to Dr. John's documents?

I knelt down and knocked the stones aside, and started digging the surface below. Not more than six inches below, I came across a small, black nylon bag which I quickly removed and opened. Inside, I found a plastic pouch containing a letter, two DVDs and five keys. I opened the letter, but despite the intense glow from the fire, I was unable to read it, apart from making out the name of the signatory at the bottom of the page – John Abromovitz. I had found Dr. John's documents! How ironic – had Alvarez not set fire to my house, I would never have found the documents. This wanton act of destruction may prove to be his downfall as now I have the weapon which may sink him.

I checked the hole just to make sure I hadn't missed anything. The ground below where the bag had been deposited was hard, showing I had found all there was to find. I stood up and made my way quickly down the woods and back to the car, clutching my precious find.

Now that I come to think about it, when I first met Dr. John in the woods, he made what I thought at the time a peculiar reference to this meeting spot. He said something like 'this is an ideal place to meet and conceal our secrets'. He must have been giving me a clue to his future intentions. Unfortunately, it escaped me; had the penny dropped earlier, I would not be in this position and perhaps Matt would be alive.

When I go to the car, Fiona was nowhere to be seen. I called her name softly a few times. A few seconds later, she emerged from the woods and came running over to me.

"What have they done, James – have they set fire to the house?"

"I'm afraid so – it's completely destroyed."

She put her arms around me and I gave her a hug. We stayed like that for a few minutes, saying nothing.

"Are you alright?" I asked.

"Yes, I'm fine thanks. Lucky I didn't stay in the car as two men who had stopped on the main road came down and had a look at the car, before returning to their car and driving off," she said.

"When did this happen?" I asked.

"Soon after you left."

"Did you recognise them?" I asked.

"No, not at all."

"We must leave now before they, or anybody else, finds us here. You will be pleased to learn that out of this tragedy some good has emerged – I have found Dr. John's documents."

Chapter Twelve

I was anxious to read Dr. John's letter and let Gonan know I had found the documents, but I was equally anxious to put as many miles between myself and my house as possible. I didn't want to stop until I was well clear of Avon and Somerset.

I decided to stop at one of the larger services along the M4 motorway as they provide banking facilities; Fiona was keen to deposit money in the boy's accounts.

On arriving at the services, Fiona rushed off to withdraw and deposit money; I followed. It transpires that she can only withdraw one thousand pounds a day, which she did; keeping three hundred pounds for us and depositing the balance equally between the boys. I couldn't help noticing how adept she was at the process, which confirms a suspicion I have had for sometime that she regularly transfers funds to the boy's accounts out of the monthly allowance I give her. The boys know my policy on handouts – I don't give them. If they have a problem or require funds to make a worthwhile purchase, they know I am approachable; I believe people must work for their income. Fiona is just too soft when it comes to the boys. It's amazing she decided to keep any money aside for us at all. The three hundred pounds we are left with will just pay for the fuel to London, a deposit on some accommodation and a little left over for food. At least we will be able to withdraw more tomorrow.

We went and bought a cup of coffee and a sandwich and sat down.

I unfolded Dr. John's letter and read it out aloud.

"Dear James,

If I am not in your presence while reading this letter, it means that I haven't made it, but am thankful that you have found these documents and can continue our fight.

I have digitally copied most of the documentation and stored them on the two DVDs enclosed. The original documents are stored in five separate trunks deposited in the lockers at Waterloo Station. The five keys are for those lockers. Please get these DVDs and keys to Gonan as soon as possible.

Once you have done that you have done everything you can, for which I am most grateful!

I hope we are ultimately victorious and any sacrifice you or I may make, will be worth it.

Goodbye, my good friend, and good luck.

John Abromovitz"

I didn't know the man well, but had a lump in my throat reading his letter. His selfless actions could be the single biggest thing in stopping the overthrow of the free world. I feel privileged to have known such a noble man, and elated that he has given us the ammunition to sink Alvarez. I will phone Gonan immediately with the good news.

I searched my pockets for Gonan's mobile phone, but it was gone. It must have fallen from my pocket on one of the numerous falls I had climbing through the woods. How annoying and inconvenient this is. I will have to phone the American Embassy in London tomorrow and try to get Gonan's number from them.

I hadn't thought much about it, but both Fiona and I looked in a frightful state. My jacket elbows and my knees were covered in mud from my numerous falls. Fiona had mud on her skirt and cardigan, acquired while sitting at the edge of the woods. Fiona is most particular about her appearance, and I don't think I have ever seen her in such a state before.

"You are looking most elegant, my dear – are those designer stripes on your cardigan and skirt?"

She looked down at the mud on her skirt and returned the compliment. "We appear to have the same designer," she said.

I'm pleased to see that through all these difficulties, she has retained her good sense of humour.

I have decided that we will stay in one of the East End suburbs, for a number of reasons. Firstly, I thought it would be a lot easier for us to 'disappear' among its multi-ethnic population, where few questions are asked of your origins. Secondly, it would be a lot cheaper, as I don't know how much longer we have to survive on our meagre resources.

We arrived in London late that evening and were fortunate enough to find a B&B open and able to accommodate us. It wasn't a B&B as such, but a single room with shared kitchen, lounge and bathroom. The establishment was run by an Indian gentleman whose accent I could barely understand. Although the place looked appalling from the outside, inside its minimalist appointments were clean and tidy. It will cost us fifty pounds per day for the room. I paid for three days but told the gentleman I was not sure how long we intended staying.

We were both exhausted and collapsed onto the bed.

Next morning, Fiona tried cleaning our clothes as best she could in an attempt to give us a little respectability; the only clothes we had were the clothes we wore.

I tried phoning the American Embassy but my mobile was not working. It kept coming up with the message 'Service Unavailable'. My telephone, broadband, television and mobile are all on the same account with one supplier, so I concluded they must have put my account on hold as all my bank accounts are frozen. That means I will have to buy a cheap mobile phone and a 'Pay As You Go' subscription. I can only do that tomorrow when Fiona withdraws more money. How frustrating it is doing nothing when you know you are sitting on such vital information.

Apart from going down to the local store to buy something to eat, we stayed in all day; I didn't want to draw any attention to us.

The television in our room, which I'm sure pre-dates the Ark, had no satellite or cable facilities, so we were reduced to watching the BBC. Rather than be bored to tears watching their endless line-up of cooking programmes and repeats, I decided to take a short nap.

I was woken by Fiona who was watching the six o'clock news.

"More bad news for us, James," she said, "listen to this."

"The Avon and Somerset police have confirmed that they have issued a warrant for the arrest of Mr. James Barton-Marshall in connection with the arson attack on his own home yesterday evening. Four charges of attempted murder and one of arson have been brought against him after numerous witnesses saw him escaping the scene yesterday evening. The police are appealing for anybody who has seen Mr. Barton-Marshall to contact them urgently. They have cautioned the public not to approach him as it is believed he is armed and dangerous.

"The four charges of attempted murder arise from the fact that he booby-trapped his house to hinder the work of the fire brigade, and in so doing, deliberately and intentionally endangered the lives of the firemen sent to fight the blaze.

"It is believed that Mr. Barton-Marshall started the fire in an attempt to claim the insurance against the house, valued at close to three million pounds.

"The police spokesperson said that unbeknown to Mr. Barton-Marshall, all his assets have been frozen by the Serious Fraud Division and that even if the insurance company paid out, these funds would have been frozen anyway.

"It is believed Mr. Barton-Marshall got into financial difficulties in attempting to implement his plans to defraud the international stock markets of multiple billions of pounds. Mr. Matt Todd, a co-conspirator, committed suicide a few days earlier as a result of his involvement in this serious crime, which would have adversely affected the lives of millions of hard working and innocent people around the world.

"The police think Mr Barton-Marshall is headed for London. If you have seen this man, believed to be travelling in the company of his wife, Fiona, then please contact the Crimestoppers number shown at the bottom of your screen now. A substantial reward of one hundred thousand pounds is being offered to apprehend this criminal."

I just sat there thinking how incredulous the whole affair is; how rich, powerful and unscrupulous people can so easily manipulate the system to their advantage. This is Alvarez's speciality – capitalising on social and system weaknesses for his own direct benefit. I realise now that Alvarez isn't going to kill me. He is going to use the system to strip me of every penny I have and to incarcerate me for the rest of my life so that I will be around when he ultimately triumphs. I haven't much chance of survival now; the entire police force, backed up by extensive media coverage and a populace highly incentivised to hand me in is what I'm up against. In court, they will produce witness after witness who will lie through the back of their teeth to bury me alive – I haven't a snowballs chance if it goes that far! I have to get these documents to Gonan, it's my only chance!

Fiona sat on the end of the bed, body bowed with her head in her hands.

"Don't worry," I said, "we may still be able to stop Alvarez before it gets to the point where I go to jail."

"Slim chance of that happening given Gonan's track record so far," she said.

"He's been waiting for the ammunition, which I now have," I said.

"Let's hope so, but I think he has been ineffectual so far," she replied.

I then explained my theory that I didn't think she or the boys were in any more danger.

"We can't take the risk," she said. "The boys must remain in hiding for a couple of weeks until we know for certain where all this is leading."

"I fully agree, but I am convinced that Alvarez is going to use the system to blacken my name and destroy me, while he walks away from the whole affair squeaky clean."

Fiona nodded her head, still sitting in the same position.

Next morning, Fiona went on her own to withdraw money and returned shortly thereafter with one hundred and fifty pounds.

"What's this?" I enquired in a rather annoyed tone.

"It's what I have kept aside to buy a mobile phone," she replied.

"I have to pay the rent today as well as get a mobile phone. That means I will have to delay getting the phone until tomorrow. I can't afford any delays; every hour I delay in getting these documents through to Gonan represents days or weeks in response time. You should have kept more money aside for us."

"James, pay Mr. Patel fifty pounds, which leaves you one hundred pounds to get the phone and a 'Pay As You Go' contract. That should be more than sufficient, provided you only get a cheap phone."

"You are right. I'm sorry if I overreacted," I said. "Would you be so good as to buy the phone for me as I need to keep a low profile?"

"I wasn't expecting you to go and get it; we have to keep you hidden. I will pay Mr. Patel and then go and get the phone. I'm sure I will have little difficulty in finding one of those ubiquitous mobile shops in the vicinity."

She returned around midday, with my mobile phone, bread rolls and some cheese for our lunch and dinner. Oh, the joys of our high life.

I wasn't anticipating any problems; it's an easy enough job phoning an embassy to get a number for one of their overseas embassies. That's the theory – in reality it was a total nightmare. I was put on hold and transferred so many times that I was giving up hope of ever acquiring the number. Finally, when I was given the number, I discovered to my horror that I only had a few pence left in my account. Fiona and I could only scrape together a few pounds, which would be insufficient to make an international call, if my recent experience in dealing with the London embassy is anything to go on. I needed a well topped-up account to make this call, which meant it would have to wait until tomorrow.

The day and night dragged on.

The next morning, Fiona made her routine call to the bank with my plea to draw more money for us indelibly stamped on her brain. She returned soon after with a measly three hundred pounds; to be promptly admonished by me.

"James, there is more than enough here for us. I will pay Mr. Patel an additional one hundred pounds for a further two days, fifty pounds on a 'Pay As You Go' contract, leaving us with one hundred and fifty pounds. Unless you intended treating me to a decent restaurant this evening, I think we have more than enough money for one day."

As usual, she is quite correct; it's just that I feel so vulnerable knowing there is so little cash between me and total poverty.

"I'm off now to pay Mr. Patel and to do some shopping; I won't be long as I know how important it is for you to speak to Gonan," she said.

After my experience phoning the London embassy, I was expecting worse treatment from the Istanbul embassy; mindful of the fact that I only had fifty pounds in my phone.

Amazingly enough, the number I had been given was correct and within a few minutes, I was speaking to David. I explained the situation to him briefly and asked that I speak to Gonan urgently. After a short delay, Gonan was on the line.

"Hello, James, it's good to hear from you again, we were getting a little worried about you. I hear you have some very good news for me – you've found the documents. I've had a feeling all along that somehow these documents would surface in time to help us."

"Yes, I have Dr. John's documents in my possession or at least the digitised version. The original documents are stored in lockers at Waterloo Station, for which I have the keys."

"Excellent, this is the best news I've heard in a long time. I will make arrangements for them to be picked up from you urgently. Can you please give me your address?"

I gave him my address and continued. "Can you please arrange to replace my mobile phone as I seem to have lost it while escaping the fire at my house? I take it that you are fully abreast of all the latest developments affecting me as they appear to have been broadcasted worldwide?"

"I certainly am, James. I warned you and Matt that you were playing with fire and could get burnt. Now that you have found the documents, my position has been strengthened, meaning I may be able to do more to help you."

"Good," I said, "one thing you can help me with straight away is providing me with a little cash as all my accounts have been frozen."

"That may prove to be a little problematic. I am well over-spent on my 'informer's budget' due to the heightened terrorist activity recently."

"Gonan, I don't really care what budgetary concerns you face, I have put everything on the line, including my family's life, to fight this cause and now when I ask for a little cash to keep my family, and I in hiding until the coast is clear, you have the audacity to talk to me about budgets. I don't care what you have to do; sell the silverware, sell the furniture and paintings, but get me some cash so we can survive. I only have a few thousand pounds for me and my sons to survive the coming months. I'm therefore looking to you and your government to help me and my family."

"Relax, James – we aren't going to dump you. We will take care of you as best we can; I know just how indebted we are to you."

"I'm pleased to hear that," I said. "I also need you to use your influence to quash all these false charges brought against me."

"As I said, James, we will do everything we can to help you, but one step at a time. Everything depends on me eradicating Alvarez first. Once that has been done, we can turn our attention to other important issues, but not before then. I'm afraid that until Alvarez has been removed, you are still on your own to a large extent. Keep a low profile and avoid detection. I will see what our London office can do to help."

"I understand," I said.

"Excellent, James, I will be chatting to you soon – well done!"

I flopped back onto the bed with a huge sigh. I felt a great weight had been lifted from me.

That afternoon, while Fiona and I were sitting on the bed eating our staple diet consisting of a cheese roll, there was a gentle knock on the door. I got up to answer it thinking it was Mr. Patel. As I opened the door, a foot was thrust through the gap stopping me from closing it. Before I had time to react, the door was forced open. I stumbled backward with the force, landing on the floor and hitting my head against the bed. Fiona gave out a shrill scream. The door was quickly closed behind the intruder. I looked up through a haze of semi-consciousness and there, standing in front of me, was Richard Petrada. My heart sank. Alvarez has found us. We are about to lose everything!

Fiona got off the bed and came over to see if I was alright; sitting next to me and cradling my head on her lap.

"What now, Richard, have you slumped to such lows that you are here to do your Master's bidding; to kill us?" asked Fiona in an angry, but trembling voice.

"My Master has sent me, but it is not the Master you think it is," said Richard, holding his forefinger to his lips indicating that we keep our voices down. "I work for the CIA, and always have," continued Richard.

"And I am the Fairy Godmother," said Fiona.

"I tried to put James off pursuing this matter so many times, yet he stubbornly persisted, and look where it has got you," said Richard.

I got to my feet and stood in front of Richard still feeling a little shaky.

"Yes, look where it has got me, I hold the vital information that can bring Alvarez, the brute, to his knees. I'm proud that I made a stand, despite the difficulties, hardships and disappointments," I said.

"I wanted to protect you from what I knew lay ahead. To protect you from a world which, until recently, you had no idea existed," said Richard.

"Well, I hope in hindsight you realise you were wrong because, if I had not made a stand, we would not be in a position where we hold enough vital evidence to be able to crush this monster," I said.

"James, I am grateful, as are many others, for your determination and strength of will, but I didn't want you to go through what you have. You should have taken your well-earned retirement when you could. You, more than anybody else, most realise that while you have documented evidence that can potentially destroy or harm Alvarez, you are not out of the woods yet and everything can still go horribly wrong for you. You have earned the wrath of the most powerful and ruthless man in the World. If you had not become involved, another scenario would have unfolded, the outcome of which we will never know. My point is, you didn't have to become involved;

your involvement has meant the story unfolded one way, without your involvement, another way, both outcomes resting on a knife edge," said Richard.

"Yes, but my involvement has at least strengthened our hand. I would like to believe that had neither Dr. John nor I become involved, another scenario would have unfolded, that is correct, but not a favourable one."

"Perhaps," said Richard, "but we will never know. I was only trying to protect you all along, that's all."

"Don't believe him, James, I don't. He has burst into our room, hurting you, making unsubstantiated claims and bluffing that he had your interests at heart from the outset," said Fiona. "He has lied to us before and will do so again. He has no compunction about lying."

"I'm definitely not handing any documents over to him until my contact in the CIA can vouch for him. And don't think I have been stupid enough to keep the documents here either," I said.

"Here, phone Gonan Mehad on the phone you requested he send and get him to vouch for me," said Richard, thrusting the mobile phone at me.

I followed the same speed dial procedures I did on my old phone and within a few minutes was talking to Gonan.

"I have Richard Petrada with me asking that I handover the documents to him, as he claims to be a CIA operative. I cannot do that as last I knew, he was an agent of Alvarez," I said.

"I do not know the man personally, but as he has given you this phone and you have come through to me, indicates that he is genuine, but put him on the phone and I will verify this," said Gonan.

I handed the phone over to Richard. He spoke to Gonan for a few minutes and handed the phone back to me.

"He's for real, James – he's one of us, I will vouch for him," said Gonan.

Suddenly, a huge sense of doubt came over me. What if this is just a big setup?

"How do I know with any certainty you are Gonan? You sound like him but I have no other means of verification," I said.

Gonan laughed, "We will make a good secret agent out of you yet, James – you are starting to think like one. Ask me a question that only you and I know the answer to, for example, what happened at our first meeting."

"Fair enough," I said, "tell me what we discussed after supper on the first evening."

Gonan proceeded to recall our evening together in great detail. His attention to detail is quite amazing.

"Does that satisfy you that you are talking to the one and only Gonan?" he asked.

"Alright, on your say-so Gonan, I will hand these documents over to Richard," I said.

"Excellent. My team is looking forward to getting their teeth into those documents. I have assembled a team of over fifty experts who are on standby right now waiting for these documents. I will keep you abreast of developments. Goodbye, for now."

Turning towards Richard, I asked him, "Why did they send you, Richard?"

"My Controller contacted me and asked me to come and see you as he knows I hold both you and Fiona in high regard. The purpose of my call has not only been to retrieve these valuable documents, but also to establish contact with you and provide whatever support we can for you. However, before any direct action is taken against Alvarez, that support may be extremely limited, but thereafter, we will fight tooth-and-nail to have you restored to your good standing in society."

"I was led to believe you worked for Alvarez together with Felicity Marchant," I said.

"That's correct, we did work for Alvarez, not directly, but through his network. However, at the time, I had no idea I was working for Alvarez or that he was behind this plot. I had, however, been recruited to work for the CIA when I left the Johnston Military Academy on completing my schooling. I have been in their service ever since. The CIA opened doors for me, and I am one hundred percent patriotic and loyal to my country," he said.

"What of Felicity?" asked Fiona, "is she too a double agent, or a victim of the network?"

"She was part of the network, but not a victim. She was in it for the money and power, and Alvarez's network provided her access to both. She is a silver-tongued, self-centred, egotistical person you are well rid of. There will be victims as the Alvarez empire collapses, and I hope she will be one of them. Needless to say that Felicity and I were never romantically involved. Her values and mine are poles apart. In truth, the whole sordid affair cost me my relationship with my true girlfriend, which I deeply regret, as well as the hurt it caused the two of you."

"Gonan said he didn't know you personally, why is that if you are here on his bidding?" I asked.

"I report to a Controller. Who they work for, or report to, I'm none the wiser. I simply act on orders given to me," said Richard.

"So how much of this affair was the CIA aware of?" I asked Richard.

"That I don't know – I have only been assigned to this task recently," said Richard.

"Did you tell them of my concerns of the potential plot?" I asked.

"I did," said Richard.

If that is the case, then they must have had all the pieces to the jigsaw in place prior to my meeting with Gonan, apart from knowing that Dr. John had built up so much incriminating evidence over the years, so why did Gonan call an emergency meeting, and ask me to do a presentation about something they already knew about? Something doesn't seem right.

Richard interrupted my thoughts. "You will need to stay low for sometime. Once Alvarez has been taken care of, we will address all the problems facing you, namely getting the criminal charges dropped and getting the Serious Fraud Division to stop their investigation into your affairs. This could take considerable time and will depend on how things pan out with Gonan and his team over the next few weeks. How are you placed for money right now, you must be pretty skint with all your accounts frozen?"

"We don't want any of your money or that of your Controller, thank you," interrupted Fiona.

"I can understand you being upset and disappointed in me, believing me to have used and abused our friendship, breaking your trust. In reality, we have always been on the same side. It is the ignominious and dirty world of espionage that we have become embroiled in which twists and distorts things until you can no longer make sense of things."

"Then you will understand why it is so difficult for us to take your word now," said Fiona.

"Just hold on a minute," I said, "things don't seem to make any sense to me. It doesn't involve Richard directly; Gonan has vouched for him. By sending Richard, somebody has either made a mistake, acted in ignorance or are attempting to flush out an enemy."

"What on earth are you talking about?" said Fiona, "that bang on your head seems more serious than I thought."

Richard also looked at me in a rather quizzical manner.

"By learning that Richard works for the CIA, and knowing that I told him my hypothesis, which he confirms he passed onto his Controller, means the CIA had all the pieces to the puzzle well before I met Gonan, so why did Gonan act as if I had provided him such vital information, and why did he ask me to stay over and do a presentation to a meeting he purported to have arranged? It was clearly a sham; one I would never have picked up on had Richard not appeared on the scene. Therefore, my question remains – has the sending of Richard been a mistake, an oversight or is somebody trying to flush out an enemy?"

"I still don't get it," said Fiona. "I can understand how Richard's role as a CIA agent has changed your understanding of your initial meeting with Gonan, but what has this to do with 'flushing out enemies' or somebody making a 'mistake'?"

"It tells me Gonan was putting on a show; trying to conceal something, otherwise he would have been totally truthful with me," I said.

"Concealing what?" asked Fiona.

"That's the Million Pound question. My mind is racing for answers. What if Gonan made a big song-and-dance about my 'revelations' to make me think we were big players; to the extent that he got me to do a presentation to his colleagues? When I did the presentation, I couldn't see the audience; perhaps there wasn't one, or only a few stooges. By getting me to think we were important and by giving me central stage at his 'important meeting', he hoped to secure my support. By securing my support, he could drag things out, and we all know how critical timing is. I always felt that Gonan was dragging his heels. It all makes sense to me now. "

"Yes, but to what end?" enquired Richard.

"Power and money do not motivate Gonan, but what if he has made a pact with the Devil himself, Alvarez, for the total destruction of the terrorist groups he so vehemently hates. For his complicity, Alvarez allows Gonan to preside over their annihilation, which is a vital component of Alvarez's plot. Perhaps Gonan is sick enough to have entered into such a pact; it would explain his behaviour," I said.

"He would have to be terribly sick to go along with such a pact," said Fiona, "as it would mean further terrorist attacks with the loss of many innocent lives, not to mention the loss of liberties in the free world and possible ethnic cleansing; the list of potential atrocities goes on and on. All this just to satisfy his lust for revenge? It seems an excessive price to pay."

"Depends on how sick he really is," I said.

"Very, very sick," she replied. "If he's on Alvarez's side, why did he go along with your proposal to launch the Internet campaign?"

"Because I don't think he thought it would be as successful as it was, and he knew we would go ahead with or without his approval," I replied.

"There could be a more sinister reason for him agreeing," said Richard.

"What would that be?" I enquired.

"He could be playing both sides. If your Internet campaign worked, then the terrorists and ourselves share a mutual enemy – Alvarez. This could potentially bring the two warring parties, namely Gonan and the terrorist groups, closer together. Getting closer to his enemies would help Gonan deliver a fatal blow to his enemy at an appropriate time. If, on the other hand, you were unsuccessful, he could argue he could not have stopped you launching your campaign and his pact with Alvarez remains intact."

"That is a distinct possibility," I agreed. "I think you need to bring these concerns to your Controller's attention. Perhaps there is nothing in them, but we can't take that chance. As I said earlier, by sending you, your superiors may have had the intention of flushing Gonan out. Whatever lies beneath, I can't risk giving you the originals. You may take the discs for your experts to evaluate, but the originals must remain with me until we have some clarity on this matter."

"That's fair enough," said Richard, "but if Gonan is playing both sides he will definitely give you up, which means as soon as I leave here and confirm that I have the documents, the police or Alvarez will swoop on you. What I suggest is that you give me the DVDs now, and that we leave together. I will find you somewhere else to stay. Unfortunately, I can't put you up as I share accommodation, and you will definitely be identified."

"How will the police or Alvarez know when to swoop?" enquired Fiona.

"As soon as I have signalled that I have picked up the documents, I should imagine," replied Richard.

"And how do you do that?" she enquired further.

"By sending my Controller a text message confirming that I have the documents."

"Right – let's pack up and leave now," I said.

"How can we trust and believe what Richard has told us?" protested Fiona.

"Very simply," I said, "I either believe Richard or Gonan, and right now I have reason to doubt Gonan, so in the absence of any other choice, let's leave now."

"Good," said Richard, "pack up now. I will leave first, taking your luggage, to make sure all is clear, then both of you leave, one after the other, allowing the first to get outside before following. Hopefully, this won't arouse any suspicions. Hurry now! Leave Gonan's mobile behind; it's bound to have a tracking device in it!"

Outside in the street, Richard bustled us along to a car parked not far from the building. We got in and drove to the end of the road. Parked around the corner and out of sight were three police cars.

"That looks like it could be your reception committee," commented Richard, "I bet there's another three cars parked at the top of the road. Looks like your doubts about Gonan maybe well-founded after all. Could you imagine what would have happened if you didn't raise your suspicions – I would have called my Controller, the police would have swooped and everything would have been over for all of us; Alvarez would have triumphed."

We carried on driving for a short time until we stopped outside the Salvation Army building. I was initially taken aback when I realised this is where Richard was going to leave us. I thought it was a case of 'from the frying pan into the fire'.

Richard explained, "We don't have many options. I've given it some careful thought and I think you will be able to hide here better than anywhere else, as your pictures have been shown regularly on TV and in newspapers. If I were to take you to a Bed & Breakfast, or hotel, you may be identified; here, nobody asks questions and they will provide you with a bed and food until I can move you to a more secure location."

Well, if nothing else, we certainly looked the part of two Salvation Army 'guests'. I gave Richard the two DVDs and my mobile number, and got out the car.

You have no idea how embarrassing and degrading it is to have to accept charity like this, but as long as they can shelter us for the night, until we can draw money and get somewhere better to stay, I am most grateful.

Inside, we met a charming young man who welcomed us warmly telling us not to worry about anything. They had a bed and food for us and that the 'love of God would protect us'. It was the latter I was more pleased to hear about.

We were shown into a dormitory and allocated two beds at the far end. Upright lockers separated the beds, where one could store one's worldly possessions. There were other people in the dormitory, but I paid little attention to them, and thankfully, they paid no attention to us. The young man told us when, and where supper was to be served, but I didn't hear him, my mind was preoccupied with the latest developments to pay any attention to him. I lay back on the bed, facing the wall, thinking about Gonan.

Next morning, early, Fiona left to go and draw money. She had been gone for some time. I sat on the end of my bed facing the wall; hoping not to be recognised. We can't stay here. With all the coming and going of people, it's just a matter of time before we are spotted. When Fiona returns, we will leave.

Suddenly, a firm hand is placed on my shoulder and I jump in surprise. I turn around expecting to see a policeman with Fiona in-tow. Instead, behind me stood the young gentleman we had met the previous evening. He came and sat on the bed next to me, asking if he could help me. He had endless questions for me which I told him I did not want to answer. Unperturbed, he asked if I wanted to go to the chapel and pray, which I thought would be a good idea as it may provide some privacy.

Eventually, Fiona returned with a rather worried look on her face.

"What has happened?" I enquired.

"I can't withdraw any more money," she said. "I keep getting the message that I must contact my local branch."

"Well, let's do it," I said, "so we can get to the bottom of the problem."

I gave her my mobile phone, and she phoned the number on one of the rejection slips.

Soon she was talking to somebody who took down her details before enquiring into the nature of the problem. Fiona duly explained this to them. After a short pause, where I assume they were checking the account, the operator spoke. "Your account has been temporarily placed on hold due to unusual withdrawals being made against it recently. This has been done to protect you from unauthorised use of your account. All you need to do is answer a few simple security questions, which you set up at the time of opening the account, and your account will be immediately opened."

"What are the questions?" enquired Fiona.

The operator then proceeded to reel them off. Fiona was unable to answer one of them. "I don't know the answer to that question," replied Fiona angrily, "all those details were in a file in my home which has been burnt down. Whatever money is in this account is all we have left."

"I sympathise with you, ma'am, but I'm sure you can appreciate that I cannot release your account until I am satisfied that the withdrawals made recently are legitimate, and I can only do that through you answering these security questions correctly."

We are totally penniless and have no other option than to stay here, despite the risk of detection being so high.

For the remainder of the day, Fiona and I sat huddled in a corner of the chapel out of the way of prying eyes.

Early that evening, Richard called in to see us.

"You have certainly set a cat among the pigeons, James. It appears that you have sparked a coup at the castle, so to speak," said Richard. "Your action of withholding evidence based on mistrust in Gonan has resulted in him voluntarily stepping down and vacating his office. Whether or not there is any substance to your allegations is unclear at this stage. Gonan claims they are baseless and is stepping down only because he cannot continue working effectively in his position under a cloud of doubt. His successor, my immediate boss, has requested that you handover the keys to the original documents so that they can continue their work.

"The risk to you will increase significantly if any of this leaks and gets back to Alvarez; the probabilities of which are high. His perverse sense of justice may see him try and take revenge on you. Our ability to protect you is extremely limited. Only when authority to act against Alvarez is issued, can we offer you the full protection of the agency; until then, you are not under our jurisdiction and at risk. If you were under our protection, I could whisk you off to a safe house right now, but because you aren't, if I did that, it would be equivalent to handing you over to the authorities. I'm afraid this means you're on your own for a while. I would suggest that you leave the city immediately and head north."

"We have no money to do that," I said, explaining our situation to him.

"It's unlikely that you will get any financial support from the agency either in the short-term," said Richard. "However, I will try and get whatever money I can from them and send it to you. Don't worry, if I have to beg, borrow or steal, I will get money to you, that I promise. I have a little money on me now to help you leave the city. When you've established a base, even a temporary one, phone me and I will mail cash to you at that address. You must leave now and keep heading north until you feel you are safe. All this turmoil should come to a head in the next month or so, when hopefully we can help and protect you. Keep on the move for the next month and you may be alright."

Epilogue

It has been three years since our harrowing escape from London.

Shortly after Richard dropped us off at Victoria Station, we were almost detained by two alert, young policemen, but managed to escape them by separating and mingling with the crowd.

Our journey north took the best part of a month. We ran out of money on many occasions and had to sleep rough. If it hadn't been for the money Richard sent us, we would never have made it. We would phone him and tell him where we were, and he would have cash delivered to that address the following morning; all his own money. This process depended on us staying at a place where we could use their address as a delivery point. As we kept moving, trying to avoid detection, this often proved difficult. It wouldn't have been a problem had Richard given us enough money to see us through the month in a single payment, but unfortunately he would only send us small amounts at a time; often only enough for a day or so. As he explained later, due to last minute changes in his department, caused through his Controller relocating to London, their accounts were not opened for well over a month, and they had no spare cash. Whatever he sent us was his own money – what he could spare. As incredible as this may sound, the mighty American government couldn't even scrape together a few pennies to help us! As you can imagine, this caused immense problems and hardships. You must appreciate that we had no change of clothing, and had to sleep rough a few times, so we didn't project an image of trust. Our deteriorating appearance also drew attention to us, making it more and more difficult for us to find somewhere to stay without raising suspicions.

We now live in a beautiful, small village in Aberdeenshire, where we eventually found ourselves and were accepted into the community as one of their own. We live under the assumed name of Gilbraith, Fiona's maiden name. We rent a small, two-bedroom cottage, which Fiona has managed to decorate exquisitely on an extremely small budget. We love the place and are happier here than we were ever in our large home in Somerset. I work in the local village store and Post Office on a part-time basis to help augment our meagre pension. Fiona started a local branch of the Woman's Institute and has become deeply involved in local affairs and loves it. I'm also very happy here but do miss a few things from our Somerset days, such as my beautiful old study and its spectacular views. Our lifestyle is totally different to that of our Somerset one, yet we feel so much happier and relaxed here. Our two sons are also well. They returned to their jobs and careers a month after our house burnt down, none the worse off, thankfully! We are also fortunate that they visit us regularly, which proves to be a tight squeeze in our small house with their ever increasing family.

It was about three weeks after arriving here that Richard informed us that a combined US force had led a surprise attack on Alvarez's island fortress. By all accounts, this attack had obliterated the island and all its occupants, including Alvarez. Gonan's successor initiated this strike, with Presidential authority, based to a large extent on the evidence gathered by Dr. John and Gonan's department. Little of this was reported in the news, apart from a brief comment that a combined US force was involved in a training exercise in the Pacific.

Richard has been so helpful and supportive over this period, often digging into his own pocket to ensure our survival. He has single-handedly campaigned, since the attack on Alvarez when I officially became part of their CIA operation, to have the criminal investigations against me involving arson and attempted murder quashed. It took him about six months before the police issued a statement that I was no longer suspected of any wrong doing in their investigation. He has also been successful in having the Serious Fraud Division drop its investigation into my affairs. However, he has been unsuccessful in getting my accounts released because at the time that the President authorised the attack on Alvarez, he also authorised an in-depth and detailed investigation into Alvarez's affairs. All accounts linked to Alvarez's trading activities were subsequently frozen pending the outcome of this investigation. As Alvarez transferred money directly into one of my accounts, my accounts have fallen within the gamut of this investigation, which could take many years to complete. Because of the power of Alvarez's networks, this investigation will be extremely lengthy due to the fears of recrimination should anybody attempt to interfere. So it doesn't matter who you are or what influence you may have, you just have to sit and wait. The likelihood of this investigation achieving much is remote, to say the least. Alvarez would never have left a document trail unless it was intentional, as in my case. Consequently, the innocent become the victims and the wrong doers will never be identified. The freezing of my accounts has left me penniless, so Richard has been able to arrange that I receive a small pension, paid by the CIA, which we live off.

The threat from Alvarez's networks does not appear to have materialised as anticipated. People have either been totally oblivious to their involvement or have just sat tight, waiting to see what happens. We thought that with Alvarez gone, the networks would still function; breaking up into locally controlled networks, which may not pose an international threat, but could still be a threat economically and socially in some regions. One of the reasons this threat may have diminished significantly is that the relationship between Alvarez and the terrorist groups soured significantly as a result of our Internet campaign, this provided Gonan's successor the opportunity to bridge the gap between the parties and get them to the table, where they are in the process of resolving their differences in an open and free manner. We have denied the new 'owners' of the networks a powerful ally.

On a more personal level, Sir Andrew Sweetman and his ilk appear to be thriving. However, Richard has informed me that his appointment to head a task force, with a brief to bring the major players involved with Alvarez to book by whatever means, will be authorised within the next few weeks. The day of reckoning for Sir Andrew, and many other prominent people around the world, is still to come. New legislation is being drafted to support this investigation so these people cannot hide behind outdated laws inappropriate for the times. Richard has asked me, on numerous occasions, to join his team, but I have resolutely declined. I'm not coming out of retirement for anything!

Little, if any progress has been made to reform our business measurement and management methods, or to change our Stock Exchange trading procedures, and yet these were the central tenets which brought us to the brink of collapse in the first instant. If only our narrow-minded business community would wake-up to this reality and realise how their continued stupidity may force us to the brink again, sooner rather than later. If only the business community could take a leaf out of Alvarez's book when it comes to innovation. I think it was Gonan who so aptly described Alvarez. He said Alvarez would take the box, within which most of us think, turn it upside down, sit on top of it while he thought of a more appropriate plan that in no way conforms to previous thinking. That is why he so nearly succeeded in achieving what others would have described as impossible; only fate was against him. If there was one thing I learnt in dealing with Alvarez – that was to expect the unexpected and to anticipate the sheer brilliance of his ideas.

I keep lobbying for change as I realise how critical it is. Perhaps we won't be pushed to the brink again, I certainly hope we aren't, but change is so desperately required I cannot understand why we continue to drag our heels on this matter. Excellent and innovative work in this area is available in the form of Modern Value Management, which deserves serious consideration primarily because it addresses all the problems facing modern business in terms of appropriate measurement and management standards.

Fiona and I have decided that when our accounts are freed, we would like to buy our little cottage and set aside a modest amount to help us meet our monthly expenditure without the necessity for me to work anymore. We would then pay off all our son's debts, including mortgages and loans, and give them a small nest egg of fifty thousand pounds each. The balance, which should then run into tens of millions, be donated to the World Wildlife Fund. Our experience over the past three years has lead to a catharsis, where we realise we don't need money to be happy. We have found happiness and tranquillity here in Scotland, living off the smell of an oil rag. We would feel so much better if we could contribute, even in a small way, to saving and preserving this beautiful planet of ours. I find it inconceivable when I read and see of the decadent waste committed around the world on a daily basis, such as in Dubai, where people are prepared to pay tens of millions of pounds for an ugly, man-made island 'to keep up with the Jones', when the world is crying out for money to protect and preserve this precious, beautiful planet. I have a very simple philosophy – invest in what supports and sustains you, namely the preservation of the world and its habitat, otherwise we have no future! People like the World Wildlife Fund have this as their brief. Therefore, they have my wholehearted support.

I often think about the past events and consider with amazement how easily things could have gone against us. In the end, it was just a matter of fate. What surprised me was the number of times fate intervened on our side. This has led to me asking myself the question, 'is good intended to prevail over evil – is there a God looking after us?'

I'm also concerned people are totally oblivious to the fact that we have only recently fought and won a war that could have plunged us into a political and social 'Dark Age'. I keep thinking people should be told about this silent war and for them to remember the bravery and sacrifice of those who fought this war on their behalf, and for us to learn from our mistakes, particularly those we continue to make. Governments of the world, understandably, want the entire affair hushed-up and swept under the carpet, after all, they don't want to have to answer embarrassing questions about how they allowed a threat of this scale and nature to slink up on them undetected until the eleventh hour. Consequently, the contributions of brave and honourable people like Dr. John Abromovitz and Matt Todd will go unrecognised, which I think is a disgrace. Richard is fighting to have them officially recognised, but this will never happen until the governments of the World stand up and tell people what really happened. The reality is – this won't happen! Consequently, I am left with no other choice than to tell the World myself!

You have just finished reading my account of a Silent War. I hope we will all heed the signs and push for change so that we never find ourselves in this position again, as then we may not be fortunate enough to have the services of brave men like Dr. John and Matt Todd to call upon!